CREATED

No Way Out

JEN ZAHARI

outskirts
press

INTRODUCTION

This book was brought to you with much personal knowledge, experience, pain, life, and growth. This is the story of a woman who has walked the trenches of life and is ready to give it all up. It incorporates some of my actual life experiences, many embellished moments, and some complete fictional moments.

Life can get in front of all of us; it's what we do in those moments, how we talk to ourselves, and what actions we take that can truly allow us to step into our personal gifts, build self-trust, and know we are in complete control to create the life we want.

For anyone struggling with self-image, lack of self-love, anxiety, depression, suicidal ideations, confidence, or something else altogether. YOU are not alone! There are options to get support in your journey. Whether through a coach, therapist, energy work, counselor, all of them, or something else altogether. Take a look and know You are worth the time to heal.

Want help directly? Contact me at 920-350-0138, jenzahari@jenzahari.com or www.jenzahari.com

If you are ever struggling or contemplating suicide, please, call the helpline at 800-273-8255 or visit https://suicidepreventionlifeline.org/

Be KIND to yourself always; the moment you are in is not the whole journey.

ACKNOWLEDGMENTS

To the love of my life, Joel, for encouraging me, believing in me, and being the rock by my side. For the life that we have built together. The learning and growth about ourselves and one another on the backend of some really hard moments. I'm so grateful that we both had the strength to make it through. Loving you forever and always!

To my son, Boe, for being the North star, shining light in my life. The bright light that I kept focus on in my darkest moments. For the continued inspiration and encouragement to bring this book to life. For your always readiness with a smile and a hug. To Infinity and beyond, much love!

For my mom and dad, to everything you provided to us when we were kids. I know it isn't always easy to hear some of the healing that I needed to do. But, you did everything exactly as you knew how to do for us kids and always with love. You raised good, hard-working kids with a great work ethic. Provided us experiences and moments that I will be forever grateful for. Thank you for everything you are to all of us!

To Christy, my soul sister, for being by my side in this process and your constant push to "read another chapter." For your words of affirmation when I needed them most and for helping me normalize so many things in life. So much appreciation that we met when we did!

To all my friends and family for the experiences, conversations, belief, love, and support.

To all my past, current, and future clients and employees. Thank you for your trust, each conversation, and everything you have taught me along the way.

Finally, to my readers, I invite you to read this book with an open mind about what you are creating for your life!

CHAPTER 1

As I was lying in bed, waiting for my alarm to sound, thoughts screamed through. *What is life in the house going to be like when I'm gone?*

Luke was next to me, sound asleep. I turned to him as the memories of when we used to laugh together swarmed in. "Why couldn't you see me for me?" I asked quietly so I didn't wake him.

An image of how he used to spoil me crossed my mind. We weren't even together a year at the time. I just finished up a 13-hour shift at the restaurant. Walking into the house, I saw rose petals all over the floor. At first I thought *really, do I have to come home to this?* Then I quickly realized what was going on as he grabbed my hand and guided me upstairs. Rose petals continued to guide our way. As we started up the stairs, I saw the line of candles leading into the bathroom. A warm bath filled with lavender and salts was awaiting my arrival.

"Why did things have to change?" I asked him quietly as he lay there sleeping.

I didn't want to wake him, yet there were so many things I wanted to say before I left. The memories of life continued in my head a short five years later from when we first met. I could barely leave the house without him questioning my every turn.

"Where are you going, when are you going to be home,

who else is going to be there?" He drilled me, one question after another, and with each one I felt the level of trust dissipate between us more and more.

"Why don't you trust me?" I'd ask time and again. I was never met with a response. He never wanted to go with me yet didn't want me to go alone either. It was a lose/lose situation every time. Most of our friends and family saw discord between us; at least I thought they did. But everyone was too nice to say anything. Our marriage, although present and good on the surface, was long over. I walked away from him countless times in my head yet still didn't have the heart to actually leave.

Why couldn't you just trust me, Luke? I would never betray you.

Turning away from him, I gazed at the ceiling again to recall the moments I tried speaking up for myself.

"Don't you talk back to me!" rang through my ears as he slammed his hand into the cupboard just to the side of my head. "What do you think, because you make the money you are better than me?"

"Luke, you know that's not true." I tried to reason with him.

"Sure, that's what you say." He stomped his way out of the house with another punch of his fist into the wall.

Laying there recalling that memory, I can still feel the tightness in my body. The twinge as I flinched when his hand hit the cupboard next to my head. The fear and hesitation it instilled. I turned back to him again. "You can finally have it all without me, Luke," I said to him quietly.

Is he going to even miss me?

I sure hope he is OK came next.

With more questions about him storming in, I changed my focus to the kids. *Are they going to be all right without me?* Tears started rolling down my eyes as I looked back to Luke. "You had better take care of my babies," I said in a louder tone.

Tears continuing down my face, I looked back up to the ceiling as the story of my life with the kids played through my mind. It was like a theater in my head. I saw the family trips, long weekends away at the lake and cookouts in the backyard. I saw the time the whole family, even the cousins and close friends, took all of the kids bowling. There must have been over 50 of us lined up in a row. We took up nearly the entire bowling alley. A smile came over me. The mini road trips, weekends at the swimming pool with the nieces and nephews. There was so much happiness created through the years. *I hope the kids always know how much I love them.*

Why did life have to get so complicated? Then my memories shifted to the last eight years. The tough parts of life came in fiercely. Arguments with Luke, holding my tongue at work, death and cancer. Anxiety and depression got worse year over year. The lack of control and uncertainty in every single area of life at work and at home. The past memories started consuming my whole body as I lay there. My chest tightened, tears falling, palms sweating, throat constricting. I could feel my body starting to close up.

"STOP" I said aloud, before quickly throwing my hand over my face. I looked over to Luke. Thankfully he did not budge. Secretly, part of me wanted him to put his arms around me, hold me and tell me that everything would be okay. Just to have that feeling of complete safety that he provided in our early years. The slight glimmer of it I would see on a rare occasion. As much as I wanted it one last time, I just couldn't handle it. Not today. Not knowing how he would wake up or respond. Worse, what would come next if he wasn't in a good state. It was the last thing I needed this morning. I just didn't want to fight anymore. It was too hard, not knowing who I was going to get in any moment. It felt like my heart was breaking on repeat, over and over.

"Stop," I said again, almost silently, trying to tell my thoughts to turn off, not wanting to relive the pain of the past anymore. I threw the covers off and decided it was time to get moving.

It was rather brisk as I got out of bed. This was the first day in years that I didn't dread getting up. Finally, all the stress and sadness were going to be gone. Looking at the clock, I saw it was nearing 5 a.m. I wanted to beat the crowds that would start arriving by 7 or 8 a.m. If I had a couple hours into my hike before they arrived, no one would know what was going on or be able to stop me.

I quietly got up out of bed, grabbed my clothes from off the dresser and tiptoed my way through our bedroom toward the bathroom. The last thing I wanted to do was to wake up Luke. I made it to the doorway of our bedroom then turned back to look at him. Watching him still laying there, I said quietly, "I've loved you since the day we met. I would have done anything to keep us whole and make you happy. I just can't live like this anymore." My legs shook as I stood there and a full spectrum of emotions filled my body. "If only you would have seen it. If only you could have tried to be happy for someone other than yourself. You can have it all now. This life is all yours, you can finally live it however you want. No more making me the dirt pile you are always kicking down."

I took a deep breath and watched him. "I wish you everything good and hope you find someone that is healthy for you."

Tears rolled down my cheeks as I shook my head. I

closed my eyes briefly, wiped the tears then blew him a kiss. "Goodbye Luke," I said just before walking away.

I got dressed quickly and made my way down the hall. Emotions began consuming me as I got closer to Jake's room. The memories of his life started filling me up. The love I felt from Luke the night we conceived him. We locked eyes after and somehow, we both knew what just happened. Quickly, four weeks went by and sure enough, it was confirmed, I was pregnant. I remembered those feelings like they were yesterday. Happiness and fear. Joy and sadness. The excitement but wondering if Luke and I were right to be raising this little one together. The feeling of question was instantaneous.

The memories of his life flashing before my eyes continued. I saw him. This little baby, this bundle of love and joy I was holding in my hands. There were no worries in those moments. My full focus was on giving this beautiful baby love and helping him build the best life possible. Quickly I saw a memory of him when he was four years old. We were laying on the floor playing with Legos. He looked at me with his beautiful face and said, "Mommy, maybe I can be a builder someday. I can build those big buildings that go all the way up to the sky."

"Sure you can, honey," I responded. "You can do anything you want to do with your life, always remember that."

"Anything, Mommy?"

"That's right sweetheart, anything."

Quickly I saw the next scene in my memories, tucking him into bed. He must have been 9 or 10. We were reading "The Magic Treehouse." The stories were filled with journeys through history. We read as though we were living the stories. With each one, we would pretend we were the characters making our way through.

Next came his first year in group sports. Jake had always been naturally athletic. From the time he could pick up a ball we started playing. Tossing around a football, playing basketball with the neighborhood kids. Getting a group together to have baseball games at the house. He was naturally inclined and good at every sport he tried. Then I saw the scene in my mind when he started drivers' education. I was so scared, wondering with every driving session, "Is he going to be okay?" Images, one after another, of every possible bad thing that could happen to him filled my cells with fear and anxiety. I worked hard to hide it, wanting him to only see the trust and encouragement I had for him. Watching the look of excitement on his face when we got him his first car was one I'd never forget. He was always responsible and grateful; I couldn't be any prouder of him.

He was so much like me in his demeanor, now in his senior year, getting ready for college. *Don't let this slow you down* I thought. He had so much potential in life and such a huge heart. Make sure he knows this had nothing to do with him Faith, I reminded myself, then slowly opened the door and peeked in his room. Instantly I was met with a smell of teenage boy and dirty socks from his football gear that was laying on the floor.

My emotions started to overtake me.

"What's up, Mom?" he opened his eyes. "Is everything okay?"

I quickly wiped my eyes. "Yeah. What are you still doing up?" I asked. Without giving him a chance to respond, I continued, "I'm heading to the lake."

"It was a weird night. I couldn't sleep. I just have a horrible feeling that something bad is going to happen today. I'm sure it's nothing," he contemplated before laying his head back down.

My heart sank further. Jake always had a keen sense of things like this, much like me. Could he be sensing what was going on, I wondered?

"What's up, Mom?" he asked again.

"Nothing honey, I'm heading to the lake and you were on my mind. This has always been our thing." I shrugged my shoulders. Then I got closer and sat down next to the edge of the bed.

"Yep, I get it Mom, but I really have to get some sleep," he said, then he looked at me and sat up quickly. "Why are you crying? What's wrong?" he said in a rather loud tone.

"Shhh," I responded. "Nothing, I'm fine. Let's not wake the house, okay?"

"I'm not buying it, Mom. Did you and Dad get into another fight?" He pressed for an answer.

"Honey I'm fine, just a bit emotional this morning, that's all. And I wanted to say goodbye before I left."

"You never wake me up before you leave. You're being weird, Mom."

"Really honey, I just wanted to see you before I left," I said, trying to convince him that everything was okay. Then I started back in. "Do you remember that time at Devil's Doorway when we got pictures for your sixteenth birthday? You were so excited that I let you make that climb." I shook my head. "And I'll never forget the first time you took me there and showed me the trails. We've had all good times at the lake, Jake," I insisted as I fought back the tears and any sign that there was something to be concerned about. "So many memories, Jake," I said, shaking my head again.

"What's this all about? Mom, you can't say *nothing*, I am not a little kid anymore. How about if I take the day off and go with you?" he asked.

"You will do no such thing, I'm fine, honey," I responded

with emphasis. Then I went in for a hug. He opened his arms. I hugged him for what felt like an hour. "All right, take really good care of you and have a great day at work." I knew in that moment I had to leave or he would catch that something was off. I kissed him on the forehead as I said "I love you" one last time before getting up.

Grabbing me on the wrist, making full eye contact, he asked again, "Mom, seriously, what's going on? You're really scaring me. Are you sure you are okay?"

"No worries babe," I said, as I leaned in, gently sweeping my hand against his face. I gave him one last kiss on the forehead.

"All right, I'll see you when I get home. I love you Mom."

"I love you too, kid."

Getting up, I made my way to the doorway then turned around and looked back at him. He looked my way, I blew him a kiss, winked and closed the door. Standing there, tears started to fall like a waterfall out of my eyes. It felt like my heart was being ripped out of my chest. *Don't hate me for this, Jake. I will always be right by your side.* Placing my hand on the door I said quietly, "You couldn't have done anything. God please make sure he knows this." I took a deep breath then closed my eyes, tilted my head back and let all of the beautiful memories of his life fill me up again.

I made my way down the hall to Doug's room. Peeking in, I saw him lying there sound asleep. I thought back to when we found out we were pregnant with him.

"How could you let this happen?" Luke had asked in frustration. Then he grabbed his keys and headed to the bar to drink his emotions away.

It was far different than the joy we both felt with Jake. I was on edge the entire pregnancy. Luke reinforced at every turn how much of a mistake I had made taking no responsibility himself.

How am I going to continue this with two kids?

My thoughts went to his fourth birthday. It was clear that Doug had a natural creative side from a very early age. We got him a set of pencils and a sketchbook that year to encourage him. He took a lot of pride in his work. I could still see the very first picture he drew for me.

"Mommy, look what I did for you," he said with pride.

It was an eagle soaring through the sky. "Wow, Doug, this is amazing. How did you get so good?" I asked him with enthusiasm.

"Do you like it, Mommy?" he asked.

"I love it sweetheart, it's perfect," I responded, then swept him up in my arms with hugs. I could still hear his giggles.

I thought about him and Luke building in the garage. They were making a wooden stool. It was his first experience with tools. I could see the pride on his face as I stood in the doorway looking at him. When he caught me in his vision, he picked it up and brought it over to me.

"Mommy, look what I made," he said with delight.

"That's great workmanship, Doug. Did you make this one all by yourself?"

"Yeah, mostly," he responded with hesitation as he looked back at Luke.

"Tell the truth, boy," Luke added with a stern tone.

He looked back up at me then quickly put his head back down and dropped his arms. The tone in his voice shifted to sadness. "Daddy helped with most of it."

I squatted down in front of him, lifted his chin and looked him in the eyes. "Honey, we all have to learn and it's okay to have help along the way, but we always still tell the truth, right?"

He nodded his head in response.

"Doug, look what you were able to do with some guidance from Dad. It's pretty remarkable. I bet you could do even more of it now by yourself than you could before, am I right?"

"Yes Mommy, I could do it all by myself now." The positive spirit came back to his tone. Then he threw his arms around me. "Thank you, Mom."

As I watched him sleep that morning, I knew he would be okay. He was the one I was least concerned about leaving without me. Doug was Luke's favorite; it was clear even though he never said it. I often felt like Luke was trying to live life through him. They had an incredibly special bond, much like the bond Jake and I always had.

"I love you, son," I said as tears dropped from my eyes. Blowing him a kiss, I closed the door and walked away.

My heart and body were feeling even more heavy with the emotions of the goodbyes.

Finally, I made it to Joy's room, then quietly opened the door and went to the side of her bed. Kneeling down, I watched her sleep. This little girl could bring peace to the toughest soul. It was hard to not be happy and joyful in her space. I knew from the minute I found out I was pregnant with her the power of her healing energy and peaceful presence that she was. The memories of her life filled me up. She was so spoiled and well taken care of by all of us. Jake and Doug were always on the lookout to protect her from everyone including Luke. I would often see the boys take blame for something Joy did just so she would not get in trouble.

Kneeling there, I cleared the hair from her face and pleaded, "Joy, keep the peace in the house. You have the ability to use your energy in a way I never learned how to.

You are the one that can keep them happy in this home when I'm gone. Stay grounded, baby girl, and know none of this was your fault. You couldn't have changed it."

Images of her first dance class came to me. I'll never forget how excited she was dancing around the house. The first time I heard her dreams come out. "Mommy, I'm going to be a famous dancer someday," she declared.

"Oh, yeah. You can be anything you want if you work hard at it, baby girl."

"Do you think I can be in movies, Mommy?" she asked.

"Baby, if you work hard and practice and keep the passion for what you do, you can do anything."

She would get so excited when I was able to break away from work and go to see her practice. Running up to me, she wrapped her arms around my neck with excitement. "Are you practicing hard toward your dreams?" I would often ask.

"I did, Mommy, I promise, I did good for you."

Each time I reminded her, "No Joy, do this for you."

I knew I had to walk away now. Joy was the youngest of the three kids. I often prayed that she would be okay when I was gone. I believed Jake would step up for me and make sure she was. "Be well, my baby girl," I started. "You're going to do wonderful things in life. I'll always be with you, Joy." Then I leaned in and gave her a kiss on the forehead. "I love you, baby girl," I said softly. I made my way out of her room, pulling the door closed behind me.

Taking one last look up the hallway all the life we had together flashed through me. Emotions stirred up the question *are you sure this is what you want, Faith?*

I quickly reasoned with myself. *It's just time, you're broken, you clearly can't fix yourself and the pain is never going away. They are better without you.*

Maybe even Luke can be happier without you here. All you do is frustrate him anyway. Not wanting to break focus, I started reminding myself why I was doing this. I thought back to how the pain, anxiety, edginess and nerves gave me constant discomfort. *Life is not meant to be lived in constant anguish.* Then I placed my hands together and blew them each a kiss. "I love you all so very much," I said just as I saw Jake open his door and look down the hall. We made eye contact. I gave him a wink and walked away.

I heard him following me down the hall.

Suck it up, Faith I said to myself. *Suck it up.* The words that had been with me since my littlest years. He can't see you like this; he'll know something wasn't right. I made it into the kitchen and started getting my things together as the coffee brewed.

Jake came in behind me. "Mom, I know something's going on. What's up?" he asked with a serious yet caring tone.

"Honey, I'm fine really, no worries. I'm just having one of my hyper-emotional mornings. It's the perfect day to disconnect from everything and re-center myself at the lake. Actually, it's divine that I'm going today. What a better day to be going to the lake than when I have stuff to let go of? I can get everything off my head and heart." As I said those words I thought *there's so much truth behind those words today.*

"Mom, why don't you let me come with you? You are always there for us. Let me be there for you," he affirmed.

"Jake you are one of the best people I know. I love you so much, thank you. But I will be okay. I need some alone time."

He stood there, watching, arms now folded. The look on his face was a mix of concern and question. I knew the look well from all the times I'd used it on him. "I'm not buying it Mom. Seriously, you're talking to me, not Dad."

"Hey now," I said in a slight scolding tone.

"It's true, and you know it."

Then I stood back, crossed my arms and mirrored the look on his face. I added a slight grin trying to lighten the mood. Then, I busted out laughing and turned to fill my mug with coffee.

He shot back a half grin and laughed. Then in a true teenager's words said, "On the real, Mom, let me come with you, I'll help. You know we would have a fun day together."

I've never said no when he had asked to join me for a day in nature hiking, exploring, and having adventures. Inside, in that moment, I so wanted to say, "Okay, let's go," yet knowing what today was for me, I couldn't let that happen. I couldn't let that be the last image he saw of me. "Jake, I really just need today alone. I have a lot to think through." I finished packing my bag. "Now, I really need to get going." I looked at the clock. "You know I like to beat the crowds. I'll text you when I get there, I promise."

Looking at me, he paused, arms still crossed. "Promise me you are going to be okay Mom?"

"Honey, I can tell you that I'm going to leave all of my fears and anxieties behind me today." Feeling the emotions building over never seeing him again, my throat tightened. *He's going to be so hurt.* My heart started racing as I felt the tingling coming up through my face. *Stop Faith, stop* I yelled at myself inside, trying to stuff it all down. *Don't do it.* Then I reached out to him for a hug. "Get in here," I said to him as I squeezed him tightly.

He hugged me back tightly, then whispered, "I love you, Mom."

"I love you too kid," I responded. "All right now, I'm out."

I grabbed my coffee, purse and keys and wrapped my arms around him one last time. He stood there watching me as I opened the door to the garage. I looked back, blew him a kiss and said, "Have a great day, babe."

"See you later Mom," he said. "I love you."

I smiled back and responded the way I did when he was little. "I love you to infinity and beyond, my sweet." Then quickly closed the door and made my way to the car.

I had had enough of the emotional rollercoaster that was my life. My strength was gone; I had nothing left. *Is this how people die? We all only get so much strength and energy in a lifetime, then when it is gone, you're done, that's it?* Sitting in the car, I pondered that question for a moment. Tears streamed down my face with thoughts of Jake still standing there in the kitchen.

He'll be okay, Faith I reassured myself. *It must end.*

CHAPTER 2

B acking out of the driveway, I stopped and looked back at the house. Jake was standing there, watching me through the living room window, arms crossed. I looked away as if I didn't see him. *I hope he didn't see the tears*. Then I drove away.

I thought back to all the projects we did on the house through the years as I made my way through the neighborhood. *How far it had come* I said to myself. What was once a little yellow dingy-colored Cape Cod house was now a beautiful two-story home. The gentle blue color highlighted around the windows. The soft grey covering the house with a bright red front door gave it the perfect splash of color. The young trees we planted when Jake was just a baby were now outgrowing him at a quick pace. All the memories of playing catch in the front yard. *God, please, hear me for a minute.* I looked up. *Keep them safe, healthy and out of harm's way. Watch over them and help them have a jubilant life. Take care of them for me.* I blew a kiss up to the sky.

Tears still rolling down my face, I got on the highway that led to the lake and turned on the radio.

Driving that morning, the memories with Luke and the kids played in my head.

My thoughts went back to the very first road trip we went on with all three of the kids. Joy was still so young. She was only three at the time. It was right after the cancer. I told Luke we needed to get away. I needed to revive myself before I went back to work in a few weeks. I was dreading that thought every time it came into my space.

We decided to take the kids to Florida for their first experience going to Disneyworld. It took me back to when I was a little girl, and the first time my mom and dad took me there. I knew it would be the experience of a lifetime for the kids. All the smiles and laughs they were sure to experience. Seeing Mickey and Minnie Mouse, live and in person...I was so excited for them. We were on the road early that Tuesday morning. We packed the car the night before to save time. It was still dark outside when we left. Luke carried the kids out, still in their jammies so we could get a couple hours of driving in before they woke. Shortly after we started driving, in excitement, Jake and Doug woke up. Joy slept almost all the way through Illinois.

About halfway into the trip our Explorer started making noises. Something was wrong. Luke started drilling me about what I did and didn't do in the general upkeep of the car. He was adamant that somehow this was happening because of something I did wrong.

"Luke, I told you a couple weeks ago that the mechanic said we should get the transmission checked out." I knew as soon as the words passed through my mouth, I should not have said it.

He looked at me with anger. "You never said anything of the sort. Don't you put this on me. And, in front of the kids. Really Faith? Why are you trying to knock me down in front of my boys?" he shouted.

"I'm sorry." I shut down and looked back at the kids with as much of a grin as I could muster. I could feel the emotions growing as I fought back tears then gazed out the window. Sitting there I wondered what would life be like if I weren't with him? *Are all marriages like this?* I quickly went into problem resolution mode and looked up a Ford dealership. "There is a Ford dealership two exits up," I said in a softer tone, trying not to trigger him more.

"What good is that going to do?" he shot back.

"Well, we should go get it checked so we don't get stranded somewhere," I responded.

"Mom, is everything going to be okay?" Jake asked from the backseat.

I went into my normal optimistic mode. "It will all be okay, honey. Life sometimes just gives us detours to deal with. It's all in how we handle them that really builds us into who we are and shows our character."

"What's that supposed to mean?" Luke replied rudely. "Is that meant to be a dig about me?"

"It is not all about you, Luke, I was referring to life and my outlook," I said, still with a calm, quiet tone, trying not to work him up. I knew deep down that comment was in part to show the kids a better way of dealing with things.

We made it to the dealership and found out the transmission was shot. After what felt like hours of back-and-forth bickering, I got him to agree to purchase a new vehicle, doing everything I could to have him take the idea as his own to help prevent future arguments. It was just easier that way. I watched Jake trying to shield Doug and Joy from seeing the conflict between Luke and me. From the time he was little he had a natural protective instinct.

The next couple of hours seemed to take forever as we got the loan and paperwork in order. When we were finally back on the road Doug and Joy were filled again with excitement. Now, with a new car on top of the trip to Disney, Jake had a look of sadness as he sat there staring out of the window.

"Honey what's wrong?" I asked him as I turned to look at him.

"Nothing," he responded with a quick glance at me before setting his sights back out of the window.

"Don't ignore your mother, son," Luke interjected.

"He didn't," I said, trying to protect Jake from any grief. Looking back to Jake, I said, "Hey." Getting no response, I gently said again, "If you want to talk about it, you let me know, all right?"

He glanced in the direction of Luke then back at me, gave a slight nod and again set his gaze out the window.

"I love you, kid," I said, gently setting my hand on his knee.

"Love you, Mom," he responded.

"Mommy, Jake okay?" Joy asked in her soft little petite voice and three-year-old structure.

"Yes baby, he'll be fine. It's just been a long day so far," I replied.

The tone for the rest of the trip wasn't quite the same after that. Luke was completely on edge and disconnected from the rest of us. He didn't want to do much. I tried my best to give the kids a positive experience whether he was with us or not. It was hard, though. I tried to have fun with them while knowing he was sitting there in the hotel distraught and upset. This was the first time I fully thought through each aspect of what it would be like if we parted ways right down to time with the kids and assets. Then it hit me. *Would I have to pay him alimony?* My heart sank as I recalled that moment.

Quickly those memories faded as I realized my final turn into the park was coming up. It felt like the fastest drive of my life. It was a sharp left turn as I entered the state park.

There was heavy fog that morning that started about

ten miles back. By the time I was at the lake it was thick. I could barely see the sign to the entrance. The path down to the parking lot was about three miles of long curving roads surrounded by steep cliffs. There were trees and boulders as far as the eyes could see. I had always enjoyed slowing down and watching the scenery as I drove in. With no one behind me, I had as much time as I wanted to slow down and take it all in. My last time coming into this most tranquil place.

The sun was just starting to peek up and shine through the fog. It was breathtaking. It appeared as though the sun was fighting to make its mark in the morning sky. Continuing down the road I saw the animals relaxed in their habitat. It was clear the chaos of the day had not started. By midday they would be well hidden from all the crowds. It was another perk of coming this early, before the crowds pushed them into hiding. The deer off to my right just stood there watching me as if knowing I was the one out of place, not them. A gentle smile came over me as I made my way down the hill and under the fog. It gradually started to lift, giving way to a glimpse of the lake.

An astonishing peace came over me as I took in a deep breath. Everything felt right being here this morning. I could feel it, it was the right time and certainly the right place.

My full attention, as I pulled up to the main entrance, was on my purpose for being there that day. The ranger had no idea. "Good morning," I greeted her with a peaceful smile, "it's a beautiful sunrise starting to make its way up, isn't it?" I looked off to my right.

"It sure is honey, that's one of the best parts of the job. I get the best view in the place. Waking up to the sunrise, there's no way to have a bad day. And you, my dear, are the first one in." She had a strong southern drawl. A happy, easy-going woman. She must have been in her early sixties. "You're clearly an early bird," she continued.

Seeing her name badge, I said, "Delilah, I bet you make everyone's day as they drive in."

"I sure hope so. Honey, when you get to be my age, there isn't anything worth having a bad day over. I lost a lot in my life. I'm just grateful for each day I get on this earth. What about you, what's got you up here today?"

"I needed to get away from all the chaos of life and do some hiking. I haven't quite figured out the philosophy like you have about not having bad days."

"You're still young darling. And if you are here hiking these hills, you sure got a strong demeanor. I'm certain you will figure it out. It's a great day for hiking, when the sun peeks the way it is. It's like the angels are playing in the sky," she said with animation in her hands. "Have you been up here before, do you know the trails? They can get tricky."

"Thanks, yes, my boys and I have been hiking up here for years," I responded.

"Oh, that's just fine honey. How old are your boys?"

"I have two boys and my baby girl. Jake is 17, Doug is 14, and my Joy is 12. Doug and Joy never enjoyed it quite as much as Jake and I do. How about you, friend, you have any kids?"

"That sounds like a beautiful family. I have six," she said before pausing. "Well, we lost our Mitch a couple years back. I also have seventeen beautiful grandbabies."

"Awe, you are very blessed too. Sorry to hear about your boy," I responded with care.

"See honey," she started again with her Southern drawl, "that's life though, you take it as it comes. If life was always easy where would the depth come in? I have learned to appreciate every minute of the time I get with my babies now. You never know how long any of us are going to make it. They love coming here just about as much as me."

I watched as she looked off to the lake and took a couple of breaths before placing her hand over her heart. I wondered what she was thinking. Before long she brought her hands together in prayer and blew a kiss to the sky. Then looking back to me, she said, "Sorry about that, dear."

"No need to apologize, I understand," I said as I tried to not show the emotions she just brought up for me. *She is a real human being. What would my life have been like if I had more people with that kind of energy around me?* "It's always a good day to have a good day," I said gently back, trying to keep some energy in the moment.

"That's a fact," she replied with the same bubbly nature.

These words I had spoken thousands of times in the past. Words I used to hide the inner discourse I often felt. "Even on our worst day, it's a good day," I replied.

"It's true," she commented.

"Well, one thing is for sure today," I said as I looked over to the lake and pointed. "With that kind of beauty and nature, it's sure to be a wonderful day for some hiking."

"That's a fact. You picked a nice one. It's not supposed to get too hot either. Enjoy your day and watch out for the snakes. We've had a couple reports of them this week." She verified my registration.

"Will do, thanks." I made my way to the parking lot.

It was completely empty which surprised me for a moment. I figured that there would have been campers here from the night before. Even better, all things considered, to have this time without any distractions. There was a clear site line from the parking lot to the cliffs, lake and sky.

"What a sight," I said out loud. If only I could live in this moment. Colors sparkling clearer than a rainbow, hues of pink, orange and hints of yellow among them. You could see a light morning dew on the trees. It was picture-perfect and would have made for a stunning print. My instinct was to grab my camera and start taking shots. For as long as I could recall, I dreamed about being a world-renowned photographer. To this day, it weighed on my heart. I often dreamed about traveling the countryside looking for new unique destinations, taking the most captivating photographs. Sights of nature from all different areas of the country. Combing the mountainsides for one-of-a-kind shots. Stopping to get tree and water shots in the most precarious of areas. And portraits of people in real-life moments, unaware that anyone was watching.

There is so much peace when there are no expectations of who you think you should be or how you think you should be acting. Just the pure trust in who you are.

Why did I set the expectations for myself so high? The one thing that always brought me joy and peace, I pushed aside. I shook my head in personal disgust. My dreams were of traveling, staying in the local towns along the way, getting to know the locals and businesses and exploring everything that the location had to offer. A lifetime dream for as long as I could remember. A swarm of self-doubt came in, reminding me why I never acted on them.

The comments from everyone along the way rang in.

"You're not good enough."

"It's just a hobby."

"You can't live that way."

"Get a real job."

And, the one that always hit me hardest, "It's time to grow up, Faith. Get your head out of the clouds."

Maybe everyone was right. I would have never made it anyway. I wasn't good enough to break into the space.

With a huff of my breath, I shook my head in self-disgust.

I blew it.

I dropped my forehead to the top of the steering wheel.

CHAPTER 3

Lifting my head back up, I yelled. "How did I let this happen?" I grabbed each side of the steering wheel and vigorously shook it. "Urgh," I grumbled as I tried letting the frustration out.

In that moment, thoughts quickly drifted back to early 1989. I was getting ready to start the seventh grade and was so excited about it. I thought for sure this was going to be the best year yet.

I remembered that summer like it was yesterday. It was one of the last times I was truly confident and had fun without the personal restrictions I put on myself. There was no overthinking or giving a care about what anyone thought. The neighborhood girls and I would often grab a boombox from one of our houses, go outside and build our own dance party. We would be in our front lawn for hours singing and dancing to Belinda Carlisle and other hits of the eighties. People were always driving by, watching and honking, but I never gave it a second thought. Even the memory of it today made me anxious.

I felt like I could do anything I wanted in life back then. The sky was the limit that summer.

As I looked back to all those years ago, I saw the people by the sidelines watching. They were making fun of me, and I never even saw it. I was oblivious to it. I saw them pointing their fingers and laughing at me. *What was I thinking? How could I have been so ignorant to it all?* I shook my head as a reminder of that thought and then reminded myself how happy I was then. *Maybe ignoring everything around you is just the right answer? But I would never do that to anyone.*

When I started school that year, I felt like nothing could slow me down. I knew what I wanted in life and there was no holding me back. *Life is a fun and exciting journey,* I thought. I had a strong belief that people were innately good and would never intentionally harm others. That year proved me wrong in so many ways. It was a huge lesson and wake-up call. I was so naïve.

I was jittery with excitement as Mom and Dad drove us to school that morning. "Who am I going to meet? What new experiences am I going to have?" I wondered. When Dad pulled into the parking lot just to the side of the school, my energy quickly shifted. I felt like I was going to be sick. My stomach churned in a way I had never quite felt before. Leslie, my sister, was sitting next to me. She never really liked me much. She was always complaining about having me around or needing to take me with her and her friends. I wanted her to like me. It never bothered me before that morning. When she shrugged me off on that particular day, I felt completely rejected. It was as though I could finally feel every comment she said to me through the years.

Fear and anxiety struck me.

"Don't come near me today," she started in with a snarky tone as she waved her hand in front of me. "I don't want anyone to know we're related. They'll think I'm weird and awkward, like you are."

"Leslie, be nice to your sister," Mom quickly snapped back.

"No, she's weird, Mom, and everyone knows it but her. Why do you pretend like she actually fits in life?" she snapped.

"Hey, don't you talk to your mother like that," Dad jumped in as he looked back at Leslie. Then giving a slight giggle, he looked back to Mom. "She's only joking. Besides, Faith could use some toughening up."

I felt my face start getting warm, and tears swelled in my eyes. Then Mom tucked in her shoulders and lowered her tone to Dad's comments.

"Create the day you want, honey," she said softly as she looked at me with a partial grin.

Leslie leaned in closely and said, "I wasn't joking." Then she pushed me on the shoulder before opening her door and getting out, slamming the door behind her. None of them said anything as she left.

Leslie was two years ahead of me in school. This was her last year at the junior high school. She was always the popular one with a group of people by her side. They would constantly be laughing and giggling at one thing or another.

In that moment, I heard the sentence she often said in a new way. It hurt in a way I hadn't let it before. I was an embarrassment to her. "No one wants to hear what you have to say. Just shut up and sit there," she would often tell me.

Shaking my head as I looked back on it, I saw things clearly. "They were laughing at people! She was laughing at me," I told myself. My heart sank.

Mom and Dad always provided for us, but they didn't have a lot of extra. Leslie often pressured Mom to get her the newest style and brand names. They didn't have the money that afforded those kinds of clothes but Mom wanted to keep Leslie happy so she still bought them. She would charge whatever it took on the credit cards to give Leslie what she wanted. It caused a lot of fights with Mom and Dad too. I saw how much it hurt Mom and I couldn't understand why she did it.

I sat there in the car as Mom looked back at me.

"Don't mind her honey, you just have a good day," she said.

"Toughen up, Faith, life's going to get a lot harder than this. You have it easy," Dad added.

Feeling that tears were continuing to build, I tried mustering up every amount of confidence and positive reminders that I could. I looked at Mom and saw her hurting. Instantly my demeanor changed. I knew it would brighten her up if she saw me happy. Pushing aside how scared I was, I looked at her. "It's going to be a great day, Mom," I said with the most optimistic tone I could find in that moment. Truth is, I wanted to start crying. I was scared, worried and anxious all at the same time. It may have been the first time that I felt scared about anything.

I watched the school out of the corner of my eye as my parents talked. I combed the lot looking for anyone I knew. *Please let me find someone.* Not hearing a word Mom and Dad were saying, I responded, "Okay, okay, I got it, now I gotta go," and then I slammed the door behind me.

"This is a whole new chapter, Faith," I said to myself. "You write the story." Just like Dad always says. I repeated it to myself over and over as I walked toward the school.

Dad was still talking but his words were a complete blur in my distracted mind.

"I have to go, I love you," I said as I kept walking.

"We love you too, honey!" Mom yelled out the window.

I looked back at her with a glare. "Mom, come on," I said. Then I quickly looked back to the school.

The closer I got, the more I felt my shoulders caving in, just like Mom. Looking up then quickly back down, my throat tightened, butterflies came and with it the churning in my belly. That feeling of wanting to throw up yet again.

"Why do I feel like this?" I asked myself. "Where is this coming from?"

Watching the kids walk up to class, random questions came to my mind.

"Love her jacket."

"He looks way too old to be in this school."

"Oh, she looks friendly." I gave her a smile and was reminded of everything Leslie said this morning as she lifted her nose in front of me and turned away as if to say, "How dare you try talking to me."

Shaking my head, I told myself in the most powerful voice I could, "Come on Faith, snap out of it. You're strong and brave." Then pulling my shoulders back slightly I continued on the long sidewalk up to the school. With my throat still tight and my chest now racing, I kept repeating it. "You are strong, you are strong, you are strong," putting emphasis behind each word.

"You got this, Faith," I said to myself.

Immediately behind it came the other voice. "Oh, no you don't!" It screamed with a stronger tone than the other.

"Just run. You're not strong enough to be here." The internal chatter continued, leaving me feeling even more uncertain about the day ahead.

I don't think I could have mustered up even a word in that moment, my throat was so tight. "How am I going to make it through the day, much less the year?" I wondered. I wanted to run and hide from everything and everyone.

"Come on Faith, pull it together," the stronger voice reminded me yet again.

I could hear Dad's voice: "Suck it up, Faith."

Then I stopped, took a breath, pulled my shoulders back and lifted my head. "You got this," I said to myself again in a calmer, more direct tone. After a couple of more breaths

I walked to the front of the school. I decided to wait by the water fountain hoping I would see someone I knew before I needed to go inside. I waited there, and watching the people and cars go by felt like forever. Where are all my friends?

Looking at my watch and realizing time was ticking away, my throat started to tighten again, and my heart was racing stronger than before. "Come on, hurry up already," I said to myself as if willing someone I knew to show up in that moment.

Then I remembered what Daddy told me. "Don't ever let them see you waver. When you do, you're done."

Watching all of the other kids go by talking and laughing with their friends, it struck me how alone I was. "Was Leslie right, am I the outcast?" I wondered. "No one wants to hear my voice."

Then a new question hit me, one I hadn't heard before. "Do I look okay?" Watching all the other girls go by in their miniskirts, skinny legs and perfect bodies, and here was me trying to play a part. Trying to look a certain way and fit in. I certainly wasn't a fitting-in kind of girl. How was I ever going to keep up with them?

"You are a heifer," came the other voice.

I had always been larger than the other kids, but it didn't hit me until that very moment. In an instant, sadness consumed my body. I could feel the heat coming up my chest and into my neck. My eyes were glistening as the tears started to fill them. There was no more shaking off what I was feeling inside. The internal critic was getting stronger and taking over.

My life flashed before me. I saw myself in elementary school, like a movie playing, but this memory was a different version. One I hadn't seen before. The other kids were pointing, laughing and whispering behind me. It was just like when we were on the lawn singing. "Have they always been laughing at me? Am I the clown?" I shook my head. "I always thought they liked me." I've been the butt of everyone's joke.

Then I thought about my mom. She was always on the heavier side too. In the second grade, I wanted her to come to school with me. It was mother/daughter day. Moms got to share what they did and joined us for lunch. The comment she made rang loudly.

"Honey," she said, "You don't want me there. All of the other kids will just make fun of you because of me. People will make fun of you your whole life, Faith. Start getting used to it. You just have to deal with it and protect yourself as best you can."

I saw how much pain my mom had recalling that. And I felt it as I stood there watching my life unload. I saw all the kids picking on me for my entire life. I heard the comments that I somehow didn't pay attention to before. My heart sank even further.

Mom went out of her way to get me the nicest clothes for the first day of school, and now I knew why. She was trying to help me fit in. She got me a cute mini skirt, pink shirt and little white tennis shoes.

"What's the point?" I asked myself. I didn't feel like me at all in these clothes. "I belong in jeans and a T-shirt. And running around getting dirty, finding new trails, not playing dress-up. Urgh, I wish I had my own clothes on, maybe then I would have more confidence."

Trying to build myself back up, it happened: the moment that shaped me and how I saw other people. My life was changed forever. There was no going back.

CHAPTER 4

"Hey fatty, go cover yourself," I heard a boy yell from the other side of the yard.

Looking around, I questioned if he was talking to me. How horrifying. *Please don't be me.*

Then I heard it again. Closer this time. "Hey, you, fatty, what are your ears blocked with, all that fat? Go cover yourself, no one wants to see you," he said as I caught a glimpse of him.

With his eyes now locked on mine, there was no questioning that he was talking to me. Looking around, I saw the other kids watching and laughing. I was mortified. Within minutes a full spectacle was starting around us, with other kids watching in. Each followed a similar pattern; they looked at him, then looked at me then back at him, and whispered back and forth. "Didn't they see me?" I wondered. "Didn't any of these kids understand how much this hurts?"

Now, standing directly in front of me, he continued. "Who do you think you are dressed like that?" With a pause he looked around the crowd then continued. "You're a poser. Someone your size doesn't belong wearing clothes like that. You're not a model. There isn't one person here that wants to see skin on someone like you. You should go cover yourself, maybe climb under a rock," he said, laughing out loud. Then he turned to the boy next to him and gave him a high five.

"Nice, dude," his buddy responded.

Clearly the cool kids, they were fit, wearing their Guess jeans, Ralph Lauren polos and converse shoes. Hair perfectly styled. They acted as though they were above everyone else. No one was possibly up to their level. They continued to snicker back and forth, and looked at me and continued.

"She's more like a beached whale," the boy's friend added.

Instantly I felt small yet in a large, oversized body. I wanted to die, I just wanted to die in that instant. What a horrible first day. "If this is what life is going to be like, I don't want any part of it," I thought. "Is this really how people treat each other?" I wondered. I could feel the sweat dripping down my back. The redness in my face, my palms sweaty and feeling like I could throw up. Then from somewhere deep inside I heard it. "Faith, don't take that, really, you're better than this. You're the one to show other people how to stand up for themselves. Don't take this." My throat tightened more. "Stand up for yourself," the voice said again, louder this time.

Then with a clearing of the throat I stepped forward. "Listen, we both need to go to school here, let's not do this," I said. Working hard to maintain my demeanor and remain unshaken, I paused and waited for him to respond.

As if shocked that I said anything, he paused and looked around the crowd. "Who do you think you are trying to tell me how to act? You are a nobody here, face it."

Taking another deep breath, I looked around the crowd trying to find someone, anyone, to get eye contact with and give me some sense of positive belonging. Then I brought the focus back to him. "Is that all you've got?" I stepped forward and lifted my hands in the air. "Dude, I have brothers. You clearly don't know what that's like," I said, shaking my head. "If you are trying to rattle me, you're going to have to bring way more than this."

It was clear he wasn't expecting me to say anything, much less stick up for myself. My whole body inside was quivering as I stood there in a Wonder Woman stance trying to stay strong. His tone shifted from cocky and in control to that of anger and frustration. Holding complete eye contact with him, I didn't move. He needed to know that I meant business and I was standing my ground. Our eyes locked, neither of us willing to stand down. He tilted his head from one side to the next as if he was about to say something.

Clearly rattled, he said in a frustrated tone, "What did you say to me?" Then he paused and looked around the crowd before starting back in. "Bitch, do you know who you're talking to? Don't you know who I am?" He puffed out his chest, again looking back to the crowd, then hitting it as though he was King Kong or something.

Maintaining eye contact, hands still on my hips, legs about shoulder-width apart, I took a couple of deep breaths as I stood there.

"Look, she doesn't even know what to say," he encouraged the crowd.

"Dude, I have no idea who you are and I don't really care, but I know your type. You're the full of himself, ego-driven, think he's all that, rude ass piece of shit, that's who you are!" Then I paused. Just before he had the chance to start back in, I continued. "You're the one that everyone's afraid of. Well here's the deal, leave me alone, you ain't pushing me around. And I'll do everything I can to encourage everyone I know to stand up to you right along with me, just watch me! To me, the way you treat people just speaks to your poor character," I said with directness in my tone. My whole body was shaking inside.

Standing there, he was clearly angry. I'd seen that look all too many times in my brothers.

"Does everyone just allow this?" I wondered.

"Who the?" he started to say, then looked around the crowd before putting his attention back to me. "Who the fuck do you think you are talking to?" He got right in front of my face.

"I am pretty certain I just answered that question. Do you need me to repeat it?" I said in a snarky tone.

Hearing giggles from the crowd gave me some comfort.

"Where are these words coming from?" I thought. Then I heard the voice. "Faith just shut up." But my whole body was telling me something else. "People need to know you don't have to stand for this," I thought.

One of the onlookers chimed in, "Girl stop, you are going to regret this."

There was no turning back now. I continued to hold my stance. I've seen that look before when my brothers and dad get into arguments. I knew at this point that there was no resolution coming out of this.

For what felt like hours he watched me up and down, looking away all but briefly, then locking eyes again. "Nobody, yes, that's you, nobody, and everyone is going to treat you as such this year, I will make sure of it. You have no idea what you started here today. I own this school; you better be ready for a rough year." He looked out to the crowd. "She's a nobody," he yelled to them. Then he turned his focus back to me. "See, the people here, they know to follow my rules, they do what I say." He waved his arms about. "You just started your sentence."

I looked out to the crowd with my arms crossed. I pointed to him. "This is who you follow?" I paused. "WHY?" I asked with emphasis. Looking out at them, I watched their expressions. I saw some of them look down. Others avoided eye contact with me yet others stood there with their arms crossed, clearly the followers of this guy.

More onlookers yelled, "Girl stop, he will bring everyone down on you."

Then I brought my focus back to him, guiding my hands outward from my chest, and said it with confidence. "Bring it, bitch!"

Oh, my goodness, Faith, what did you just say to this boy? Did I really just call him a bitch?

"She's fucked," I heard from the crowd.

"Yeah, but brave as shit," came from someone else.

"Or, dumb as shit," came yet another.

He's not one of your brothers, Faith, you have no protection on this one.

His face turned multiple shades of red as he stepped closer to me. The look on his face was one that said he wanted to punch my lights out. His friend quickly grabbed his arm and pulled him away.

"Come on man," he said as he looked at me, shaking his head.

The other boy pulled his arm away from him. "Let me go," he said, as he tried walking back by me.

Then I heard it from off in the distance: "Ryan, Mike," in a solid voice. I looked off to the right to see a beautiful brown-haired woman walking in our direction. Her strong stride said she meant business.

"Thank God," I thought. The crowd must have been over a hundred people, everyone watching in suspense.

At least I know their names.

It was Ms. Fritz, the principal. She looked at the boys, arms crossed, then looked at me. Her eyes clearly told all of us to stop. She brought her focus back to Mike and Ryan. "Is this really how you want to start the year after finishing the way you did?" She gave them a moment to think. Then, before they had time to respond, she continued. "If you want to start detention early, I'd be happy to write out an annual slip for you."

"Miss Fritz, we're not trying to start any trouble this year," Mike said as he pulled Ryan toward him. "You're not going to see any trouble from us this year."

Ryan's eyes were still locked with mine.

Mike was tugging his arm trying to get his attention off of me. "Dude, let's go," he said.

"How about you?" she asked Ryan in a firm voice.

Standing there with his eyes still locked on me, his face red with anger, I'm not sure that he heard a word of what she said.

She asked him again, in a firmer tone. "Ryan how about you?" Still, met with no response. She stepped in front of him, breaking the eye contact between the two of us. "Really Ryan," she said.

With his arms now crossed, he looked around Ms. Fritz, lifted his arm and pointed at me. Loud enough for the crowd to hear, he said, "You are going to regret this, little girl."

"Hey, you best leave this young lady alone, Ryan. That isn't the way you want to start the year off, young man. Walk away, Ryan," she said again, forcefully yet calm.

He briefly looked at her then abruptly pulled his arm from his friend before turning around and heading into school.

Ms. Fritz turned back and looked at me. With her arms still crossed she asked, "And who are you, in the middle of all this ruckus on the first day of school?"

"Um," I said, pausing for a moment, "Um. My name is Faith ma'am, I wasn't trying to cause any trouble," I said with a respectful tone. Then I raised my hand to shake hers as a proper introduction.

"I sure hope I'm not going to see trouble like this from you for the next three years, young lady. You sure do know how to make a first impression," she asserted.

I quickly responded, "No ma'am, I'm not a trouble starter. But I do believe in sticking up for myself."

"Well, I'm going to trust that that's the case. But I'll be watching you. I don't expect to hear about you again unless it's in a positive light. Now go on and get to class. It's sure to be an interesting first day for you," she said as she gently put her hand on my back guiding me towards the school.

Walking away, in that moment, I felt a wave of confidence. *You did it, Faith. You stood your ground, and everyone saw your grit and tenaciousness.*

Without another second to enjoy it, the reminder of what Ryan said came to mind: "You're going to regret this."

"What did he mean by that?" I thought as I made it to the front door of the school and started walking in. I had an odd combination of anxiousness and excitement in that moment. Down the hall I could see that all eyes were on me. I watched as they whispered back and forth, looking at me.

"There she is," said one girl.

"That's the girl that talked back to Ryan," said another.

"Better stay away from her or Ryan will make us a target too," came from yet another girl.

"Who is this boy everyone is so afraid of?" I asked myself. "Ugh, Faith what did you do?"

As I continued down the hall, I finally saw a familiar face. It was Beth. My best friend since kindergarten. We had been basically conjoined at the hip for all of our activities. We lived in the same neighborhood just three doors down from one another. Over the years, even our parents became friends. Beth was a petite young girl. She was often dressed in whatever style was popular at that time, but she wasn't ever rude or above everyone else. She was friendly to everybody. She started running toward me. As she approached, she threw her arms around me for a hug.

"Where have you been, Faith? I have been looking all over for you," she said.

"I was waiting outside, Beth. You'll never believe what just happened."

"Wait Faith, what are you wearing? I mean, don't get me wrong you look great, but you don't look like yourself at all."

"I know!" I said with emphasis, then paused. "My mom got me this outfit for the first day. I think she was trying to solve some type of insecurity in herself on me and help my first day go well. But with the way my day has gotten started, I sure wish I was dressed like me." I shook my head. "You're not going to believe what just happened outside." We started walking to class as I tried telling her what happened with Ryan and Mike. The hallway seemed double the size of our old school. Lockers lined both sides between the classrooms. As we walked, I heard comments and saw kids pointing at me.

"Look, that's the girl." Came from a girl off on my left.

"Girl, you are going to hate this year," came from another girl standing by the lockers. "I feel so bad for you," she continued, "you have no idea what you did."

Beth leaned in. "What are they talking about, Faith?"

"I was trying to tell you. I had a bit of a run-in with one of the ninth graders outside," I said.

"Faith, wait. What?" she asked. "That was you?"

"Beth, all I did was stick up for myself."

"Faith, why are you always doing this?" she asked in

frustration. "Can't you just keep your mouth shut? We're new to this school. We're supposed to just fly under the radar and play the game." Her tone got louder just before she said something I never expected. "Can you just for once keep quiet and know your place?"

"Beth, what are you saying?" I asked. "We always speak up for ourselves. If we don't stand up and hold our ground, no one would do it for us, right? That's the pact. And if not now, when?" Before giving her a chance to say anything, I continued. "Beth, you clearly have no idea what happened outside. What was I supposed to do, just let him stand there and pick on me?"

Watching her and knowing Beth, I saw the look on her face. It was one of care and concern, but that look didn't at all match the words that I heard next. Placing her hand on my shoulder she said, "I can't be with you today. I'll see you after school. You should have kept your mouth shut, Faith." She looked down and shook her head back and forth, clearly disappointed as she started walking away.

"Beth, where are you going?"

"You need to deal with what you did on your own," she declared in an even louder tone, clearly wanting the other kids to hear. Then she came in close to me and whispered, "You know, I'm not as strong as you are, Faith. He was right and you were wrong. That's it, bottom line."

My heart sank as I fought back tears. The one person I'd always counted on just turned her back on me. I could see the other kids watching and listening as two of the ninth-graders approached. Both girls were in the most current fashions. Their hair was done to style, with heeled shoes, short skirts and perfect slim bodies to match. It was clear they were the popular girls in school. "Great, now what?" I said aloud with a tone of frustration.

Standing directly in front of me, they scanned me up and down as though they were judging every part of what they saw. Then they looked at Beth with a smile, turned back at me, again with disgust, then finally back to Beth. One of the girls started in with her high-pitched snotty tone. "I'm Sarah and this is Amy. Want to walk with us to class?" Looking back to me the one girl, Sarah, she lifted her nose up as if saying without a word, "You're not welcome." They joined arms with Beth and started walking.

"Come on Beth, really?"

She looked back at me, again with eyes clearly saying something different than the words I heard next. "You shouldn't have disrespected him, Faith." Then she continued walking with Sarah and Amy.

The conversation outside with Ryan replayed over and over in my head. Back and forth my thoughts went. On the one hand, I was confident and grateful for being able to stand up for myself. On the other, I second-guessed every word I said, and shamed myself with disgust over it. "I just don't understand why no one has my back? Not even one person gave me an 'Atta girl.' I'm proud. Do these boys really have that much control in this school?" In that moment I just wanted to run away, never to be seen or heard from again, and then wondering, "How am I going to do this?"

As that memory passed my heart, thoughts were brought back to the present time. Tears rolled down my face. All I could see was that young girl who needed someone to have her back. She needed a friend yet was all alone once again. That little girl wanted to be seen, heard and appreciated for who she was, yet everyone was dismissing her and shaming her for using her voice.

Sitting there sobbing at the memories, even more swarmed in. All the other times in my life I felt dismissed and shamed in moments that I used my voice. My body sunk into the seat of the car. "You gave it your all, Faith," I said to myself, "it'll all be over soon. You don't have to feel it anymore, no more being unseen or unheard."

For a second, the thought of how brave I had been with Ryan came in. I stood up for myself. "What if only I would have built on that?" Not wanting to find any potential good in life, I recentered myself to why I was there today.

It was time. No more feelings of pain and unworthiness.

CHAPTER 5

S itting there, I basked in the sadness that I felt when Beth walked away that day. Random flashes came to mind of other times I stood up for myself. The other times when I felt strong and confident. With each one that came in, I actively deflected it as I looked for the negative that it caused. The people I lost, the looks, the disregard from others and all the anxiety it caused when I used my voice. It wasn't worth it, I reminded myself yet again. Going through my memory banks of life, I started looking for every instant I felt those feelings to further reinforce what I was doing here today. I saw it; one flash of the past after another when I felt completely unseen and unheard. "See, proof," I said to myself. "You don't belong here, you never have, you are a nobody."

And, in that instant, my emotions shut off like a light switch. "No more pain," I reminded myself yet again. "Not today."

Taking a deep breath, I brought my attention to the beautiful sky in front of me. It was as if I was looking at a picture, perfection. The circle of the sun shone with bright red, pink and deep orange hues. The sky around it was a tidal wave of colors on either side in all tones and depths. The water below gave the most magnificent reflection, as if the sky was looking back up at itself. Then with another breath, I took in the fresh morning air which offered a hint of s'mores and campfires from visitors the night before. The smells instantly brought me back to when Mom and Dad took us to the lake as kids. Weekends spent camping, swimming, playing baseball and singing by the campfire. A smile came over me in recollection of those weekends.

I continued to allow my thoughts to drift in those memories as I watched the scenery around me. It reminded me when I got my first camera and what sparked my love of photography. Since the earliest time I could remember, I was out exploring and watching out for the unique shots that other people missed. Then the freedom when I turned sixteen and got my first car. I was always out looking for new destinations. But with all the traveling and everywhere I have been, nothing ever quite compared to this lake, Devil's Lake, in the heart of Wisconsin.

Shots started coming to mind that I could get of the sky right now. These were the moments photographers waited hours for. Then I reminded myself, "That's not why you're here today, Faith."

Instantly my thoughts were taken back to high school.

It was 1995, my senior year of high school and I was so ready to be done. It had been five years since my first encounter with Ryan and Mike, and it was rough. They held to their word and kept people in my path to make sure I never forgot what I had done. There was so much pain that came from me standing up for myself, it made it hard to see any good around it. Even after they finished school and had moved on, their legacy was present. They made sure everyone in school knew I was not to be treated kindly. With each month that went by it seemed that they got crueler in what they said and did. I did my best to shut off the emotions, but the words hurt. Even worse than that was the feeling of utter loneliness.

Food was my escape. It helped me cope and felt good when I was on the cusp of chopping down a pizza or indulging in a bowl of ice cream. They were some of the only times I felt good. All the eating and hiding away in my room led to gaining even more weight. By the time I graduated I was nearing 300 pounds, giving the other kids still more reason to ridicule me.

College wasn't my path after high school. I didn't want anything more to do with school or the people in it. And I knew that I wanted to get as far away from this city as I could. When a conversation about moving out West was brought to my attention, I got attached to it quickly.

Here is your chance, Faith, start over.

I envisioned starting fresh in a place where no one knew me. Somewhere I could build a new name for myself. I thought for sure that people would be nicer and I would be free of the criticisms and bullying.

Boy was I wrong!

I was always a hard worker and saver. When I made the decision, I was even more focused on saving everything I could to make it happen. By the time I graduated, I had just over $7,800 in savings and a fully paid off car."

Before I knew it, my graduation party and official send-off had arrived. Mom and Dad invited everyone. All our closest family and friends were there. Throughout the morning people were coming in and out, wishing me well. It was interesting now as I looked back, I heard the compliments in a way I hadn't then.

"You are always so brave, Faith," said my Aunt Ginny.

"Oh, honey, if anyone can do it, you can. You are one of the strongest ones in this family" came from Grandma May.

"Faith, I would be so scared, doing this all on my own. I wish I could be more like you," one of the cousins said quietly so the others wouldn't hear.

I remembered thinking *why didn't they say these things sooner?* I shook my head. *I could have used the boost a long time ago.*

When my Aunt Betty arrived that morning, it was clear that she had been crying as I saw her walking up the driveway. I started walking in her direction to meet her. I greeted her with a huge hug. It seemed like it lasted for hours.

She abruptly grabbed each of my arms and looked at me. "Honey, I can't believe you're doing this," she said strongly. "How can you leave your mom and dad?" Then before giving me a chance to say anything, she continued. "First they lose two of your brothers and now you. Don't you understand that the girls in the family are supposed to stay behind and take care of their parents? Who's going to be here now to take care of your mom and dad as they get older?" Continuing eye contact, she paused, then gently placed her hands on each side of my face. In a more softened tone she continued. "Faith, you can't leave. You're the light in this house, don't you see? You're the balance that keeps everyone together. I know it's not always easy but good things are often hard."

"Aunt Betty, I'm not going to be gone forever. I'll come home and visit as often as I can, and Mom and Dad have each other. Besides, Leslie and Matt are still here. They'll have plenty to do when I'm gone, trust me."

It was interesting, sitting there in the car, present day, watching the sunrise and reminiscing this memory. I didn't recall any amount of hesitation or second-guessing as I spoke to her that morning. I was all in.

I continued to recall how Aunt Betty and I both paused as we looked around to the rest of the people stopping by.

"Where are you going to stay?" she asked.

"I found a nice apartment, a flat just off the Seattle Bay.

It's beautiful and I'm in the perfect spot to capture shots and quickly get around the city. I'm sure I'm going to meet some supportive people while I'm there too," I said with confidence.

"Don't you realize how much crime is in that area?" Betty insisted.

With a slight giggle, I responded, "Aunt Betty. I'm going to be okay. I know how to take care of myself," I reassured her.

She opened her arms and came in close for another hug. I saw the tears rolling down her cheek as I hugged her. Then I gently locked arms with her and started walking over to Mom.

Just then I heard Leslie walking up behind us.

Instantaneously, I felt myself starting to tense up as she approached. I don't think she ever liked me much, even when we were kids. I always felt like a burden to her. Nothing I ever said was right and if I took time away from her and Mom and Dad, I was sure to pay later. I always hoped it would be different as we got older but somehow, I thought it got worse. Even after all these years, I just wanted her to like me. She was my sister, after all.

Perfectly put together for the day, she started in with her snarky, better-than-everyone else tone. "Who do you think you are, Faith? You're not the type of person that can just move away and become a success. You're the one who's supposed to stay in the background and help everyone else shine. You are the puppet, always have been, always will be," she said.

Standing there, my heart started racing wondering if everyone else overhearing the conversation was thinking the same thing that Leslie was saying. *Is she right?* I recalled thinking.

Then she continued. "You're going to crash and burn, mark my words, you'll be home before winter." Looking to the rest of the family standing there she sought agreement. "I'm right, right? You guys might as well tell her, save her the agony of trying. She is just going to fail anyway." Then looking back to me she continued. "People who look like you," she said as she waved her hand in front of me, "Well, no one is actually going to take you seriously, you don't even take yourself seriously." As she chuckled, she added, "Well they may pay attention to how out of place you are. It doesn't matter where you go, Faith, you can't outrun who you are, irrelevant." She nudged her nose up in the air.

Once again, feeling worthless to her words, I stood there, speechless, my heart racing, on the brink of tears. I wanted to hide from everyone. *What if I just leave now?*

"Leslie, you stop that right now," Aunt Betty said with force as she stepped in front of Leslie. "Can't you just be nice for a change? Why do you always have to be such a bitch?" she said in a blunt tone.

"Betty," Aunt Ginny said with a scolding tone.

Shaking her head to Ginny, Betty continued speaking to Leslie. "Someday you are going to regret the way you treated your sister Leslie, you mark my words."

"Yah, that will never happen," Leslie replied.

Continuing to stand there in silence, I waited.

Mom, setting out more food close by, overheard the conversation and jumped in. "Seriously Leslie, you are going to do this today? Your Aunt Betty is right, just like I've told you before, someday you're going to regret treating people like this, especially your sister."

Leslie continued, "Don't count on it, Mom. She's a loser and always will be. No one has ever liked her, and no one ever will. I'm just the only one with the nerve to say it."

Still stuck, standing there, uncertain what to say, I wondered *why do I care so much about what she thinks? She has no care for me, she's a bully just like the kids in school.* Suddenly, it hit me. "You know what Leslie," I looked at her with directness, "at least I'm trying, at least I'm going for what I want in life. I'm taking the chance that you never did and you're jealous. That's what's going on here. What have you done since high school?"

Instantly I could see sadness come over my mom's face, and I quickly wanted to backtrack. I didn't want to hurt her. But the dichotomy was, I still wanted to stand up for myself. Looking back at this moment, I couldn't even imagine what Mom felt or what she was thinking. Her daughters head-to-head against each other.

Watching, I saw Leslie's face starting to turn various shades of red just like Ryan's did back in junior high. How dare I challenge her in front of the whole family, I'm sure was close to what she was thinking.

Then she started in again, quieter now than before. "Whatever, you know I found my love and got married."

"Ha," I remarked without another word, everyone around knowing it lasted all of six months. Still, deep down, I wanted her acceptance and didn't want to hurt her. I tried turning the conversation around. "Look, can we just have a good day with each other? You are my sister and the last thing I want to do is leave things like this," I pleaded.

"Whatever, I've seen what happens when people hang around with people like you. I don't need that image. Good luck," she said in a snarky tone as though implying there was no way I would make it.

Shaking my head, I turned my attention back to Aunt Betty. "See, it's time I get out of this town," I said.

"Honey, it's just your sister being herself, it's not a reason to leave all of us," Aunt Betty defended.

Before I had a chance to respond, Jamie arrived. Standing about 5 foot 9 with long, beautiful brunette hair, gorgeous blue eyes, Jamie was the one person who since the day I met her, I could always count on to have my back. Even when all the other kids in school were picking on and ridiculing me, she would stand up for me. She took on the wrath of the other kids, brought about by her association with me. Through it all, she was still right by my side. An avid sportsgirl, Jamie was fit, toned and often found herself in a pickup game of volleyball or soccer on the weekends. We first met about halfway through the seventh grade. She watched month over month as the other kids called me names, pushed me around, threw food at me in the lunchroom, and poured paint down my shirt in art class. I'll never forget the day she came and sat by me at lunch. Many of the other kids looked on with *oohs* and *aahs*. Jamie was one of those people who was accepted by everyone. As she sat down with me that day, I warned her of the possible repercussions. She quickly assured me that she knew what she was getting into. Watching her walk up the driveway that day brought a huge smile to my face.

Overhearing some of the conversation with Leslie she immediately started in. "Don't let her get to you, Faith, she is just dealing with her own insecurities is all. You and I both know she is not worth your time, energy or fight. You have far better things to focus on. Now get over here and give me a hug," she ordered.

"Whatever!" I heard Leslie say before she stormed off.

"Jamie, I'm so glad you made it," I responded as I put my arms around her.

"Of course. Did you really think I was going to miss

sending off my best friend? That would never happen," Jamie responded. "Can I steal her from you, Aunt Betty?" she asked as she turned to Betty and gave her a hug.

"Yes, of course dear," Aunt Betty responded with joy. Jamie grabbed my arm and pulled me over to her car.

"What are you doing?" I asked her.

"You'll see," she said as we made our way to her car. She started in with all the reasons I shouldn't leave. She tried persuading me with possible adventures together and trips now that high school was over. She brought up the idea of opening a spa, like she had so many times in the past.

I simply grinned and reminded her, "Maybe someday, Jamie."

"All right so, since I know I am not going to change your mind about all of this, I wanted to get you something to remember me. I'm going to miss you so much, Faith. Not sure what I am going to do without you here."

"Jamie don't even start with me," I said in a sassy tone. "This isn't a forever goodbye. Besides, you'll be off at school in Denver doing your own thing meeting new people and building new friendships."

"Yah, I know, but I sure hope we find our way back to each other someday."

"OK, OK, hold up, so here's the thing," I said. "I for one don't plan to lose touch so where is the problem? I'm going to Washington and you'll be in Denver. It's a short flight. And I'm sure we will be doing plenty of talking and texting. Besides, you are not getting rid of me that easy, girl. You're stuck with me."

Jamie laughed before coming in for another hug. "See this is why I love you girl; you can always set me straight." She hugged me yet again before opening her car door and pulling out a rather large rectangular box. Holding it for a moment, she said, "I hope you like it." Then she handed it over to me.

"What did you do Jamie?" I asked.

"You're moving on to big things in Washington, Faith, and I wanted you to have something. Well," she started, then abruptly stopped herself. "You just need to open it," she directed me.

I opened the box to a beautiful portfolio. Instantly a smile came to my face. I turned it over, and sewn in on the front was an inscription that simply read, "Have Faith." I felt my eyes start to well up as I stood there.

"Look," Jamie started back in to break the silence. "It has dividers so you can keep everything nice and organized just the way you like. It even has a pocket in the front for your business cards. You are going to be all fancy sharing your work," she said in a fun, light-hearted tone. "Faith, you do the most amazing work. I wanted you to have something to protect and carry everything in. Besides, you'll need something to store everything for when you visit me."

"Jamie, I love it, it's perfect." Then I paused and took a breath. I had so much I wanted to say yet held myself and the tears back, so I simply responded. "I'm going to miss you."

Before I could continue, she jumped in. "I know," she said, as if reading my thoughts.

We both opened our arms at the same time for another hug. "I love you girl," I told her.

"Ditto that, Faith."

"All right, I need to get to work. Call me when you get there?"

"Yes of course," I responded.

Then she quickly got into her car and blew me a kiss as she started down the road.

Standing there watching her leave, I asked myself *are you sure, Faith? Can you do it without her?* She was the one person whom I could always count on, my trusted sidekick. There to lift one another's spirits when the jerks of the world were tearing us down. The one person who always stood up for me in ways that no one else did. And someone who actually wanted to hear what I had to say. My voice mattered to her. In the swarm of memories, a tear started rolling down my eye. "I'm going to miss you girl," I said to myself. Memories of our friendship flooded my mind.

The rest of the party seemed to go quickly. Before I knew it, it was time for me to get on the road.

I gathered the attention of everyone still there. "A'right you guys, it's time for me to get going." Within minutes they were coming up to give me hugs and well wishes.

Dad jumped in as Mom packed me some snacks for the road. "Can't you leave in the morning? Get a good night's rest before you go. There are a lot of crazy drivers out there and you don't need to be out in the middle of it all. You're not in a rush to get anywhere, are you?"

"Daddy, the sunrise in South Dakota is supposed to be gorgeous tomorrow. I would wait but the rest of the week is going to be cloudy and overcast. I don't want to miss it. This is a great opportunity to get some new shots before I get to Washington. It's the perfect starting off point to build my brand," I pleaded. "I don't want to miss the chance; you understand right, Daddy?" Before he had a chance to respond, I continued. "I love you and I promise I'll be okay. You taught me well."

"Faith, the Badlands will still be there if you leave tomorrow. You could always stay for a few days until the weather passes to get a morning sunrise. At least then you are driving on a full night's sleep," he persisted. "That would give us the rest of the day together too."

As a daddy's girl through and through, the last thing that I wanted to do was disappoint him or tell him no, but this time, I needed to stand my ground. I gave him a gentle smile that reinforced my answer without a word. "Daddy, I'll be safe, I promise. This is the easiest stretch of the trip and besides, I am excited and wide awake."

Daddy was a strong man; he didn't show his emotions often. He served in the military late into WWII then served nearly thirty years on the police force. When you live the kind of life he did, you build a certain grit about you. A bit rough around the edges. Dad had seen more life than most people will ever get the chance to. I didn't see him cry often, only when he lost people he loved. In this moment as I was getting ready to leave, I saw the tears rolling down his eyes and I knew how much I was hurting him. I knew this was a tough one for him. He didn't want me to move but he also didn't want to hold me back from my dreams.

"All right honey," he simply said, then turned and started watching the kids playing in the yard.

"Dad!" I said in a rather firm tone before moving in closer with a smile on my face.

He turned and looked back at me, trying to hide the tears in his eyes.

As I got in front of him, I opened my arms for a hug and said aloud, "I love you Daddy. I promise, I'll be okay. And I'll come home and visit as often as I can."

He squeezed me tightly for a moment then let go before putting his hands on my arms. Then he locked eyes with me. "Faith, you have so much potential. If there is anyone in this family that can make her dreams come true it's you. But don't tell your brothers and sisters I said that," he whispered in my ear.

I giggled.

"You have everything in you to build the life of your dreams. You have more grit than most anyone I have ever seen. Maybe even more than me," he joked. Then he hugged me one last time before pulling a card out of his back pocket. "Here honey, this is for you."

I felt how thick it was and started to open it.

"Not here, Faith. Open it later after you leave," he ordered as he placed his hand gently over mine. I could see the crowd watching us. "Just a little something to make sure you are okay until you find work."

"Daddy, I'm really covered," I pleaded.

Before I could say another word, he interrupted. "Enough, what's done is done." He placed his hands on my cheeks and kissed my forehead. "Keep my baby girl safe," he said as he looked up to the sky. Then he briefly looked off to the guests still at the party, giving them a wave, and started walking into the house.

As I watched him walk into the house, his head hanging low, my heart sank at the thought of not seeing him every day, not talking to him while he was drinking his morning coffee. Missing our daily conversations of good humor and laughs after a long day of work. "I love you, Daddy," I said one last time, loud enough for him to hear.

I watched as he lifted his hand with a wave. He pulled the door open and went into the house.

Feeling the eyeballs of everyone still watching me and overhearing the conversations, I made my way over by Mom and quickly threw my arms around her. "I'm going to miss you, Mom. I promise I'll visit as often as I can. I'm worried about Daddy, though. Is he going to be okay?"

"Sweetheart, don't worry about your father. He'll be fine. Just be sure to call him every now and again, okay?" Then she gently took my hands in hers. "Honey," she said, "I'm going to miss you. Remember, you might have some hard times. Things may not always go as planned and it won't always be easy. But if you stay focused, you can do it. You, my sweet, sweet, baby girl," she said as she feathered my hair back, "you are going to do beautiful things with your life. And don't worry if it becomes too much, you can always move back home. There is no shame in that. At least you will know you tried."

Mom often gave me an out for not pushing myself. I remembered in elementary school when we had to run the mile. She thought I couldn't handle it because of my weight and the occasional asthma attack. She got my doctor to write an excuse so that I didn't have to do it anymore. I often wondered what would have happened if they would have healed the real pain and I would have learned how to push through the discomfort. Gritting through things now may have felt a bit less uncomfortable. I knew she was coming from a place of love when she did it.

As Mom and I stood there and said our goodbyes, I assured her. "I got this, Mom. I am strong enough to push through anything that comes my way."

She jumped in again. "Well honey, just know people are going to judge you. You are going to get picked on and laughed at. Protect yourself. It's easier if you just don't put yourself in situations that give them a chance."

In that moment I wasn't quite certain what to say. Every part of me wanted to push back and tell her that life is so much better when you are not living in fear, no matter how much discomfort it brings. I wanted to tell her how capable she was of using her own voice. All too often growing up I watched as Mom made herself small and backed down in the moments when I knew she had more to say. I saw the pain in her so clearly that day. I didn't want to hurt her anymore then I knew she already was, so I simply said, "I'll be okay, Mom. No one can say anything to hurt me anymore. I've heard it all," I said again, this time with emphasis. Then I put my arms around her and hugged her as tightly as I could. "I love you, Mom. Thank you for everything you have done for me growing up." As soon as I said it, she hugged a bit tighter.

She let go then gently pushed me backwards and gazed at me. She scanned each part of my face as I smiled at her. "Mom, what are you doing?" I asked with a slight giggle.

"I'm taking a mental picture. I want to remember every part of you right now so that I can lock it in and bring you up in my mind daily. I'm going to miss you, sweetheart," she said before putting her arms around me again. Then she placed each of her hands on my cheeks and pulled my head down to kiss me on the forehead. I watched as the tears started to roll from her eyes. "Be sure to call us when you get there, okay honey?"

"I will, Mom," I quickly responded.

As I walked to my car, I saw Daddy watching out of the window in the sitting room. His face resting in his hand, I saw that he had a look of sadness. I locked eyes with him then blew him one last kiss. Then a sign, first pointing at my eyes, then my heart, and then at him. "I love you, Daddy," I said, before turning around, opening my door and getting in my car.

I was so proud of that car. It was the first one I ever bought and I did it all on my own. I bought it brand new and paid for it within a year. A little pink Ford Aspire. I packed everything I could fit into it for my move. And sitting right next to me were my most important possessions: cash, my music and my trusted Canon with all the lenses. They were all I needed; well, and clothes, of course. As I sat in there getting situated for my drive, I opened the sunroof and the windows, and threw on my sunglasses. Digging through my music, I landed on Reba's McEntire's album "Starting Over" for the start of the trip. A perfect choice in reflection of my starting over.

Then with my music playing, I reached my arm out of the window and gave one final wave to everyone before I headed down the long, narrow driveway. Mom was standing there watching with tears rolling down her face. Aunt Betty had her arm around her, consoling her. As I got to the very end of the driveway just past the front porch, I thought *I knew he wouldn't let me down*; *he never does*. Daddy was sitting on the porch swing with red eyes and what clearly was a heavy-handed wave. I watched as he seemed to look directly into my soul. Then I stopped for a moment and blew him a kiss and nodded my head as though saying *I'll be okay*. "I love you, Daddy!" I yelled. "I'll be home soon."

Driving through town, I saw all the memories of my life. The old diner where Jamie and I would go and have milkshakes after school, dreaming big about being movie stars or singing on stage in Hollywood. The old tattoo parlor where I got my first tattoo. Mom and Dad were so mad. Lakeside Park and Main Street...oh, how I remember all the hours upon hours of driving that path on the weekends. In that moment, I asked myself *am I really doing this?* It was a wave of excitement and anxiousness all in one. Approaching the interstate, I took a deep breath as I turned on my blinker and started up the ramp. "It's my time," I said aloud, "nothing's going to stop me now." I turned up the music, hit the gas and headed up the highway.

Wahoo!! I yelled.

CHAPTER 6

B ringing my thoughts back, I felt a smile come over me recalling the excitement that I felt that day getting on the highway. Just as quickly they shifted as other memories came behind it.

My innate drive was to go enjoy the lake and get some pictures. The combination of nature and photography always had a way of taking my mind off the stress. My anxiety and life overall always seemed lighter after a day of shooting.

"That's not why you are here, Faith," I reminded myself. "Besides, you don't have time for that today."

"It's your last day, shouldn't you enjoy it however you want?" came the other voice.

"Don't forget why you are here, Faith," I reminded myself again.

In that instant, I saw beautiful flowers in bloom off to my left. The sunrise was hitting them perfectly, giving way to what could be a delightful shot. "Fuck it!" I reached in my back seat, grabbed my camera, put my sunglasses on and hopped out of the car.

Walking down to the beach, snapping pictures of the flowers along the trail, I thought *you spent way too long rushing your way through life. Enjoy this one, Faith.* As I approached, I looked up to see a swarm of eagles overhead. Stopping to watch them, I closed my eyes and put my head back. My hands naturally came into prayer form in front of my heart as Daddy came to mind. I could always trust in the fact that the eagles were right here and Daddy right along with them. I could feel his presence around me. There was no wondering if he was watching over me; I knew he was there.

"I gave it my all, Daddy, I really did" I said out loud as if he were standing next to me.

Then as if hearing what he would say in response, I heard it: "Suck it up and find your fight, baby girl." Those were words he said all too many times when we were growing up.

"I tried. It's just too much, I don't have anything left."

Not wanting to give more thought about how disappointed he would be with me, I gently blew a kiss up to the sky and started cleaning my lens. Feeling heavy, I fought back the desire to cry. Avoiding the emotions, I started snapping pictures of the sights in front of me and above me. The eagles somehow looked like they were watching me as they got closer. "I know you are there," I said as I felt the presence of love around me. Continuing to shoot, I thought about the messages I'd leave on the camera to explain each one. *I'll always be watching from overhead,* I thought as I changed my view to the sunrise. Continuing to breathe in the peace of that moment, I took more shots. The sky was radiant, all the colors of the rainbow coming through giving way to another message. "You were here with me today, for my final sunrise. Always know how loved you are."

In that instant, I crashed down to my knees as I thought about the love I had for them and yet the pain I instilled on myself with each mistake, each unsaid word and every missed moment.

My thoughts drifted back to the move out to Washington.

With my music turned up high and wind blowing through my hair, I had so much excitement about that move. I remembered the anticipation and adrenaline of it all like it was yesterday. The further I drove the more my perspective of life started to shift. Perhaps it was the realization that I was on my own. Or the wonderment about what life was going to be like in Washington. We drove this route a handful of times as a family but this time it looked different, somehow. I appreciated everything so much more intently. It wasn't just the drive, it was the experience, the emotional aspect of what I was doing. In what felt like minutes I was coming up on a beautiful large bridge that crossed over the Mississippi River, water on each side as far as the eyes could see. Big green bluffs covering everywhere in the backdrop. The sun was just starting to turn down from its peak; it was flawless. Nearly three hours had passed since I left the house, and it was still so surreal that this was actually happening.

Driving into that sunset, I felt the power of my dreams throughout my entire body, envisioning my life as one of the most famous photographers of all time, traveling the country fulltime to find some of the newest shots for my work. I could see it vividly, my photos hanging in homes and businesses across the country. Watching as I accepted the IPA award in the Nature category.

"Oh my gosh, it's really happening," I said out loud.

Continuing the vision, I watched my reaction as I got a letter notifying me that I was being featured in National Geographic's "Top 5 Travel Photographers" issue.

"There is no better place to make this happen than Seattle," I reminded myself. "They have one of the best art districts in the country. You are building your dream, Faith!"

With all the daydreaming, the drive to South Dakota

breezed by. It was nearly 12 a.m., yet it felt like only hours since I left home. The drive in was like a ghost town. Straws of hay blowing around in the warm summer breeze. Rustic wooden benches lining the walks, tie-up stations for the horses and the old swinging doors outside of the local tavern. The closer I got to my hotel the more eerie I felt. As I pulled up, my nerves were heightened even further. The old hotel had chipped paint, broken latches on the shutters and a flickering light out front.

"Okay, Faith, this is one of those moments. You need to turn off your creativity!" I said to myself as I sat there in the car wondering what I was walking into.

Possible scenarios started playing in my head. "What if I walk in and am never heard from again? Or a kidnapper grabs me from behind the garage? Or a bear behind a tree attacks me?"

Then I laughed out loud. "Oh my gosh Faith, seriously stop it." Shaking my head in those thoughts, I started getting out of the car. "This is really happening. I'm really here." I felt the excitement. "Ha!" I said out loud with emphasis. Nothing could stop me now.

As I opened the door to the hotel, a strong musty smell hit me. The interior looked like it was stuck in the 1970s. The walls were covered in lime green paint with diamond carpeting and a rustic-looking orange couch. Although it was dated, I was impressed by how well-kept and clean everything was. Then I felt it, the fun and laughter those before me had in this place. My creative imagination was sparked again in wonder of who it may have been. Perhaps it was the adventurous ones out hiking and nature-seeking. Or maybe the local couple that came for date night, or possibly the fellow dreamers before me, making their way through town.

"What stars were built from right here?" I pondered. Lost in thought as I soaked in the surroundings, the clock caught my attention. Shoot. It was already 12:30 a.m. "I really need to get some sleep," I said to myself, continuing to my room.

I laid my head down and as fast as I did the alarm sounded. Sitting up, it felt a bit surreal. "It's really happening," I said again. Working to wake up and get my bearings back about me, I stood up and started stretching. Arms out wide, letting out several big moans, I felt a smile come over me. Then the excitement rebuilt from the day before. Knowing the sunrise would come quickly, I got ready and was down at the receptionist's desk to check out.

I was met by a sprightly older woman. Looking at her name badge, I asked, "Sally, are there any good places around here to grab a cup of coffee?"

Looking at me for a moment, clearly wondering how I knew her name, she paused, then grabbed her badge as if just realizing it. "Sure thing Sugar, where are you heading?"

In my anticipation of the day, I shared, "I'm moving out West. I'm a photographer and am going to start my career in Seattle. On my way through, I wanted to get some shots of the sunrise over the Badlands. I've always loved this area and what better start than here?" I asked as I raised my arms, as if showing where I was.

"Well, there are some great places around here. You're probably in one of the best spots for it," she said.

"Do you know where the best spots are for the sunrise?" I asked.

"Sugar, you'd better talk to Bill and Joe about that one." Then she looked at her watch before looking back at me. "By now they should be down at the Stony Brook Café, just up the road. We're all early risers around here," she said.

"And, well, Bill and Joe," she added with a snicker, "those old-timers have lived here for as long as I know; forever, I think. If you're looking for the best trails, they're going to have some good suggestions for you. When you get there tell them Sally sent you."

"That's great, thank you, I really appreciate it," I responded.

She nodded her head. "What made you decide to move so far away from your family? I'm sure they're going to miss you."

I took a deep breath, gave a small smile as I looked down, then back up. "Well, I just, um," said with hesitation, "see, I felt like it was time for a fresh start. I just finished high school and I have big dreams. And to be honest, it wasn't the right place for me to get my start. Besides," I continued, "what better time than now to take a chance on me."

"Sounds like you have some big dreams," she responded. "You know you don't have to have it all figured out right now, right? You are still so young; you have your whole life in front of you."

"I know but, no time like the present, right?" Instantly I felt it, that doubt. *Is it right?* I thought as she questioned me.

"I guess, you do have to try," She responded.

"Yes."

"Well, honey, you better get on your way. If you don't get on the trails soon, you're going to miss it," she said before walking around the counter, putting her arm around my shoulder and walking me to the door. "The Stony Brook Café is just up that way." She pointed down the road. "Good luck with your trip."

Good luck I thought. *Is she doubting my ability?* I speculated.

"Come on Faith," came the other voice, "trust that she was wishing you well."

Shaking off the internal doubts, I started walking to the café. This little touristy town had so many unique opportunities for pictures along the way. I couldn't help myself but to stop and capture each one that called to me. I could feel the history here. There was just enough light coming through to get a good shot. The old wooden wheel leaning up against the side of the corner store. The old penny flattening machine. And those beautiful laid bricks on the road. There was no mistaking this town's history. Walking into the diner I felt so much nostalgia in the surroundings. For a brief second, I thought I was walking into the old diner from back home.

When I walked in, I was immediately greeted by the very friendly owner, Ginny. She welcomed me to have a seat wherever I chose. With her silvery gray hair, thin metal-framed glasses, she reminded me of my great-great grandma. "What will it be, honey?" she asked.

"Coffee, black, to go please," I responded.

Ginny was a lively woman, running around that diner as though she was a teenager. "What brings you into town today?" she asked as she buzzed by.

Again, telling my story to Ginny, this time about my trip out West, I was met with more questions about leaving my family before I jumped in and shared that Sally sent me to talk to Bill and Joe about the best hiking trails.

"Oh, this area has some great hiking trails," she added, "but you better get moving or you're going to miss it," she said as she handed me my coffee. Then she pointed to the corner table where two older gentlemen were sitting. "They're right over there," she said as she pointed to Bill and Joe.

As I turned and made my way to the corner booth where they were sitting, I passed several of the other townies having breakfast. In that moment, I sensed it. "They're watching me." Feeling judged, my confidence shifted. Instantly, I felt out of place and did my best to shake it off before getting to the table where Bill and Joe were sitting. "Hello, I'm Faith," I greeted them. "Sally from the old hotel said you may be able to recommend hiking trails to watch the sunrise."

"Oh, she did, did she?" Joe started in before turning his head back over to Bill and taking a sip of his coffee. Looking down, he shook his head back and forth.

Joe reminded me of my Uncle Dick. With an old camouflage jacket on you could smell the hint of tobacco and Old Spice. One change of his facial expression could take him from lighthearted to angry in a matter of seconds. Joe had a sarcastic yet firm tone in his voice. Not knowing him, it was hard to decipher if he was being serious or not.

He started back in with that rather serious tone. "Young lady, Bill and I've been in this town forever. There ain't no parts around here that we don't know about." He looked back up at me, then looked me up and down. "I assert you'll want a lighter trail," he said as he waved his hand up and down in front of me as though saying *the way you look, I'm not sure you can take some of the more intense trails.*

Immediately my heart started pounding again. I wanted to run, yet I didn't want him to see what I was feeling inside.

In that moment, an image came across my mind. It was me in the fourth grade. We just finished running around the track. I was the last one in by a large margin. Walking towards all the other kids as they waited for me, I looked up and saw them, pointing and giggling.

Bringing my focus back to the conversation with Joe, I instantly went into defense in that thought. "Well sir," I started, "while I appreciate your perspective, there's nothing that can hold me back. The more intense, the better. It builds grit," I said with force. "I know I have a few extra pounds on me but looks can be deceiving, sir. I can handle almost anything," I stood there with my hand on my hip trying to maintain a strong presence. I felt just like that day back in high school with Ryan and Mike.

"Well, all right then," he quickly responded, then went back to drinking his coffee.

"Don't mind him young lady," Bill jumped in. "So, what brings you around these parts?"

"Well sir," I started, "I'm a photographer. I'm headed out West, moving to Seattle. I've always loved it here and I wanted to stop to enjoy the sunrise and capture some pictures before I get on my way."

"So, you're a photographer, that's a fun hobby to have. But what do you plan to do for a living out there?" Bill asked.

Joe quickly chimed into the conversation. "Are you one of those hippie folks that actually thinks you can live without working? Girly," he continued, "haven't your parents taught you anything? Hobbies are all fine and good, but you can't make a living doing your hobby," he said in a stern tone.

I watched Bill sitting there, shaking his head. "Young lady, Joe's right. We all have to support ourselves in the world and make our own way. Do you really think you can make your own way doing this photography thing of yours?" he asked as he made quotes with his fingers.

Standing there I took a breath. Uncertainty was building again in my stomach, tightness shooting from my stomach through my heart and right into my throat. I felt my throat tightening as I tried to clear it. Before I had a chance to say anything, Joe jumped back in.

"See," he said with a rude tone, "you don't even have

enough confidence in yourself to talk about your ability to do it. How are you going to actually make a living doing this photography thing that you can't even talk about?"

I took another breath, thinking to myself, "You got this Faith, you got this, Faith." Then I turned back to Bill. With all my attention on him, I said, "To answer your question sir, I do, I really do, I'm good at it. I have a great eye and I know how to capture pictures in a way that brings in emotion. It may take me time, but I know I can do it. NO, NO, NO," I added with emphasis, "I know I will do it! I know without question, I can make a good living actually doing what I love and I believe more people should try." Pausing for a moment, I put my head down, then brought my attention back to Joe. "Sir," I started, "with all due respect, I do have confidence in myself and still, when we're doing something new it can be a little intimidating and I'm not afraid to admit that. You mark my words, I'm doing this. And, I will make a good living from it." In that moment an internal contrast of thoughts came to mind. Knowing in my heart that this direction was so right for me but wondering in my head *can I really make it work? Or, are these men right and I am totally full of shit?*

Joe jumped in again. "Well girlie, let me tell you this, if you're going to make it in this photography thing of yours, you best get more self-confident. Ain't no one going to buy something from someone who doesn't believe in themselves. And, another word of advice from someone that's been in this world for a lot longer than you," he continued as he points to himself, "people don't want to buy from someone looking like they don't even take care of themselves."

My heart was pounding at this point.

"You best start taking care of you first," he said as he waved his hand again up and down towards me. Then he turned back to his coffee.

The emotions inside me were growing rapidly. I was ready to scream, cry and run out of the door all at the same time not quite knowing how to respond.

Bill turned and smacked Joe on the shoulder then looked at me and said, "Don't mind the likes of him, young lady. You stay focused on what you want to do. You may never make a living at it but hey, what do we know."

Just then Ginny walked up. "Joe, why do you always have to be such a jerk?" she scolded him. "Just because you didn't go after what you wanted in life doesn't mean everyone else should have to live with it. And the two of you old grouches, seriously, not even being able to see the possible with this young lady."

"Look at me for example," she said boldly before pausing for a minute. "How many people told me that I would never have a chance with this café?" she continued in a loud overtaking tone as she reached out her arms out as though saying *look at this place.* "Forty-two years ago, everybody told me I was crazy. "See honey," she looked at me and said, "you just gotta be all in with whatever it is you want from life. You have to believe in yourself and stick with it. It'll come." Turning to Joe and Bill she continued. "Now come on you two, let's help this young lady get to where she's going so she doesn't miss her sunrise."

"Oh Ginny, calm down," Joe said before turning his focus to me. "And, you young lady, suck it up, you don't need to be getting all emotional on us. I'm just giving you real talk the way everyone should. I love people of all sizes but no sugarcoating. I've been around this world way too much to sugarcoat shit." Clearly still stewing in Ginny's comments, he shook his head. "Now tell us some more about the view you're looking for."

As I stood there trying to collect myself and hold it

together inside, I thought, "It's no different than it was back home. Is this really going to be how life is? Am I always going to be labeled as the fat girl with everyone looking down on me? Why should I even bother?" I asked myself. Then a little voice inside even deeper kicked in. "Stop It, suck it up and let's do this, Faith." Then with a breath, I turned back to Joe. "I'd like to find somewhere that gives the view of the full Badlands. I envisioned the sunrise coming right up over the top. Maybe if there's a spot that has a unique rocklike structure or even spots of water. Are there any places similar to that?" I asked.

Bill turned and looked at Joe. "You should tell her about Castle Point Trail," he said.

Joe looked back at him, clearly still salty. "What, you think I don't know what I'm doing either?" he asked. Then turning back to me, he asked, "Did you get a map of the trails, girlie?"

"Yes, I have one," I said as I pulled it out.

"Castle Point is the best trail 'round these parts. It's about a mile and a half in from the entryway of the park. The hike is a bit tricky with some steep drop-offs." Looking at his watch, he added, "I am not sure you can make it there at this point."

"We have a lot of memories hiking out that way, don't we Joe?" Bill chimed in. "Remember that time in 1972 when we took the girls out there?"

Joe quickly interrupted him. "Bill, this girl doesn't care about our stories."

"Actually sir, if I had more time this morning, I'd love to listen in," I responded with a soft smile at Bill.

"Now girlie," Joe said directly, getting my attention, "listen here and listen closely. There are a lot of scary things that happen along these parts. You need to watch out for yourself. And don't trust anyone, except for yourself." He stopped as he pointed at me. Then he finished drawing the line on the map to Castle Point as he gave me the directions.

Standing there trying to listen, emotions about how small I felt continued to build. How insignificant my voice was, and how fat I was. Every thought of disempowerment screaming through my whole body. I just wanted to run. "Come on, come on, get on with it," I thought. The enjoyment of why I was there that morning faded even faster as I felt the eyes in the café still stuck on me. I pictured them behind me laughing, giggling and pointing just like all the times in school.

"Did you catch all that?" Joe asked.

Being met with no response, he asked again. "Did you catch all that? Hey, where you at?" I finally heard him as he snapped his fingers in front of my face. "Oh you're one of those, a daydreamer too, huh."

"Joe, would you leave this young lady alone already? She doesn't need any of your shit," Ginny said.

He asked yet again. "Did you catch all that?"

"Yeah, yeah, yeah, I got it, I got it," I told him as I looked at the map and saw the track he had drawn out for me. Clearly knowing that was all I needed and still fighting back the tears and emotion I was feeling, I held it all back just as I had so many times in the past. "Well thanks for all your help. I'm going to get on my way then."

Clearly hearing something was wrong, Ginny asked, "Are you okay, honey?"

"Yeah, I'm good," I said as I smiled and started folding the map. "I just don't want to miss the sunrise, is all."

She freshened up my coffee as she said, "Don't mind those old-timers, honey. They got something to say about everybody. It doesn't make them right."

Wanting to believe her words I knew my faults; they were just telling me what I already knew which made it easier to fall into the negative self-talk. I wanted so much to tell her how scared I was and yet held back for the sake of not wanting to be judged even more. "She's too soft," I heard another comment come in, as I recalled my grandma yelling at my mom about me. "You should trade her in for one that works," came another comment. Trying to stay present to the moment and just get out of that place, I thanked her again as she threw her arms around me.

"Good luck honey, you're going to do great," she said, encouraging me.

My thoughts continued down the rabbit hole of despair. *Am I kidding myself? Is any of this really possible?* I asked myself. My confidence was being tested from this experience. I walked out of the door and made the short walk back to the hotel as I went back and forth in my mind trying to reason with myself about what was right or wrong. *Am I kidding myself or not?*

With what felt like an emotional daze, I got back to my car and made my way to the entryway of the hiking trails. When I got there and saw the beautiful view in front of me, I was instantly reminded of why I was here and what I was out to achieve. This was the view everyone should see. Badlands spanning on both sides in front of me. The glimpse of light starting to shine slightly from underneath was nature's sign that the sun was getting ready to rise. I got out of my car and took a deep breath as I stood in the peace of it all, the negative thoughts dissipating as I did. After a few minutes, I threw on my sack, laced up my tennis shoes and started making my way down the trail.

Although I didn't want to admit it, Joe was not kidding about the terrain. In the dark morning skies I carefully made my way down the short declines then climbed up larger inclines. The soft light of the moon led the path on the trail. From one rock formation to the next, around one curve through the beautiful boulder archway just as Joe mentioned, it was a great way to keep my mind off the emotions of life. One last jaunt upward before making a left turn and arriving at Castle Point. The view when I got there was breathtaking. The rock formation was like a large picture frame with a flat rock underneath. It was the perfect place to set up my tripod and camera. Another rock behind it left for the perfect stoop to sit on as I waited for the sun to peak.

I put my elbows to my knees then followed with my hands in a prayer position, gazing into the view before me. For a moment, my mind was free of any thoughts, simply lost in the view.

Then without warning, I felt the tears start rolling down my face. Joe's words rang through my mind. They were words I had heard hundreds of times before yet still stung the same. As if in rapid fire, I heard them over and over from each person, stacking one memory on top of the next.

"Fatso," came one.

"You should go on a diet." Yet another.

"Why would anyone want to give you attention, you don't even give yourself attention." And, yet another.

"Fatty fatty two by four can't fit through the kitchen door." Seemingly friendly people and foes alike.

"You are worthless, Faith." From some of those closest to me.

As the words kept hitting over and over, I wondered what everyone in the café was saying as their eyes were fixated on me. *Were they the same judgmental things as the others?* I wondered.

Then I felt it, the throat tightening, chest pounding,

face warm with the emotions, hearing that voice, yet again: "You are so insignificant. A big fat nobody." I said to myself, "What's the point in all of this, really? You aren't fooling anyone, Faith, it's clear."

"Stop." I tried to shut off the voices.

Stronger than I was in that moment, they continued. "You should have believed Leslie, she said it, she has for years, you're worthless."

"Faith, come on, let it go. You are doing it, you are here." I tried again to remind myself.

Then I heard it, one I don't remember hearing before. "There is no point in living, you are never going anywhere. No one really wants you here, anyway." Tears streamed steadily down my face.

Wait, what? Faith, come on, pull it together!

"Maybe I should just end it all, be gone," came the louder voice again.

Then in that moment, it happened. All my thoughts broke away as I watched the sun rise over the Badlands.

CHAPTER 7

S itting there on the beach, I watched the eagles. "I didn't remember that." I recalled wanting to disappear and end it all, even back then.

"I bounced back so quickly that morning." I reminded myself of the grit and strength I brought behind that morning sunrise in the Badlands.

Did I really ever let all of the negative stuff go? Have I been hanging onto it this whole time? Maybe I wasn't as strong as I always thought myself to be?

"Huh," I said, out loud.

Then quickly a smile came over me as I reminded myself of the no-fear attitude I had when I decided to move out West. The "watch me" conversations I had with Joe and Bill that day not to mention all the others like them. The experiences I built in that period of my life. Pulling my knees in closer, I shook my head. "I felt alive back then."

"The train has left the station, Faith, you missed the chance, it's gone forever," I said out loud, not caring who may be listening in. "I gave up on myself and my dreams a long time ago." I realized that I'd stopped trying. With tears starting again, I sat with that thought.

"It's time to be done, get moving Faith," I told myself, then I looked up to the sky and put my hands in a prayer position. "If anyone's listening, watch over them for me." Then I blew a kiss up to the sky and headed back to my car.

Other memories of the grit, strength and determination I've displayed in life filled me up. "Where did it go?" I asked myself. "Did I ever really have it?" Reaching into my car and grabbing my phone, I was quickly reminded of how little of a fight I had left as I saw seven missed calls from Luke. "You're not taking this day away from me," I said out loud with emphasis as I felt my heart starting to race. "I let you fill my head and heart for way too long. Today is mine, you can't have it," I continued with conviction. The confidence I had in my voice was a rush. "Why can't I be this strong when I'm with him?" I wondered, shaking my head. "Great, now I feel empowered. I'm done feeling like a puppet to anyone. No more being told to shut up or how wrong I am every time I use my voice. He can be a miserable old man without me by his side."

Yet, still caring about his health, happiness and well-being I asked, "Will he be okay?" Then I reminded myself, "This is why it needs to be this way, Faith. You'll never leave. This is the only way to be free of the pain." With another deep breath, I unlocked my phone and turned on the video so he could see my pain for a change. "Good-bye Luke. If only you could have loved me as much as I loved you." Shaking my head, I stopped the recording and quickly hit send.

Instantly I saw more messages coming through, one text after another. "What do you mean? What are you saying?" he asked.

Now you care I thought as I shook my head before putting the phone back in my sack. Then I grabbed my camera, propped it up on top of the car and aimed as best as I could at myself. With my remote in hand, I started by putting my hands in the shape of a heart, then snapped four pictures, one pointing at my eye, another at my heart, yet another pointing back at them and finishing with the blow of a kiss. I quickly wrote a note to Jake asking him to develop the pictures and leaving my thoughts about each before taking the camera and the note and setting them on the driver's side seat. Then I grabbed the envelope meant for whomever found my car and set it on the steering wheel. Written on the front were two words, "Open Me." Inside were instructions on where to find me, who I was and how to get in contact with my next of kin.

Reaching over to the other side of the car, I grabbed the rest of the letters before making my way to the mailbox. Looking around, I thought *where is it? I know I saw it around here somewhere.*

Still looking, I heard my phone ding, ding, one after another they continued. I stopped, took the phone out and saw 13 missed calls and two more texts. They were coming from everyone, Luke, Jake, even Mom. Shaking my head, I turned it to silent, cleared all the messages and kept going. "What's done is done," I reminded myself. "They will know everything soon enough when they get the letters. There's no turning back now." I walked towards the gate, still looking for the mailbox.

Holding the letters close to my heart, I made prayers over each.

"God, I know I haven't exactly been present to you often but please, hear me on this one," I said.

First, for my kids leaving, a blessing and wishes for their wellbeing, stories about our lives together, memories of the fun times, reminders of how much they mean to me, and reassurance that I will always be by their side in spirit. Included in it, a plea to them: "Please know none of this was your fault. I simply did not have the strength to carry on anymore." Each one was signed with love.

"God, please, they need to know this had nothing to do with them."

Then a letter for Luke, the love of my life, even in our worst times no matter how bad things got, he was the one I would never leave until, well, as committed by marriage, till death do us part, reminding him how much good I know he had inside. Asking him to look deep, get outside of himself and support my kids as they continued into adulthood. *I love you Luke, always have, always will.*

"God, he needs to know, I created this, it wasn't his fault, it was always my choice."

Next, a letter to my boss and the owner of the company. Recommendations for a better work strategy. Stronger support for the humans behind the work. Letting them know all the times I showed signs, I was screaming for help and nobody cared. All the pushing for better numbers and more performance, losing sight of the impact on people along the way. A simple message: do better.

"Lord, he's pretty sure of himself, he will know it's not him, but my ask could help him to realize the people behind the work, that's who need attention. Show them empathy and care."

Finally, one for my mom. A request that she finally forgive herself and start seeing all that she could do if she wanted. Letting her know that I always believed she did the best she knew how with us kids. Asking her to finally work through the pains she felt in life.

"God, give her the gift of forgiveness."

Each letter was signed with love and my reasons why it needed to happen this way. Telling them that one day they would understand. Holding them tight by my heart, I said one final prayer over them. "Lord hear me, see over my family, help them see the light and the joy that life really is. Let them know how much I care, how much I've always cared. Help them understand that this hurt was all mine to bear. Let them know, let them feel, that I will always be with them." I gently wiped away the tears rolling from my eyes and kept going.

Deep down I knew how much I was letting them down and hoping that at some point they would forgive me.

Anxiousness and emotions started making their way up my chest right into my face. It must have been bright red at this moment. The decades of memories playing through my mind. Reminiscences with the kids playing and reading, childbirths, growth in my career, marriage. "Am I really ready to step away from it all?"

Do I really want to put it all behind me?

Will they be okay?

The other voice arrived. "They'll be fine, Faith, they're old enough to fend for themselves now. It's time to go."

With a tear rolling down my face I knew that I didn't want to fight anymore. A sense of support came over me. It was as though something or someone was there with me. I had a strange sense of someone holding me, which gave me peace.

Then I saw the mailbox and was reminded of how close it was to the ranger station. "Shit," I thought. "Pull yourself together" came next. "This one is smart and cares. If she senses anything, you're in trouble." Breathing deeply, I thought about the serene day, the sunrise; these thoughts could always center me. "You are a strong, healthy woman. Let her see your energy and stamina. She will never suspect a thing," I said to myself.

I saw her waving out of the ranger station as I approached. Peeking her head out, she yelled, "Everything all right, honey?"

"Yes, just have a few letters I forgot to mail on my way in this morning," I responded in a clear, patient tone.

Looking closer she said, "Honey are you okay?" She had more concern in her tone. "You look like you've been crying. I know that look well from my own girls."

"Tell her, Faith, tell her what is really going on. Maybe she is the one to help." Quickly I redirected that thought and started in with an answer to assure her that I was okay. "Yes, ma'am, I am fine, just worried about my aunt, I heard she was in an accident."

She got out of the ranger station and made her way over to me. "Is she going to be okay?" she asked with concern.

"I sure hope so," I continued the lie. "She was in a pretty severe car accident. It sounds like some broken bones, ribs, she's out of ICU, but it sounds like it's going to be a pretty long road ahead for her."

"Well honey," she started again, "the good news is that we can repair bones, we can replace cars, at least she's alive. And no matter the road ahead, I'm sure you'll be there to support her."

"Of course." I responded with as much conviction as I could muster in that moment.

"Can you go see her? Is she close?" Delilah asked.

"No, she's down in Louisiana. I'll be able to go in a couple weeks. My mom is there with her now. We have a lot of family down in those parts."

"Well, I'll keep her in my thoughts," she genuinely responded.

"Thank you. I'm going to get on with my hike." I pointed in the other direction towards the eastern trail.

"You stay safe out there, honey, and don't let the emotions get the better of you. Those trails can get rough," she pleaded.

"I'll be good, thanks. Have a good day." I threw the letters in the mailbox, blew a kiss to the sky and walked away.

"Why is it in the hardest of times some of the nicest people come out?" I wondered as I made my way to the east trail entrance. "Where was this type of care and support for the last thirty years? All the years I had hoped someone would be there to pull me off the ledge, now in my final hours she appears." The years of loneliness had taken way too much toll. "There is no turning back now."

Coming up on the entrance to East Bluffs, I knew it was time to start building some stamina and energy if I was going to make it up all the way. The initial incline could get rough and rocky fast. I knew without the right mindset it would be a challenge. I wished I would have brought my headphones so I could crank up some music and get lost in the climb. As the incline was starting, I stopped for a moment, then turned around to get one last view of the water. The sunrise was climbing even brighter above it. I took it all in for a second, then with a deep breath brought my focus back to the trail and started stretching out my legs.

Standing there, I worked to stretch each side. First the left, then the right, then changing to a wide squat formation working more to loosen and warm things up. Transitioning into a boxer shuffle I started shaking out my arms and did some side twists to finish up. Just as I did, I heard someone coming up from behind me, unexpectedly.

"Looks like you're getting ready to start up the trails, huh?" a nice man's voice came from behind me.

After a brief pause, I looked at him. I turned back around, kept stretching, and responded with my back towards him. "Yes, just warming up."

"It's a great day for it," he continued, "and this hike, well it's worth every step. Have you done it before?"

"I have, quite a few times," I responded with a slight

giggle as if implying that he should have figured that out on his own.

"Nice," he responded with emphasis. "It's only my second time up here but it's going to be a regular occurrence moving forward. I enjoyed it so much the first time. It took all of my stress away." He looked around. "It looks like you're alone up here today too. Would you like some company?" he asked politely.

He was a rather good-looking man, about my age and easy on the eyes for sure. Well-built, 6'3" and maybe 210, all muscle, with beautiful hazel eyes. My heart got a patter when I looked at him. I was certain in that moment that he would have made good company. Thoughts quickly came in about what the day would be like having someone to listen and chat with. Maybe even genuinely care. "Thanks for the offer, I appreciate it, but I'll be writing here today. And I have a lot of stops to make. Another time perhaps," I offered, fully knowing today was my last day here.

"Um," he said with a long pause, "are you politely blowing me off, or do you mean that?"

Shocked at the fact that he was bold enough to ask, I turned around, looked directly at him, then shook my head. Letting out a brief sigh, I responded, "Fine. We will probably never see each other again. Okay?" I said with a snarky tone.

"Why are you so fast to turn down company?" he asked.

I continued to lock eyes with him. "Why are you so fast to ask for the company of a complete stranger and a woman nonetheless?" Then being bold, I added, "is this your normal pick-up spot on the weekends?"

"Touché," he responded. "No ma'am, it's not like that at all, I just felt like we could make good company for each other today. That's all, no motives, nothing else."

Looking at him again with confusion in silence, I thought, "What should I do?" Then it came to me. I wondered, "Did he not see the wedding ring on my finger? Did he not care?" I knew I put it on this morning, then I looked at my hand, then again back up to him.

As though reading my mind he jumped back in with emphasis. "Really, there is no motive, no ill intent, just good company."

Without a response, I gave him another strange look, then started making my way up the trail. "So, what's your name, stranger?" I asked with my back towards him.

Hearing him following me, he responded, "I'm Matt. What's your name?"

Looking back at him then focusing again on the trail, I responded, "I'm Faith."

"What a great name," he said with conviction.

"Yep, I get that a lot," I responded.

In silence we made our way up the incline. For a moment, I lost sight of the fact that this man was still behind me, remembering the last time Jake and I were up here. We talked about college, the military, traveling and which direction he wanted to go in. Snickering for a moment as I lost breath, I thought, "No matter what shape I'm in, I always manage to lose my breath on this part." I stopped to catch it before making the rest of the short jaunt up. Instantly I was reminded of this man behind me. We both started laughing as we stood there trying to steady our breathing. I looked back at him for a second, gave another half laugh, then continued. I had a sense of peace fill me just then. There were no doubts, no negatives, it was just me and this climb. Well, and this rather handsome man climbing behind me.

We got to the first break which offered a large, flat boulder to rest on. I often wondered how it was formed;

perhaps the decades of people trampling over it. The trees offered a slight opening to see the water below. As I stood there, hands on my knees and catching my breath, my eyes gazed in that direction. Then I heard Matt behind me also trying to catch his breath.

"Look Faith, I don't want to sound weird or awkward, but I believe in my intuition and I just feel like we could have some great conversation today. What do you say? Can we hike together?" he asked yet again.

Looking straight at me, it seemed like I could see right into his soul.

He continued. "I get you want to be alone, and I respect that. If you don't want to hike together now, perhaps we could meet up for lunch," he offered.

Still unsure of what his motive was and not knowing yet if I could trust him, I looked at him with a simple smile then caressed my lips against each other. "Why is this man interested in having time with me?" I asked myself. "A 40-something woman with clear time written on her face in the wrinkles?"

"I have a lot of stops to make and I plan to do the entire hike, not just a portion of it. I don't have time to be slowed down."

"Wow!" he said with emphasis.

"What?" I responded with equal emphasis.

"Well, it sounds like I've been shut down twice, ouch, in less than an hour," he said as he made a motion of getting stabbed in his heart.

Letting some of my guard down, I gave him a snarky laugh and then shook my head. I felt my shoulders gently relax as I started biting on my thumbnail, my true sign of either creation or flirting. It was clear to me which it was in this moment. I had an attachment to this man already, and

I wasn't quite sure how or why. I tilted my head and looked back at him again. "Well," I started with a deep breath, "I suppose, since we are both going the same direction, at least for now, if you want to hike together, that would be fine. But I'm going to be stopping and making some videos and I don't expect you to wait. I really need privacy for them. I'm here with a purpose today and I have a lot on my heart that needs to get out," I said as I looked down in a softer tone.

He looked at me again with a look that I hadn't seen often from people other than my boys. It appeared as if he had genuine care and honesty in his eyes. He seemed completely present in our conversation. "I get it, Faith, I know those days very well. How about we just see where the day goes and if you want to tell me to buzz off, well, just let me know. I may not take it easy, but I'll understand," he asserted.

Watching him, I said nothing, then turned around and continued on the trail.

CHAPTER 8

Thoughts drifted back about my life in Seattle. It was 1997, and I was starting to build a real life for myself there. Some days felt like I just made the move, yet others seemed more like it was taking forever to get seen. I didn't have any big breaks yet, but people were starting to notice my work. I would sell a piece here and there. Month after month it seemed to get more consistent. Occasionally I would get requests to do special shots around the coast, which I never anticipated but it gave way to some great work. I wanted it more than ever before, yet I still doubted myself around every corner. There was just something holding me back from going all in and doing it full-time. When I checked in with the family back home, they would often ask in snarky tones: "Have you made it big yet, Faith?"

It would send chills through my body. "Why did they doubt me so much?" I often wondered.

I was working as a restaurant manager at a little pizzeria called Milo's to help pay the bills as I got my art career established. It helped to keep my stress about money out of the way. All in all, it was going pretty well. I was coming up on my two-year mark with the company and making some hefty performance bonuses.

I had a beautiful flat right in downtown. The view out the front bay window was stunning. It was a straight shot of the bay overlooking Pike's Pier. I would often grab my coffee and get lost in my daydreams as I gazed out at the sunrise.

The combination of working long restaurant hours while trying to establish my name in the art district and the consistent redirecting of my own self-doubt were really taking a toll. My spare time was dedicated to finding new coffee shops, gift shops and art shows to promote and sell my work.

"They aren't going to be interested, anyway." I would often hear the internal dialogue even before I stepped into a store. Anxiousness about how to approach it also grew. "Am I doing it right?" I would often ask myself. I started second-guessing most everything. I wanted to do everything right, prove to everyone that I wasn't the mistake they said I was, and build the name I dreamed for myself. Yet, each time I would put myself out there I could hear the comments as if they were happening in the present moment.

"You're a loser."

"No one wants to hear what you have to say."

"You have no control over yourself. Look at you."

I could count on that voice from deep down to always help out: "Just do it, Faith. You got this." But some days, it was hard.

I habitually found myself eating my feelings away; it was how I coped with all the anxiety and stress. When I wasn't out shooting, food was the only thing that redirected all the emotions.

Looking back at that memory, I realized it so profoundly as I headed up the hiking trail. "I was reinforcing those beliefs the whole time," I thought, shaking my head.

"What did you say?" Matt asked me from behind.

"Nothing," I responded as I let the flashback continue.

I was questioning myself more and more. *Am I ever*

going to make it? was frequently my internal discussion. It was taking me longer and longer to control the internal chatter and I found myself looking for reinforcing experiences to back up those negative thoughts. This was my last chance to prove to myself that I was worthy.

It was the biggest time of the year for artists in the area. Seattle's annual art show. People came from all over the world for this. It was one of the biggest in the nation. I applied on a whim as soon as they started accepting applications, never really expecting to get chosen. Most artists waited decades to be invited. I'd heard about tenured artists being rejected year after year. It was a huge surprise when I got the letter congratulating me for my spot. Additionally, I was offered one of the larger spaces right up in front, a prime spot for any artist. Opening the letter that day, an instant picture came to mind. I saw it clearly, the people walking through in awe of my brilliant photography. Closing my eyes, I went into a daydream, feeling it, seeing it, imagining everything that day was going to bring. I could hear the comments.

"Wow, this is gorgeous."

"Are you the artist? I have to shake your hand; I've never seen anything like this before."

I could feel it, the joy in those comments. The fulfillment I felt. "You did it, Faith!" I heard.

"Who are you kidding?" came screaming from deep down.

"What are you going to say to them?" I wondered.

"STOP!" I said out loud, trying to quiet the chatter.

"What if they hate my work?" came next.

That dream quickly faded and turned to uncertainty. "This must be a mistake," I thought. "This must be for someone else."

The months since I originally got the letter went fast. The anticipation, anxiety and uncertainty were building stronger and getting more prevalent day after day. I tried to ignore it and often coped with food to avoid the feelings. But now it was here, less than 24 hours before the show. There was no more avoiding it and I felt even more insecure knowing the extra weight I was carrying.

It was Friday night, and I was closing the restaurant with my team.

I had the whole crew with me that night: Kim, Gena and Andy. It was busy to say the least, nonstop, your typical Friday. The best part about working at a downtown pizza pub is the constant traffic. It would generally keep my mind from wandering to dark thoughts. But that particular night, with the expo starting the next day, it was very hard to avoid. Most of the night internal chatter kept showing up.

"What am I going to say?"

"What if I forget something?"

"It will be perfect, Faith." The other voice often came quieter behind the first.

"What if they hate my work? Ugh!" was showing up more and more frequently.

And, worse, "What if they just walk by with no words or acknowledgements, nothing? Urgh."

"Breathe, Faith," I reminded myself. "The people who love your work will keep loving your work and at least you have an income," I assured myself.

"I want this so much," I reminded myself frequently.

Walking the final guests out for the night, I closed and locked the doors behind them.

"Good luck tomorrow, Faith," they said as they left.

With a simple shake of the head and another deep

breath, I made my way to the bar and poured myself a drink. "Come on you guys, let's take a break before we clean up," I called out to the team, inviting them to join me. "We have a lot of work still ahead of us."

"I'm in, what a night!" Andy yelled quickly as he threw his towel on the table.

Andy was a rather handsome guy. Standing about 6'2" and 175 pounds, he was all muscle and enjoyed showing it off every time he got the chance. He had your typical gym rat vibe, always flexing his muscles. This one time, I caught a look of his abs when he was changing after shift, and instantly I was turned on. None the matter, there is no way a man like him would ever go for a fat girl like me. His demeanor would often remind me of the jocks in high school that would throw around remarks about my weight even knowing he never directly said anything.

"When does your show start Faith?" he asked as he sat on the other side of the bar.

"We start setting up tomorrow morning," I responded.

"Did you get a good spot?"

Looking at him with a slight smile, I felt myself blush before looking down and pausing for a moment. I took a little breath and felt the joy on my face when I responded, "I have a great space, in fact. I'm right up front in a double booth."

"Get out!" he said in a shocked tone. "They think you're that good, huh?" he questioned.

In utter shock by that remark, I asked myself, "Did he really say that?" Glaring at him, I responded, "Wow, Andy, what the hell does that mean?" I knew I didn't want him to hear any amount of self-doubt.

"Oh, um, nothing," he replied unconvincingly as he turned and looked away.

Getting more frustrated with him, I asked again,

"Seriously Andy, what the heck was that supposed to mean?"

Looking back up at me, he said with a slightly arrogant tone, "I just know how hard it is to get into this show. My sister has been trying for years and still hasn't been accepted."

"It's because your sister's a tool and believes her shit doesn't stink," Gena chimed in. "Don't get me wrong, she has some real talent, I'll give her that, but she disregards the feedback from people trying to help her be better. Worse even, she disregards it then does the complete opposite. People know what they like, Andy, and art directors know what the public likes," she said as she shook her head. "Ya know, it's not as if they're asking her to completely change her work, a few small shifts. Then she could easily be in the show, but she's too into herself to listen to anyone. Her ego gets in the way. Besides, she's just mean. Urgh," she said with frustration as she slammed her hand on the bar counter.

"All right, all right," Andy slowed her down. "You don't need to get so fired up all the time when you talk about her."

Looking back at him with a glare she responded as she stood up from her stool. "Well maybe one of these days you will stick up for your girlfriend the way you do your sister."

Andy attempted to put his hand on her arm as she quickly pulled it away from him.

Trying to break the tension, I jumped in again. "Okay, well art is abstract, let's just leave it there. Now, what does everyone want to drink?"

Clearly frustrated, Gena and Andy looked at each other, neither willing nor ready to back down.

"Come on you two, enough! Tonight is about fun, not adding to my nerves. Can you just set aside the argument for now?" My thoughts quickly fed into Andy's comments and impressions about getting into the show.

"Why on earth would anyone buy this fat girl's art?" I asked myself.

"Who am I fooling anyway? This is never really going anywhere; it'll never pay the bills."

Trying to change my thoughts, I brought my attention back to Gena and Andy, as they sat there still nagging at each other. "I said enough, you two," with a louder tone. "Look, art is abstract, everyone sees things from a different perspective. At least she continues to go for it, you must applaud her for that, Gena."

"Why are you defending her?" Gena responded quickly.

I shrugged my shoulders before responding, "Everyone deserves a chance when they're leaning in and going for it."

Andy, clearly puzzled by my response, looked back in silence. Then he said, "I guess I just figured it takes everyone that long. I saw how hard she works and how much it hurts her every time she gets another rejection letter."

With my heart now racing and arms crossed, I continued to look at him with a firm tone in my eyes. "Call it luck, call it skill, call it whatever you will Andy, I've worked my ass off to get here. How about if you just say *congratulations Faith!*" Working to hold my confidence, I felt the same energy I did when I stood up to Mike and Ryan. It felt good for a minute, then I quickly started second-guessing what I had said.

"All right, all right, Faith, calm down, I was just asking about your show is all." Andy clearly recognized that I was now getting frustrated with him.

"Don't let him get under your skin," Gena said as she sat back down. Then turning her attention back to Andy, she scolded, "You're such a jerk," and smacked him upside the back of the head.

"Yah, a jerk you love," he replied as he got up off his stool and tried pulling her in for a kiss.

Gena, a well-built woman standing about 5'9", knew how to hold her own. She quickly backed away from Andy and responded, "Whatever, why are you saying these things the night before her show? You're so mean." Then turning her attention back to me she took a sip of her drink and asked, "Which pieces are you showing tomorrow, Faith?"

I let her question sit with me for a minute as I continued to wipe down the bar. Images of all my pictures ran through my head. Truth be told, I had them all set and ready to go but at that moment was starting to question my choices. "Well, I have a full set ready to go, but as I think about it, I might switch out a few pieces. I plan to bring a good mix of everything, people shots, nature pictures and other random moments. I'm hoping that way I reach everyone's interests."

"That makes sense. I mean, all of your pictures are amazing," she said as she looked up smiling at me, then shot a glare back at Andy. "Faith," she continued, "I don't think you can go wrong with anything you decide to bring. Oh, do you still have that one with the big oak tree right in the middle of it?" she asked with excitement.

"Do you mean the one with the sunset behind it?" I asked as I recalled the day I captured it.

"Yes, that's the one, it's my absolute favorite. I could lose time looking at that picture." She closed her eyes and took a deep breath as though imagining it in her head.

"I know how to make you lose time," Andy chimed in as he placed his hand on her thigh.

"I swear that's all you think about!" Gena quickly responded as she shook her head.

With a sarcastic laugh and shake of the head to Andy's comment, I avoided fully answering Gena's question. "Yeah,

I'll have to see about that one. I only have space to display 12 large pieces and six small ones. Then I can replace them if someone purchases something."

"Wait, what?" Kim jumped into the conversation. "Seriously Faith, have I taught you nothing, it's 'when,' not 'if,'" she said, shaking her head.

Kim, a petite woman, stood about 5'4", had gorgeous blonde hair and blue eyes, and was beautiful in every sense of the word. She was always aware of how people were talking about and to themselves. Very intuitive and empathic, Kim was a bit of a hippie.

I grinned and looked back up at her. "Thanks Kim," I simply replied, then continued to answer Gena's question. "So, I want to make sure that I'm bringing my Midwestern vibes to the show. People in this area seem to be very drawn to my tree and nature pictures. But," I added with emphasis as I waved my finger, "I also want to bring in some of my skyline, city and sunsets pictures."

"Well," Gena added, "the big oak with the sunset behind is your number one in my book." Then she took a sip of her drink before standing up and wiping down the chairs.

"That one is gorgeous Faith, I agree." Kim chimed in.

Little did Gena know I was framing that one for her birthday. I knew she loved it.

As we continued to talk and clean the bar, I started feeling the anxiety building again. The mere thought of the show made me want to throw up. Questions were coming in quickly yet again: "What do I say? What should I wear? What if I forget something? Urgh, what if nobody likes my work? What if I leave having sold nothing?"

I could hear it from everyone, all the "I told you so's" coming back to me after the show.

Urgh, I don't want to have to tell them I failed. That's

exactly what they've been expecting of me, a failure, unnecessary and irrelevant. I could hear the people pointing and laughing at the show as they walked by; I bet they'd be thinking, "Look at that fat girl." I wasn't looking forward to the snickers and smirks that I was certain would be present.

Stopping for a moment, I asked myself, "Are you sure you want this, Faith? Is it worth it?"

Kim, in her usual intuitive nature, jumped in. "Faith," she said in concern, "are you all right?"

Gena added instantly, "Faith, you are always so confident and sure of yourself, I know you are going to knock it out of the park just like you do everything else."

With a small smile and a "Hmm," I shook my head and continued wiping down the keg toppers. Then I looked back up to her. "Thanks Gena. But —" adding a long pause, "How is it that people see me that way? Strong, I mean?"

"Wait. Crap," I said to myself, "did I just say that out loud?"

"Seriously, Faith?" Gena responded.

"Nah, I'm good," I quickly responded, hoping she wouldn't ask more as the internal discourse continued. *Why can't I see it? Does my outside really look that bold and confident?*

She got closer, then grabbed my arm and looked me in the eyes. "For real, are you actually asking that question?"

Kim got Andy's attention now.

"Guys seriously, I'm good," I said with emphasis, trying to redirect their attention while questions still filled my head.

What if you're the only one that doesn't sell anything? That would be horrifying.

Gena, standing with her arms crossed behind me, was still focused on the comment I made. "Are you ready to talk to us about it?" she asked with a parent-like sternness in her tone.

I looked up and saw the three of them standing in a row, watching me. They stopped working. Leaning up against the jukebox, I crossed my arms to mirror them. I brought a large smile to my face. "I love you guys. It means the world to me that you care this much. And –" I continued with emphasis, "I am really okay. I just had a moment of question. It's completely normal."

"Okay, fine," Gena started with a tone of uncertainty. "But you really do know why, right?"

"Yes, Gena, really, I got it!" I said while placing my hand on her shoulder.

"Gena, she said she's good, now let her be," Andy chimed in.

Kim was standing back watching, and tilted her head, observing me. "How about some tunes?" she asked.

"Oh my gosh, yes, I'm on it," I quickly replied.

Gena followed behind me, then wrapped her arms around me from behind. "I'm here when you're ready to talk about it," she whispered in my ear.

"Faith, you should take off, we can finish up," Andy yelled from the other side of the bar.

"Yah," the rest of the team chimed in.

"No way, we'll finish this as a team," I replied just as I caught a glimpse of myself in the reflection of the window. As I stood there, I saw all three hundred-ish pounds looking back at me. *No one is going to want to buy anything from me.* I placed my hand on my belly.

"What's the point?" I said, shaking my head, as I continued working.

CHAPTER 9

Bringing my mind back to the present as we continued along the trail, I contemplated why this man wanted anything to do with me. Oddly, he was providing me with a feeling of comfort that I hadn't felt in years. "Was there really no one there for me before?" I asked myself, "Or, did I push everyone away like I tried doing with Matt today?"

I made my way up the incline of the trail as I watched the beauty of nature unfold. I was seeing and feeling everything differently than before. There was an energy coming from the trees firmly rooted in the ground. Walking by them, I waved my hand, touching the leaves off to my right. "One last time," I thought. The sounds were crisp. I was hearing everything – snakes hissing deep in the trees, birds chirping all around, the water from down below. My senses were heightened as I was present to everything and breathing it all in.

In that moment, I remembered this man following me. I looked back at him. We had instant eye contact. I asked, "If we're going to be together today, we might as well get to know one another. Tell me more about you."

Continuing to look at me, he paused, then clapped his hands and rubbed them together. "Okay, finally."

I chuckled briefly as I shook my head and continued along the trail.

"Well," he said, with a brief pause again, "I grew up in a little town in Indiana outside of Kalamazoo. It's beautiful there. We were always out in nature doing something, usually hiking. Mom was very nurturing. She constantly found ways to make us feel important. Dad was tough. I couldn't ever do anything right by that man." He let out a brief huff as he shook his head, looking down. "Nothing was ever good enough and watch out if it wasn't done his way. Looking back, I realize he must have had a tough life. He didn't trust anyone. He would often remind us that we're alone in life and that we should watch our backs and 'never trust anyone, they'll rip you off.' It's too bad. I lived with that mentality for all too many years."

I could feel the emotions as he spoke. Watching him, it was clear how much pain this brought him.

Clearly wanting the attention off him, he threw the question back to me. "How about you, Faith; where are you from?"

"Hmm," I had a small grin on my face. "I was born and raised in a little town just northeast of here called Fond du Lac."

"Oh, yeah, Foot of the Lake, right?" he asked.

Looking at him with surprise I responded, "Ha, yes, that's right. Most people don't know that history. Mom and Dad were good providers. They always did the best they knew how. They provided a safe household and a lot of community. There were always people stopping by to visit. To them, everyone was family, and everyone was welcome. Mom always came across as 'go with the flow.' So long as our chores were done, she didn't really care what we did. I didn't realize it until I got older how insecure she was in herself and her voice. It brought a lot of perspective when I got older and started working through my own shit. I took on insecurities that were never really mine."

"Yeah, when we're little, we don't always know how to interpret what we see and hear," Matt chimed in.

"Isn't that the truth," I responded. "Then there was Daddy. Ahhh, one of the best men I've ever known," I said with conviction in my tone. "Of course, being a daddy's girl, I may be somewhat biased," I said, looking at him with a smirk. "Daddy grew up in the midst of the Great Depression. I can't even imagine the life he saw and lived. They worked hard to provide for us and teach us a strong work ethic, instilling a 'grit it out' attitude." I pictured Mom and Dad in my mind. "I know they always only wanted the best for us and honestly, I wouldn't take the values of inner strength and the work ethic they gave me away for anything. There were eight of us kids and it's fair to say we all took on those traits. I was the dreamer and creative doer of the bunch." Pausing again, my siblings crossed my mind, then I turned to Matt and asked, "How about you, do you have any siblings?"

He hesitated, then stopped and took a breath.

Not catching that he stopped, I turned around and saw him standing there. Watching his tone, I could see that his presence shifted. Waiting, I watched and stayed present for him.

Getting closer, I placed my hand on his shoulder, "Matt, are you okay?" I asked.

Breathing deeply, he waited, then looked back up to me. "I had a sister; her name was Sarah." In silence he started walking again.

We continued in silence as I saw that question clearly impacting him. I wondered what happened to her. They must have been close, I thought. "I bet she was beautiful Matt," I said softly. "She is still here with you, yah know," I assured him. Seeing that he was clearly distraught at this conversation, I asked, "Do you want me to change the subject?"

"Yes, yes I do," he said with immediate conviction.

In that moment, I recognized how much Matt needed me today, perhaps as much as I needed him.

"So," I took a brief pause, still thinking about what happened to Sarah. "I've been in the staffing industry for about twelve years. What do you do?" I asked him.

Seeing that he was still in a space of emotional pondering, I waited.

"I wouldn't have guessed that Faith. I thought for sure you were a writer or photographer or something creative," he responded.

"Nah, I just do that for fun, you can't make a living at it," I said with a disheartened tone. "I sure did try though; I wasn't good enough to make it work. My family was clearly right," I added, shaking my head. "Doing what you love clearly doesn't make a living, that's why they call it *work*," I said with a snarky tone.

"What!" he said with emphasis. "Why the hell not? I was a corporate business attorney for about fifteen years when I finally made the move to open my business. It was the best decision I ever made. The long hours, constant arguments and debates with clients, and worse, having to represent people that I knew were not ethical," he said, shaking his head. "It finally became too much to handle."

"How long have you been out on your own?" I asked.

"I started doing it on the side about nine years ago, and finally left my day job five years in. The first year was a struggle. I had some savings but not enough to get me through. I ended up selling my house and living in the shop for a while. My dad was so mad and disappointed. I know he just wanted what's best for me, but the thing is, he didn't realize what was best for me is to do what I love."

Listening to him, I could hear the emotions behind those

years but oddly enough they sounded more joyful then stressful. "How did you know everything would be okay?" I asked.

"Well, I didn't Faith, I just trusted myself, that no matter what happened, I could handle it. All I knew was that nothing could possibly be as bad as me living the life I was living in constant stress and anxiety."

"But didn't that bring as much stress, not knowing how things would work out?"

We continued to talk as we worked up the next phase of the trail. This was the longest and biggest one on this side. The elevation was building quickly, and there was a gain of nearly 1000 feet over the mile. This stage of the hike was always the hardest for me but somehow today it was easier. There was a new focus and attention on it. There was no worrying or second-guessing today, just me and the hike, and well, Matt by my side.

"What was your tipping point?" I asked in the middle of breaths as we continued up the hill. There was no stopping on this part of the hike. Once you stopped, it was a challenge to get momentum back.

"You're going to ask now, in the middle of this climb?" he asked in a lighthearted tone.

"Sure, I might as well get to know what you're like in stressful moments," I responded.

"Ah, I see what you're doing, Faith," he said as he stopped walking.

"Matt, what are you doing?" I asked with a slight giggle.

"Waiting for you to stop and listen," he responded, half out of breath.

Standing there at an angle with his feet about five feet apart on the steepest part of the climb, he waited. I stopped, turned around, then slowly caught my grip and leaned against one of the rocks peeking out from the hill. After I got my balance, I looked back at him.

"Faith, I finally realized that me, my health, what I wanted, were the most important things. I realized the longer I went on with not living into my true self, the more I was getting away from happiness. And, well, as with most things, something happened that really just pushed me too far; it was my breaking point. The company started asking me to represent people who were breaking every value I have as a person, and I couldn't do it anymore."

Quickly, I jumped in. "Yeah, but how do you deal with all of that stress and worry without letting it break you down?"

He came in closer, then closer still. With each step in, my heart started racing faster. I tried to back up, to increase the distance between us, yet he came even closer. Feeling so connected to him in this moment, I thought, "Why now, after everything, why now do I finally find someone that cares?"

He got within inches of me as he balanced his back foot, placed one hand on the rock just beside me and leaned in. "Faith," he said softly, "in those moments of stress and anxiety and worry, I stop, I breathe, and take a look at what it is I really want in life. I look at what fight I want to win. And I've learned to take the time my body needs to reset." Then, he grabbed my hands with his and stood up as he pulled me up with him. "All of this," he said as he waved his hand around the park, "this, right here," he said, "this is resetting. And this climb today, it's proof and a reminder of what we can do when we get out of our heads. It's proof of how strong we really are." Working to keep his balance, he pulled me closer. "It's keeping people in my space who support me and that I can be myself around. Strengthening together, building ties, that's what we are meant for as people."

Heart racing, palms sweating, I could feel the tears starting to well up in my eyes then start down my face. I shook my head for a moment as I pulled away from him and leaned back against the rocks. Wiping the tears from my face, I looked up. He was watching me and hadn't moved. "You're right, Matt, all of it, that's exactly what we need." Then I turned and started back up the incline. He quickly grabbed me and pulled me close, then wrapped his arms around me. Standing there on the side of the rocks as he held me tightly, tears started welling up again. Fighting the urge to allow them, I put my hands on his chest and had eye contact with him. Without a word, I felt as if he knew what I was thinking, then quickly I pulled away and started again back up the incline.

Slightly ahead of him, I got to the next landing and quickly made my way to the opening that showed a beautiful view of the lake and skyline below. Getting as close as I could to the edge, I wrapped my arm around the side of the tree and leaned over as I pulled my head back and took a deep breath into the sun.

Tilting my head, I felt the cool breeze from the morning. The sun beaming down felt like pure energy being sent from the heavens. "Why couldn't life have been easier?" I asked myself as I closed my eyes, took a deep breath and leaned forward.

CHAPTER 10

The day of the expo flowed quickly back to my mind. I laid in bed that morning, daydreaming about what the day was going to be like. The director of the expo was expecting art connoisseurs from all over the country. I envisioned a flood of orders coming in following the show.

"They finally see me," I thought. "This is it, I'm here"

Then just as quickly, another thought grabbed hold. "I wonder if the director will finally see me?"

Closing my eyes, I imagined the responses from people who doubted me through the years. How their tone had shifted now with words of encouragement. "We always knew you could do it, Faith." *Finally, they see my worth*, I said aloud.

A peaceful excitement came as I recalled my experience at Milo's. I felt appreciation and gratitude as I embraced Jean and Jeff, the owners, who supported me since the beginning. I observed their excitement for me. Then, watching, I saw a line building around the corner of the booth. People were waiting with anticipation to get their hands on my newest prints. I felt the joy and absolute bliss in the knowledge of my worth as I talked to the crowds. Continuing to lay there watching the scenes play out, I saw what the expo was doing for my career.

Then it hit me as if a freight train were coming in fast, the little voice from deep down. That little voice mimicking what Leslie said so many times growing up: "You're nothing, worthless."

"Don't listen, Faith." I tried to fight it.

"They don't want to see your stuff, you're a fake, a fraud." I could hear it just as clearly today as the first time she said it.

The words stung and, in an instant, my energy shifted. "Don't do it, Faith," I said again out loud with even more force this time as I jumped up off the bed. "You are stronger than that. It's time to show her. Show everyone." I threw on my clothes then started getting my makeup on. Looking in the mirror, I reminded myself, "You've got this! You worked hard to get here and deserve it. No one can stop you."

"Well, you can stop you," came a thought from deep down. "Is it worth the risk?" I asked myself.

"Come on, don't do it, you got this, Faith."

Then, louder this time, that voice came again. "Look at you. They're right, you clearly don't take care of yourself." Then putting my hands on my stomach, I jiggled it around. "It's not like you can hide it. What an embarrassment," I said to myself.

Seeing my broad shoulders in the reflection of the mirror, I continued to criticize myself and the jiggle and fat on my body. "No one ever takes the fat girl seriously."

Then all the fat comments I've heard through the years started in. As I stood there, it hit me: I had accepted those criticisms and owned them as if everyone was right. I stepped into the story of who they said I was. Shaking my head, my eyes started welling up.

"Look at you, you're so gross," came the next voice.

"I love you, you're beautiful." I combatted it.

"You're ugly, who are you kidding?" came the other voice yet again.

The internal argument between the two voices played back and forth like an orchestra.

"Enough!" I finally said out loud. I could hear the echo across my apartment when I yelled it. Throwing my mascara back in the case, I blew myself a kiss in the mirror and said, "You're going to crush it today, gorgeous!" Then I finished getting ready.

We were required to check into the Expo at least two hours before opening. My flat downtown was just a few blocks from the pier. I could be there in a matter of minutes. It was nice not having to deal with downtown traffic.

I grabbed a cup of coffee and quickly checked to ensure I had everything from my list and was ready to go. "You can do this, Faith, just keep moving forward," came into my thoughts, those words Daddy used to tell me all the time. Bert, my 100-pound husky, came running up in that moment.

"Hey boy, where you been?" I asked him in an excited tone.

With a light howl, he showed his good morning greetings back. As I petted him, everything else about the day stood still and a smile came over me.

"Mommy will be home later," I said as I handed him a treat from off the counter. "Wish me luck today buddy," I finished, then I grabbed my purse and portrait case to make my way out of the apartment.

Walking to the pier that morning, an excited peace came over me for all a second as I saw the Expo being set up. For that moment, I had complete faith that everything was going to turn out perfectly.

Just as quickly, I heard the question, "What if you're not ready? Maybe you should wait until next year."

"Stop it, you're going to crush it," I reminded myself yet again out loud.

Actively working to get out of my own thoughts, I observed the people as I walked. The old veteran sitting on his usual bench, a newspaper for a blanket, with an old coffee cup being used for money. In my usual fashion I threw a couple of dollars in as I walked by. The runner passing by with her beautiful black lab by her side. The man in the suit yelling to someone on the other end of the phone, off in his own place as if no one else was around. Watching everyone in that moment reminded me that we all had our own life stuff going on.

"Does everyone have the kinds of thoughts I do?" I pondered.

I approached the corner and waited for the light to change as I continued to watch the people around me. In that moment, a sharp thought came in as a bus whizzed by. "You could jump in front of it, no one would miss you."

"What?" I thought.

Then just as fast, the thought passed, the light changed and I made my way across the road to the entry of the Seattle waterfront pier, home to the infamous Seattle Space Needle, Pike's Market, the Seattle Aquarium and so much more. I was down there at least weekly since moving to Seattle and yet the enjoyment and appreciation hadn't faded a bit.

Breathing in deeply, I told myself, "Here we go" as I looked around for the registration booth. Within seconds of arriving, a young boy greeted me with a smile and a lot of enthusiasm. He couldn't have been more than fifteen years old.

"Ma'am, I'm here to help the artists carry in their work. Are you an artist in today's show?" he asked. Before I could even answer, he continued politely. "Can I get that for you?" he said, pointing to my portfolio.

This young man was all of a hundred pounds soaking wet, and maybe 5'3". "Is he really going to be able to navigate my large awkward bag?" I wondered. Not wanting to deflate this boy's desire to help, I said, "Sure, of course, that would be great." I handed him my bag. As he took it in his arms I asked, "Are you okay with it? I know it's a bit awkward and heavy."

"Yes ma'am," he replied directly.

I could hear the uncertainty in his tone as he did.

"I am in weight training. I can handle this." He puffed out his chest and pulled his shoulders back.

Walking down the pier, I introduced myself. "I'm Faith DeWalt, what's your name?"

"Me, oh, I'm Skyler," he responded, with surprise in his tone that I asked.

Speaking with this young man, I felt my body starting to shift as we got closer to the booths. The nerves were sinking in. Trying to escape my mind, I kept attention towards Skylar and the conversation. "So, what else do you do here, Skylar?"

He bashfully looked back up at me. "Nothing much, I'm just helping my dad over the summer so I can buy a car in the fall. Dad always says we need to learn the value of hard work."

"Well, I can't disagree with that, hard work is important," I responded.

With certainty in his tone, he looked back up at me. "I'm not going to be doing this forever, that's for sure. I'm going to school for architecture when I finish high school," he said boldly.

"Nothing is wrong with honest work like this in the meantime," I reminded him. "What type of structures do you want to build?" I asked.

As though uncertain why I was engaging in a conversation with him, he hesitated. "I want to bring the character back to buildings. You know the ones where you look at it and say, 'I wonder what the story is behind that?' and watch as people stare in awe of my work," he said.

I could hear the conviction in his tone and what he was saying. He knew clearly what his dreams looked like. "That sounds amazing, Skylar. I for one would love to see your work." I paused briefly. "If you stay focused, you can do it," I assured him.

We quickly got to the entrance of the expo and I saw my name on the very front booth.

"Faith DeWalt, that's you, right?" Skylar said.

"Yes," I said with a slight grin.

"Wow, this is a great spot. You have the best one here," he said with excitement. "You must be really good."

Immediately, I felt it. It was like a knot in my throat. "Hm, hm, hm." I tried clearing it. I could feel the heat climbing from my belly all the way up my chest, jittery all over.

"You can still walk away, Faith," I thought.

"Stop it, you got this," I quickly reinforced.

"Faith, are you okay?" Skylar asked. "You don't look very excited right now."

Not wanting to acknowledge how scared I was in that moment to this young man, I postured. "I'm just getting a sense of the surroundings, is all." I set down my things and handed Skylar a couple of dollars for his help. "Thanks Skylar, I appreciate you."

"Thanks Faith. Good luck today," he replied, then quickly ran to help another exhibitor.

Standing there in thought of this young man, his confidence and optimism at life, I caught a glimpse of the sunrise over the bay and captured a few shots. With the boats in the harbor, it was the perfect view as if the sun was rising up above all of it, perfectly placed between the ships.

"You got this, Faith," I reminded myself again. "You're finally here. Stay focused, you're going to do great!" Encouraging myself over and over, I wished I had someone here with me to share in the experience. Turning back to my booth, I started setting out my pictures. As I did, the memories swarmed in, each one telling a different story about the excursions I had so far in life.

"Are they going to understand the stories behind it?" I wondered.

"Will they care?" came next.

"Are the shots as impactful without the true experience of it all?" I pondered.

As I finished setting up, a woman stopped by the booth. Reaching her hand out for a shake, I watched as her eyes looked me up and down several times. Then just behind it was the look of disgust on her face. Putting my hand out, I met her with an extra tight squeeze. "Hello, I'm Faith, who are you?" I asked in a rather cold voice, making it clear that I witnessed her judgments toward me.

Pulling her hand back, I watched as she rubbed it and grinned slightly. I thought, "You don't treat people like that."

She started in with, "Oh, ha," with a perky voice. "I'm Misty. You must be really good; this is the best spot here," she said in a high-pitched tone. Then again, looking at me up and down, she asked, "How did you get this spot?" Before giving me a chance to respond, she continued, "How long have you been shooting?"

Taking a deep breath, thinking to myself, "Don't do it Faith, don't do it" and trying not to allow my emotions to get the better of me, I responded, "I simply submitted an application and samples of my work, is all. Then I got notification of my acceptance." I locked eyes with her to ensure she knew I was not taking her judgmental looks or comments. "I guess they liked my work," I added with a sassy tone.

Watching her, I saw her discomfort growing as she tried to break eye contact with me. Wanting desperately to make her feel as uncomfortable as she made me for a moment, I instantly shifted, realizing that was not who I wanted to be. Changing my tone slightly, I continued talking as I went back to setting out my shots. "My dad got me my first camera when I was eight, and I've been shooting ever since. I took that camera everywhere," I said with a grin. "And, as an obsessive dreamer, I was always imagining going off to far-off lands to find new shots.

"Sounds like you had quite the imagination when you were young," she added, with another giggle.

With a patient smile and pause I locked eyes with her again. "Yes," I said with conviction. "Imagination, it's a beautiful thing. The dreams we have in life, well, I'm so grateful I've always gone for it. The last thing I want is to be old and know I never tried. No one should feel that way." Watching her, she started looking uncomfortable again with my comments, then she broke eye contact with me, looking down. As I watched her, I wondered, "What dream have you given up?"

"Well then, do you have anything you need from me?" she asked. Before I could answer, she continued, "Looks like you're all set."

"No, I'm good, thanks. How many people are you expecting out today?

"There will be about fifty thousand during the whole show."

In that comment, I felt it, my nerves growing at the thought of it. "Fifty thousand people," I repeated.

With another sassy giggle as if acknowledging her looks and thoughts from earlier, she responded, "Yes, it will be great," with a sway of her head.

"Holy shit, Faith," I thought.

"Run!" came the other voice. "There is still time to leave."

"You got this," I reminded myself yet again. "Gosh, I hope they like my work," came next.

Doing everything I could to hold myself together so she didn't see the nerves, I focused back on Misty. "Wow, that's great, I'm excited to see what the day brings."

"I'll be around, just let me know if you need anything. And there will be helpers making their way through if you need a break," she said.

"Thanks." I replied.

"Good luck," she said in a long, drawn-out snarky tone as she looked me up and down one last time before nudging her nose up and walking away.

Without a word, I stayed focused on my work as I set out the story behind each shot, saying to myself, "Let it go. You're going to do great."

The expo was opened, and people started funneling through. I watched one person after another slow down as they walked by my booth gazing at my pictures before looking at me, then doing the usual up and down scan just as Misty and so many others had done in the past. Each time I made eye contact and greeted them accordingly. I didn't want to show even a small amount of uncertainty in myself. Internally I heard one thought after another: "You're a loser" and "Everything Leslie and other people had said throughout the years was right," came the next. "They are not going to buy your work. Why even bother?"

Hearing those words, I felt the anxiety building, my

palms were wet and a drop of sweat rolled down my back. "Why won't someone just stop?" I thought as I worked to maintain my composure. "Someone just stop already," came next.

Looking around I saw people stopping and interacting with the other artists, creating more self-doubt. Then Andy's comments from last night screamed through. Who was I to get a chance here, anyway?

Then it happened, as all those thoughts went to the side. A nice younger calm-looking lady stopped by. "Good morning," I started, "what brings you out today?"

"Enjoying the view," she responded as she waved her hands towards the bay. "It's gorgeous, right?"

"It sure is," I replied, then to my own surprise I asked, "Is there something specific you're looking for?"

"Nothing specific," she responded with a smile. "Checking everything out."

"I hear that," I responded. "Well, if you have questions, just let me know."

She continued to observe my prints then asked, "Did you take all of these?"

"I did," I responded with a smile.

"They are breathtaking," she responded. "Where are they from?"

"Thank you. I have pieces from all over. Most of them are from the Midwest area. I'm from a little town in Wisconsin where I got started."

After some light small talk, she was quickly on her way.

That interaction lifted my self-confidence and gave me some much-needed energy in the moment. Through the rest of the day, traffic was steady. There were people consistently at my booth. I sold most of the Wisconsin prints early in the day. Many of the visitors asked about the prints. They wanted to hear the stories about where they were taken, what brought me there, and if there were other unique stories behind them. In each conversation another print would go. It's as though they heard my emotions and were instantly drawn to my photos, wanting the same experience.

It was the end of the day when a middle-aged couple stopped. I didn't realize at the time how much this couple would change the direction of my life.

I could see clearly when they walked up that they were well off. "Hello," I greeted them. The woman looked at me. Slowly, as if not caring how obvious she was, she looked me up and down. I could see the judgment in her eyes. The man then turned his attention from my prints to me and mimicked her observation. His facial expression gave way to the internal criticism in my head. "See, I knew it, everyone is judging me for my weight." Wondering what they were thinking, I assumed it was something like "there's no way this fat girl could possibly be the artist who took these pictures."

"Good day," the gentleman finally said, as his lady lifted the side of her rather large hat. Without saying a word, she simply nodded. Then he continued, "Are you the artist here?"

"Yes, I am," I responded.

"Huh." He said with disbelief.

"Don't do it, Faith," I thought. "You've gotten so many compliments today, don't lose sight of that." Trying hard to distract myself from the negative thoughts, I simply said, "Let me know if you have any questions." Then I pulled out my portfolio to fill in the empty spots from my most recent sales. I had several from the day at the Badlands. As I looked through them, the lady came over my shoulder.

"Those are stunning," she said with a bold tone.

Not realizing that she was behind me, I jumped and quickly turned her way. "Oh," I said in surprise. "Thank you," then I reached out my hand to make a proper introduction. "I'm Faith." She looked at me, looked at my hand, and then looked back to the prints without even a gesture of who she was or the respect of a handshake. "Who are these people?" I questioned.

She continued to observe the prints as she nudged me out of the way. "Where exactly did you take these?" she asked.

"I was hiking in South Dakota; those are near the Badlands," I said as I boldly reached around her to grab one of them and place it on the easel next to its proper description.

"You," she said with disbelief, "you took these? How did you get there?" she asked while eyeing me up yet again.

Looking at her, I thought, "Seriously lady, are you really that oblivious to how rude you are, or do you just not care?" Wanting desperately to ask them to leave, I knew that would leave a terrible impression on the show directors, so I resisted. Taking a deep breath I responded, "Yes ma'am," in a firm tone. "These are all mine, I hiked to each and every destination," I said with emphasis.

The man joined her side again. "These pictures here?" He pointed to the ones she was looking at. "You shot these pictures and climbed there?" he asked in disbelief.

Shaking my head, I could feel my heart beating as tears started welling up. "Stop Faith. Don't do it. They're not worth it," I reinforced to myself. "Yes!" I said firmly. "As I've already mentioned, I did all of these." Pulling my shoulders back and looking at him square in the eyes, I attempted to tell them both through my demeanor that I had enough of their disrespect.

"Were you smaller then?" he asked boldly.

"Did he really just ask me that?" I questioned myself in disbelief.

The lady backhanded him as though scolding him.

"Look," I started in, as I reminded myself internally to be nice. "I know I am a bigger girl but that doesn't stop me or slow me down from anything, hiking, adventures, whatever it is." I stepped slightly forward to them. "My weight does not define me. And, I would appreciate it if you stop acting as though it does," I said with conviction as I gently set my hand on my heart.

Both of them looked at me with disbelief. The man simply nodded as though appreciating my directness as the lady continued to look at me with questions.

"Is there something else I can answer for you about my prints specifically?" I asked, yet still wanting to ask them to leave.

"Yes, are you putting these out for sale?" the woman responded.

"I am," I answered as I finished prepping them.

"I'll wait until those are ready. They're stunning. Ron, did you have any you were interested in?" she turned and asked the man.

"Whatever you think, dear," he quickly responded.

I finished prepping the prints and set them out as fast as I could in order to get them out of my booth.

As she continued to look at them, she asked, "If we want them in a bigger size, can you do that?"

"Yes ma'am," I responded as I stood back and watched her look at my work and read the stories.

"These are the accurate prices?" she asked with a pretentious tone yet again.

Shaking my head, I responded, "Yes, everything is as listed."

"You should really value your work more. These pictures are worth far more than what you are asking. If you don't value yourself, the right people are not going to value you or be interested in your work," she said boldly. "And," she continued looking me up and down again, "you should value yourself more too. You are incredibly talented and clearly have a good eye. This is a tough business. If you are not valuing yourself enough you are never going to make it," she insisted.

"Did she really have the audacity to say that?" I asked myself. "Well thank you for the advice," I simply responded.

"You're a loser, Faith," came that voice again from inside my head. "She's just being honest like everyone else has been through the years. When are you going to start listening and just give it all up?" Working hard to not feed those thoughts I reminded myself in a less confident tone this time, "You're worth it, Faith. You got this," as I wished they would just leave already.

"I will take this one," she started, "and that one," she said, pointing to another. "I would also like that one but in a bigger size. Here are the measurements." She handed me a piece of paper. "Ron," she said, calling the man over. "What do you think of that one in the foyer of the Park Street building?"

"Whatever you think, dear," he swiftly responded without looking.

"You are really no help with this at all," she responded brashly. "Okay, we will take this one too, in these measurements."

"Did you want these two today or would you like me to deliver them with the others?" I asked.

"You are going to deliver them?" she asked, yet again looking me up and down.

"Grr, the nerve," I thought. "Yes," I responded assertively. "Me, right here, me," I said this time as I waved my hand up and down my body, tired of the judgment. "I deliver them personally. Just let me know the address."

"Well," she said with a huff, "I suppose you can deliver them to our Park Street building. But," she said with a pause, "I would appreciate it if you dressed a bit more, well, appropriately, when you do. If you are interested, I suppose I can also give you a tour and see if you can help with some other prints."

"Is it worth it, Faith?" I thought. "Am I willing to deal with this lady to get seen?" I asked inside.

"Yes, I have a good selection of professional clothes for the proper occasions. And a tour of your building would be great, thank you," I responded, trying hard to be respectful to her.

"Give her your card, Ron," she turned to the man and directed him. "Here is my card too."

It read *Shelly Hyatt*. She was the owner of the Hyatt buildings in all of Washington. Instantly my nerves sparked as I realized whom I was talking to.

"When you have them ready just send me a note and we will arrange it. You have potential, Faith," she continued. "See more value in yourself and what you do. You can do better," she finished.

Amazed at the fact that this woman even remembered my name, I simply said, "Well thank you for your feedback. I will look forward to connecting with you soon." The man paid their bill, and they were quickly on their way.

Standing there, in that moment after they left, I was filled with a clash of emotions. "Someone that upscale recognized me and my talent." Then I thought, "And made very clear all my faults."

Speechless.

CHAPTER 11

Continuing to lean forward, enjoying the sun and breeze of the morning, I felt as if my energy banks were filling. I asked myself yet again, "Why does it have to be so hard?" Just as I did, Matt grabbed me gently from around the waist and pulled me back.

He asked with a frantic tone, "Faith, what are you doing?" Before giving me a chance to say anything, he continued. "That's way too close. What if you would have slipped? What if you would have lost balance? There is no coming back from that. Urgh!" he said with frustration in his tone.

Watching him, I paused. Wondering again *why? Why now?* as I shook my head. "Matt, clearly nothing happened," I said with a feisty tone. "I was enjoying the space and view," then I paused to breathe deeply again. "Ah, and all the memories of life." Yet another pause. "I told you earlier I have a purpose and thoughts of being here today. If we are going to keep hiking together you need to understand that."

Seeing my frustration, he came back in closer. "Faith, I'm sorry." I saw his expression change to that of concern and care. "I get it, I just don't want anything to happen to you," he continued as he grabbed my hand. "We only just met and I'm not ready to let you go."

With a puzzled look, I continued to lock eyes with him as I thought, "Why do you care? I wish Luke cared this much." Without a word, shaking my head, I looked down, then made my way around him and continued on the trail. It was another short incline up that brought us to a large opening giving way to a full panoramic view of the entire park and for miles as far as the eye could see. I knew that was the place it needed to happen.

Hearing Matt get closer from behind me, he said, "I really am sorry Faith; I wasn't trying to overstep. Can we start again?" Then he grabbed my hand and attempted to gain eye contact.

I glanced at him, looked back to the trail, then back to him. Our eyes locked and I instantly felt safe in his presence. "Sure," I responded.

After a short time, walking in silence, he asked, "So, what memories were you thinking about when you were on the ledge?"

Instantly, the expo came back to my thoughts as I grinned. "I lived in Seattle for a few years when I was trying to build my photography business. It was my dream to be a prominent figure in the space."

Without hesitation he asked, "Why did you give it up?"

"I wasn't good enough, and everyone made it very clear," I said, shaking my head as I kicked around rocks from the path. "Yah know," I continued with conviction, "it's funny, though, how much we learn through the years. Looking back, I'm certain that most of what I was feeling were my own insecurities. Sure, people would say things, they would look at me a certain way, and I always read those as not being enough. I always made myself bad and wrong for being obese and for not having more control in my life. And when it came to my voice," I paused, "well, that was a whole other thing. But honestly, Matt, it doesn't matter anymore, that was decades ago. There's no sense in mulling it over now. Fact is, I blew it and I can't change it, so we move on."

"Faith, seriously, I can't keep listening to this. First, even if you were overweight at some point, which has no bearing on someone's ability by the way, but even if you were, look at you now." He paused as he waved his hand up and down in front of me. "You're gorgeous, toned, fit, you clearly take care of yourself. And, the fact is, we learn a lot over the years. They are lessons to help us grow, that's it. You do know you can start again, right?" he asked with emphasis. "Look at me. I completely recreated my life. My business is thriving, and I get to do what I love every single day, the way more people should if they could get out of their own way."

Shaking my head, I let out a "huh" as we continued up the trail. "Matt, I appreciate what you're saying but I gave up those dreams a long time ago. There is no sense in getting my hopes up again. It hurts too much. Besides, I'm not 20 anymore, I don't have the hustle in me." Lingering in that thought, I waited.

"Look, I get it, it takes time to build anything, I hear you. When I was working at the law office, I spent every second I could in my shop. It took me years of playing around with different metals and woods to learn what I liked and what really felt like me. But notoriously I would lose time doing it. I'll never forget some of the comments that I heard along the way. Huh," he said with emphasis. "Even some of my closest friends and colleagues, they would razz me all the time about why I was doing this, why I didn't spend more time on my cases. None of them understood why I enjoyed it so much. And when I talked about selling my work..." He stopped mid-sentence. "Well, let's just say I got very aware of who I should share things with and who I shouldn't. Let me ask you this, Faith," he said with honesty in his voice. "Do you love it? Do you love it when you're out somewhere capturing shots?"

"What kind of a question is that, Matt? Of course I do," I responded.

"Then why not just try? There are so many great ways to get your name out there now. It is far different than when we were in our 20s and the hustle you mentioned. Faith, we both know when we love it, it's a different kind of stress."

I diverted his attention as we arrived at the large lookout area. It was one of Jake's favorite spots in the park. I remembered back to the first time he climbed out on those rocks. He made it look effortless, fearless, like me in so many ways when I was his age. Yet, he was confident and secure in his abilities. I turned and looked at Matt and asked, "I need to do a video. Can you give me some space?"

"Are you okay?" he asked with concern. "We were talking."

"I know Matt, but I need to do this, and yes, I'm okay," I responded. "It's one of those moments I mentioned earlier that I need space for. One of my reasons for being here today," I said with stress in my voice.

"Can we come back to this conversation?" he questioned.

I smiled without responding, then started making my way to the tall rock off on the right. It was Jake's favorite spot to sit and reflect. It was about a 2500-foot drop if you lost your balance yet worth the climb out to it. We would rest there for hours talking about life. Making my way out there today, I had no hesitation in my footing. It all came so freely. As I lightly jumped from one rock to the next, I paused and looked back to see Matt standing there, watching me, looking at me as if ready to run out to help.

"Are you okay?" he asked with an apprehensive tone.

"Matt, I'm good. Go," I responded.

Still watching, he got closer and said, "I'll just be up the way at the rock-climbing site. You're not going to bail on me, are you?" he asked in a sassy tone.

"Matt if I was going to do that, I would have already. Now go."

Keeping focus, I made my way across the other two rocks to get to my destination. This was one of the most beautiful structures on this side of the park. Tall and rich with colors of the earth. Brown, tan and reds mixed in. The sun brought out more colors of yellow and orange. "It's no wonder why Jake liked this spot so much," I thought.

I was finally there and pulled out my phone. Sixteen missed calls and too many texts to count. Clearing all of them, I propped my phone up against the rock formation that peeked out just across the way. I turned my camera on and sat in front of it for a minute as I looked at the view, waiting to build up the courage for this one. After some time and thought I hit record.

Watching for a moment at the camera, my eyes welled up. "Hey babe, by now you know what happened. Jake, I tried, I really, really did. I gave it everything I had in me and the last thing I want to be doing today is leave you here alone. The pain, it's just too much, I can't do it anymore." Pausing, I watched the video as if speaking without saying a word. "Jake, you, my beautiful son, are one of the most intuitive, creative, caring people on the planet. I'm so grateful for you. I gave up my dreams a long time ago. The fact is, I wish I had the strength to start again. I wish I would have never given up. I can't take that back but what I can do is ask. Please Jake, stay focused on all the things you want in life. Go for ALL OF IT," I said with emphasis. "No matter how hard or how big the risk, I know you can do anything you set your mind to. And please, please know, I will forever be looking over you and rooting you on from the heavens.

You have big things in front of you. Don't let this weigh you down. I know you knew when I left this morning that something was wrong, baby. It's not your burden to bear." Taking a deep breath, I wiped away the tears from my face. "Jake, I'm sorry, I'm so, so sorry for not having your back every time he didn't let you have a voice. I hope, I pray that you keep your voice to him. Some days might be hard, but you need to know, he really is a good man. He has simply had a tough life. And remember, whatever he says, whatever happens, it is not about you. It is his pain, not yours. Jake, I love you to the moon and back and beyond," I said with a smile as I blew him a kiss. "When you come here in the future don't remember the pain, okay? Remember all the love that this place holds for us, remember the good times and the memories. Remember all the love I hold for you and know that you can always come here to talk, right here, in your favorite spot. I will be here, and I'll always be listening. I love you," I said again, choking up on my own words and then blowing him a kiss, I smiled again and shut off the video.

Sobbing, the tears started falling fast. I sat there thinking about our memories together, every conversation we had out on the trails. The laughs and the tears.

Breathing deeply, I kicked my legs out over the ledge.

CHAPTER 12

With my legs over the ledge, I reached my arms out, up then across and then back behind me as I pushed my chest forward slightly. My thoughts drifted back to the expo.

I finished the week strong, making more money than I did in two months at the restaurant. Meeting and talking to hundreds of people, I was filled with energy. There were two very distinct conversations I'll never forget.

Sitting there on the cliff in recollection, I saw it all so clearly. Those two conversations were huge opportunities. If only I would have seen it at the time, I could have been somebody.

Watching that day, I saw it clearly, the day I decided to move back home.

I was scheduled to go see Shelly at her hotel. She wanted me to do an entire redesign of their pictures. I was trying hard to be excited but all I could hear were her comments from the day of the expo. "What am I getting myself into?" I questioned.

Heeding her warning, I had on a blue and grey pantsuit with a bright white blouse underneath that Mom got me for graduation. It was the best outfit I owned. "Maybe now she will stop judging me," I thought.

"You're still fat," came the other voice. "How much weight have you put on now?" came next.

Shaking my head in my own self-criticism, I tried to encourage myself. "It's not about the weight, Faith. You're beautiful. It's about your talent. You got this. It's your chance."

"Shelly's right, successful people control what they eat. And you have no control," came the other voice quickly after.

With no rebuttal, I told myself, "Let the work shine for you, Faith."

"Are you really good enough, can it compensate?" I asked myself silently.

Tugging down the bottom of my suit jacket and pulling each side, one after the other, I was trying hard to stretch it out just enough so my belly wasn't making the buttons bulge. I could hear Shelly silently criticizing me with each look and I was trying to prepare myself for whatever she had to say this time. She was not a woman who held back from her feelings, that was for sure. I still was uncertain why she was giving me this chance, knowing how she treated me that day.

"Is it a massive joke on me, like high school?" I wondered.

"Stop, Faith," I said to myself.

Looking back through the rearview mirror, the cab driver asked, "So what has you going to this part of town?" I could see he was clearly judging me like everyone else.

"I have a meeting with Mrs. Hyatt," I responded as I looked out the window.

"Umm," he said with slight hesitation. "That's a pretty high-end lady," he said slowly and methodically. "You do know what you are walking into, right? Have you ever been there before?"

"No, I haven't, and yes thank you, I am well aware of who I am meeting with today." I thought, great, even the cab driver is questioning me. "Stop it Faith," I said to myself again. "You've made it here three years, no family, no support, just you, doing it!" I continued trying to give myself the pep talk I needed. As we started getting into the richer side of town, I breathed deeply and continued to reinforce myself. "You deserve this, Faith. Who cares what they think? You're a brilliant photographer, one of the best. They loved your work at the show, and you deserve this," I said again.

Suddenly we arrived at the hotel. I looked at the driver and paid what was due as he looked back at me.

"Are you sure?" he questioned with a protective type of tone again. He reminded me of my uncle, always trying to talk me out of going for it.

"I appreciate your concern. Thank you, I got this," I assured him.

Turning fully around this time and looking back at me, he slowly and methodically looked me up and down yet again, then said, "Good luck, young lady."

I got out of the cab, tugged my jacket down again and thought to myself, "She's not going to approve of this" as I shook my head. "Forget her," came next. "I love this suit and I feel confident in it. I'll show her what I'm capable of. No one is going to tell me what I can or can't do or be."

"Bullshit" came next. "You know full well she is going to tear you apart."

"Faith, stop." I said so loudly in my head that I questioned for a moment if I said it out loud. I definitely didn't need everyone around me examining my sanity today.

Standing there outside the door of the hotel I watched as one person after another walked in and out, dressed in their $2500 suits and $1500 handbags. I felt clearly out of place. Each one watched me as they walked by, scanning me up and down. I was certain they were wondering, "What are you doing here?" I thought, "Stop it, Faith. You have as much right to be here as anyone else," I thought, in a slightly less confident tone.

Walking up to the doorman, I felt my legs shaking. He was an older man, grey hair, and he reminded me of my grandpa. Well put-together, but clearly not the life he was brought up in. "Good day, sir," I greeted him.

He looked at me with a quick glance, seemingly non-judgmental, then came in close. "Honey, are you sure you're in the right place?" he asked with a caring tone. "This can be a tough crowd," he continued.

"Thank you, sir, I understand, I've already encountered it a number of times. I'm here to deliver some prints for Shelly Hyatt," I replied.

He looked at me again, eyes now widening. "You are here for Mrs. Hyatt?" he asked with an inquisitive tone. "Might I suggest that you assert yourself and be confident in your tone with her? It will go much further for you, young lady. Ms. Shelly really does mean well. I have known her for a lot of years. She has a great big heart; it just comes out differently than it does for other people."

Questionably looking at him, my head slightly tilted, I asked, "Really?

"Honey," he responded, "I've been the doorman here for nearly 28 years. I watched her grow up. That Mrs. Hyatt, she is a good lady. She may have high expectations, sure, but look where it's gotten her. She clearly knows what she is doing and is a good person for you to learn from. She obviously sees potential in you or you wouldn't be here. All you have to do is listen and keep up with her."

I felt the grit, determination and strength in me as I pulled my shoulders back and stood slightly taller. "I am a strong woman," I responded to him with sureness and confidence in my tone. "But, sir, I must say, I believe you can be kind and respectful towards others while being strong, determined and getting things done."

"Fair enough," he responded. "Good luck to you, honey, you better get in there," he finished as he opened the door and nudged me inside.

I walked into the grand entryway of the hotel. Everything the eye could see was perfectly placed, from the curved couch to the glass high-top tables. Making my way to the reception desk, I worked to hold my posture, shoulders back, head held high. The closer I got the more I felt my throat start to tighten. Clearing it as I approached the desk, I stood there waiting for someone to help. There were three receptionists and each was clearly avoiding me. Not so much as a comment from them, it was as though I did not even exist. Yep, high school all over again. "Excuse me," I tried to get someone's attention. With disbelief, I kept waiting as none of them acknowledged me. Clearing my throat and getting slightly irritated, with a more assertive tone, I asked again, "Excuse me." Louder this time. All three of them suddenly looked at me, dressed all prim and proper in their Hyatt attire. The first, a woman with long brown locks, black glasses, bright red lipstick and the shape of a supermodel, looked me up and down before turning and helping the next person in line. The next, a shorter woman, blonde hair, clearly older than the others, glanced at me, nodded her head slightly then went back to the person she was with. Finally, the last woman, in her four-inch heels, perfectly hemmed skirt, hair pulled up in a high bun and designer glasses sitting towards the end of her nose, approached me.

"Can I help you?" she asked with a pretentious tone.

Seriously, I thought, *is this really the type of service they provide to everyone?* I took a deep breath, looked down, then quickly looked back up as I said directly, "Faith DeWalt here for Mrs. Hyatt."

She looked at me, tilting her head in disbelief, then pushed her glasses up her nose before regaining eye contact. She started again to look me up and down. Before allowing her a chance to say anything I jumped in again.

"Can you please ring Mrs. Hyatt? Let her know Faith is here for her."

"Um, are you sure you have the right name?" she asked.

"Look lady," I started, "I was quite clear, thank you very much." Matching her rude tone, I said it yet again. "I'm here to see Mrs. Shelly Hyatt, if you'll let her know I'm here." Standing there trying to embrace the directness I was communicating at that moment, I felt every part of me wanting to run out of the door. "You got this, Faith," I reinforced to myself. "Don't let her see you shaking." Quickly the other voice came in again. "You don't belong here. Even the receptionists know it."

I watched as she went to ring Shelly. "It will all be over soon enough, Faith," I tried assuring myself again.

She hung up, looked back up to me then over to her colleague and back to me again. "Well, I guess you can go up. The elevators are around the corner to your right. You will ring up to the penthouse. They know to expect you." Then with a slight chuckle in her tone she said, "Huh, and good luck" before turning to the first woman and snickering as they stared at me walking away.

"There is no way I'm going to let this lady defeat me," I thought. "I'm not sinking to her level."

Quickly up the elevator, I was met by the security guard just outside the door reading a magazine. He quickly came to his feet. "Seriously," I thought, "they have security? Who are these people?" Not knowing what to expect from him, I greeted him with a simple nod and a smile.

"How's your day ma'am?" he asked.

Perhaps one of the kindest people I've encountered since getting here, I responded, "My day is good. How about yours?"

"Well, it's another day, not too much goes on up here," he said. "You're Faith, right?" he asked. Before I could get a response out, he continued, "Mrs. Hyatt said you would be here. She really likes your work. She showed me some of it after the expo. You're really good."

Surprised, I hesitated for a moment. "She, umm, she showed you my work?" I asked in a puzzled tone.

"She did. Mrs. Hyatt knows talent, maybe even more than anyone I have ever known before. She may not show it well, but she really does support people and is very excited to have you doing more work for the hotel."

Speechless for a moment at this young man's comments, I looked back up at him. "Thank you," I said just as Shelly opened the door.

He looked at her and nodded his head. "Ma'am."

She nodded back without a response then invited me in and closed the door behind us. Standing in their front entry she slowly looked at me, up and down, then shook her head ever so slightly before starting to walk down the hall.

"Okay, wait a minute," I said in a semi-firm tone. "I don't want to be disrespectful, but this is a nice professional suit. Why did you do that again? Why must you judge me?" Instantly I regretted it, knowing I may have just given up my chance at this project.

Stopping mid-step, Shelly looked down, turned around, then looked back up at me before coming in closer. Now directly in front of me she shook her head again. "Faith, is this really you? Let me ask you this, if money was not a factor, if you had unlimited resources and knew you were coming here, how would you show up? Like this?" she said in a patronizing tone as she waved her hands up and down in front of me.

Connecting eyes with her I said, "Shelly, I don't know, but what I can tell you is that I would be respectful and kind to anyone no matter how much money I had. I felt really good when I left my house today. This is the best suit I own, and it may not be a $2500 Neiman Marcus suit, but we all have starting points. Fact is, even if I had that kind of money, I wouldn't go spending it on a suit."

Then there was silence for a moment. I questioned myself. "Did I blow it?"

"Be honest, Faith, did you really feel good about yourself this morning?" she asked as she crossed her arms and leaned in slightly while maintaining eye contact with me.

As I stood there in front of her, I was reminded of all the comments I thought looking in the mirror this morning. The criticisms about my belly. The big wiggly arms. Avoiding the question, I said to her, "Look I don't know how you grew up, but I have worked hard for everything I have and a suit isn't going to ever make or break what I am able to do in life."

She looked at me with what felt like a look of respect before continuing up the hallway. Then briefly she stopped, connected eyes and said, "Maybe you just don't have what it takes, Faith. If you are not willing to take care of yourself, respect your body and your mind, why would others respect you?" With a pause she continued down the hall before stopping yet again. "I have to believe you want more for yourself," she said in a firmer tone this time, then turned back around and continued.

Following her, I pondered that thought. *"I have to believe you want more."* It stung through my head as I felt my hands getting sweatier, a beam of water dripping down my back, heart beating fast. I could feel it coming straight up through my neck and face, the nerves and anxiety that I had felt so many times before. She was right. I wanted so much more, but how? "Suck it up, Faith, suck it up, don't let her see you like this," I told myself over and over.

During the rest of the afternoon Shelly showed me the entire hotel as she shared her vision. She expressed her thoughts about my prints and other new shots that could enhance the space. She was very clear about her expectations, too. If I was to be in her hotel my appearance and demeanor needed to change. I asked myself, "Can you do it? Do you have the strength to be who she expects you to be? The person you really want to be for yourself. Is this what you want?" With each word she spoke, I criticized myself even more, feeling smaller and less significant than ever, reckoning why I wasn't able to be that person.

Getting ready to leave, she walked me to the front door of the hotel, then reached out her hand for a shake. "You have so much potential, Faith. I was very clear on my expectations. You let me know if you can rise up and give me what I need. If you can, I would love to have you growing with the rest of the team that supports me. But I only bring people onto my projects who have respect for themselves and align with me."

"Shelly, I don't get it. Please explain why you would bring me here, show me all of this, just to tell me in order to work together I have to change who I am?"

Looking at me, she shook her head yet again. "Because I believe in you, Faith, that's why. You have some real gifts, ones you haven't even realized yet. Something I do not see all that often. You just don't see it. I sure hope someday you do. If I am not holding people to a higher standard, who will? If I allow those around me to be less than they are capable of, what does that say about me? Let me know within the week if you are interested. I sure hope you are up for it." She finished, then walked away.

Reaching for the doorknob to leave I felt the rush of tears coming to my eyes.

CHAPTER 13

Still sitting there with my legs hanging over the side of the cliff, I let the memories fade as I thought about the video to Jake. As I did, I glanced off to my right. Matt was sitting Indian-style with his chin resting in his hands next to the rock-climbing area, watching me.

"Who is this man?" I asked myself again. "What's his motive?" came next.

Placing my attention back to the view, I put my hands behind me, laid back and looked up to the sky then breathed in the morning air. "I love you, Jake," I said out loud, not caring who heard me. "I will always be here, right here, with you every step of the way." Looking up I saw my trusted eagles right in front of me. They looked close enough to reach out and touch. Feeling my heartbeat faster and tears coming down again, my throat tightened as I tried to hold them back. "Take care of him for me," I requested as I blew a kiss up to the sky then got up to make my way back to the trail. I saw Matt still there in the distance, anxious to see what my next move was going to be.

Taking my time, I climbed back over to the trail and started making my way to reconnect with him. Tears continued down my face as I thought about the kids. "Will they be able to get past this and move on?" I asked myself. "Don't do it, Faith" came quickly after. "They are going to be just fine," I assured myself with a partial smile. "You built them to be strong." Images of them played in my mind as I saw Matt quickly approaching.

He looked at me and slowed down as he got closer. "That was a tough one, huh?" he asked with a pause.

Then, without getting a response from me, he continued. "Are you okay?" He placed his arm around my shoulder from the side as we kept walking.

I looked over to see him watching me. Without a word, I laid my head on his shoulder as I wrapped my arm around his lower back. "Thanks Matt," I simply said as we walked. Feeling safe, the tears started to subside.

Walking in silence, arm in arm, I felt like we were connecting without any words needing to be spoken as I listened to nature fill in the sound. It was calming in so many ways.

Letting go of him, I wiped my face and took a break for some water.

He stopped to wait and asked, "Are you okay, Faith?"

"Yah know, the thing about life, it's emotional, and well, hard sometimes. Looking back, I realize how insecure I had been with the things I wanted most in life. I sold myself short over and over." Shaking my head, I continued. "I really hope my kids don't follow that same path."

"Is that what your video was about?" he asked.

"No, that was something else. Actually," I said, "now that you mention it, I guess in the big scheme of things, it was part of it," I said with a pondering tone.

"So, is that what brought you back from Washington, because you doubted yourself?"

"Wow, aren't you full of questions," I said in a playful tone looking up at him as I thought *he really does care.*

"That's a pretty bold question considering we just met, Matt," I said to him.

"Come on. It feels to me like we have known each other for years," he replied playfully as he bumped my shoulder with his.

Shaking my head, I thought, "I suppose it won't hurt. It's my last day here anyway. Who cares if I get judged at this point." Yet, something inside told me I didn't have to worry about that with him. Feeling uncertain about why I trusted him so much already, I hesitated, as he jumped in.

"It's all right Faith, I get it if you don't want to share with me," he said.

In that comment, it instantly made me trust him even more. "Matt, bottom line, it's like I said before, it was never about anyone else. Ultimately, it came down to my own lack of confidence. As a large girl, from the time I was little, everybody made it really clear that I had no self-control and I owned that story. I accepted everything everyone said about me as if it was the truth. I kept it as part of me, true or not. Fact is that my move to Washington was just my way of getting away. I never dealt with the issues that needed to be dealt with. I never dealt with the fact that I couldn't even stand looking at myself in the mirror. When I tried to be happy looking at myself, there was always an underlying critic. Even reminding myself how good of a human I was, it never mattered. All I saw was that fat girl whose voice didn't matter. It was exactly how my sister said, the whole time we were growing up."

Pausing for a moment, I took a deep breath. I stopped and placed my hands on my knees, squatting down slightly. Then shaking my head, I continued. "When I got to Washington, the judgment from people in this new place I called home, people who had no idea who I was, well, let's just say it kept building and I kept adding to that story." Looking down I picked up rocks from the trail and started tossing them off to the forest area as we walked. "It's easy now to look back and see all the good things I did, how strong I was at that time. Man," I said, "the grit I had through the years! But it's true, the hard stuff is always easier to believe. The criticisms, the judgments, well, I accepted them as mine, so that's what they became." Tears started rolling down my face again.

Quickly grabbing my arm, he stopped me. "Faith, you've changed that story, right? You know that's not you anymore, don't you?"

Waiting for a response I met him with silence.

"Look Faith, we've all had moments in life when the self-critic takes over. It doesn't mean you quit. Adjust maybe, decide if you want to own the comments, pivot if you need to, then move on," he said with emphasis as he looked me in the eyes. "But listen, whatever you decide, it doesn't mean you quit on yourself."

"I already did, I gave up on my dreams a long time ago. It's fine, it just wasn't meant to be."

"Perhaps you could just call it a long break," he said. "My second year in pre-law, things were going fine, I was getting great grades, on the surface it looked like all was well. But I wasn't happy. In fact, I was quite miserable. I knew early on it wasn't what I wanted to do with my life. Dad was pushing me hard and constantly bragging to his friends. *My son the lawyer* he would say with his chuckle at the end.

"It was as though I was some type of trophy. He pushed me constantly to get specialized and go into something that made the 'big bucks,'" Matt said as he made quote marks with his fingers and imitated his dad's voice. "Every time I tried talking to him about it, he shut me down. But I was so drawn to creating things. I wanted to make unique sculptures that people couldn't find anywhere else. For summer break that year I decided to buy my first welding machine. I went to the junkyard and found some different pieces of metal to work with. I made this cool little bohemian man with gangly spring arms for my mom. She loved it. She still has it in the yard too," he said as he looked at me with delight. "All of my friends and the guys at school gave me crap. They said my work sucked and to stick with what I was good at. Dad was adamant. *That's not the life for you* he often said. It didn't take long before I gave it all up and stopped."

Glancing his way, I asked, "Did you keep playing around with it afterwards?"

"Nope," he responded with a shake of the head. "I told myself, life wasn't meant to be fun, you're not supposed to enjoy what you do, life is about having a job and working hard." He waved his arm half bent in front of him. "I didn't pick up that welder again for years. Then I was cleaning out Mom and Dad's garage one day and there it was. I fell in love with it all over again and haven't looked back since. When people had opinions that time around, I didn't care, I just stayed focused on what I wanted. They could keep their thoughts. I was not owning them this time. See, the passion never left. Let's just say I put a pause on it, and when I was ready it was ready for me."

"Fine Matt, I'll give you that but, you have to agree, it's a bit different. I was all in. I had it, I was right there, I had the best show of my life. Three years I dedicated out in Washington, building, growing, experiencing life, getting some shots of places most people never even get to see in their lifetime. Then when I finally got my big opportunity at two large jobs, I caved to the critics. I listened to what they were saying and didn't believe I was up for the challenge."

Abruptly he interrupted. "Is that true? Is it really?"

"Excuse me?" I responded curtly.

"Come on, Faith, I for one am not going to let you bullshit yourself. So tell me, is it true? Were you really all in, or were you looking for a reason to give up?"

Did he really have the nerve to just say that?

After a moment of stewing in that thought, it hit me; I never really believed I could do it. "Oh my gosh, you're right, I was always looking for a reason to fail. The criticisms and comments were what I was looking for to acknowledge the fact. Those were my out," I said, shaking my head, feeling my heart sink at the thought. "I'm sure it was just never really meant to be."

"Come on, Faith, I'm not having the pity party anymore," he said with emphasis. "If you love it, if you enjoy it, start doing it again, bottom line. Even if it's on the side to start, what would it hurt?"

Annoyed and yet appreciative at the same time, I thought about what he said. "What would it feel like to start shooting the way I used to?" I wondered as I imagined some of the shoots I could go on and new places I could explore. *Stop, Faith* I quickly redirected myself. *You made your choice.*

"What's done is done, Matt, I've already made the decision." I responded to him knowing what was to come at the end of my day.

"Just hear me out, okay?" He kept pushing. "Just play with me here for a minute." He continued with an excitable tone. "Let's run it down. I mean, what is the worst thing that could happen if you started shooting again? For real, if you started promoting yourself and your work the way you did in Washington, more so even. Maybe set up an Instagram account, a Facebook and post pictures of your work. I can even help you build a website; it won't take long, a few days if that. I could have it ready for you in a weekend."

Looking at him perplexed again I asked, "Matt, you just met me, why do you even care this much?"

Avoiding my question, he asked again. "Come on, what's the worst thing that could happen? The absolute worst?" Stopping, he crossed his arms and looked at me. "Go ahead, hit me with it."

With a huff, I stopped and mirrored his look, crossing my arms, staring him down. "Fine!" I said. "It's the fat girl trying all over again. She'll never make it, she isn't strong enough. Yep, I can hear them already, Matt, I don't need it again."

"I'm so over this whole fat girl thing, Faith. Give me another, you must be able to do better than that," he said boldly.

Shaking my head again as we stood there staring each other down as if we were having a duel, I continued. "This would not go over well at all with my husband. As far as he is concerned, I just need to stay focused on work to keep making him money and taking care of the kids. Life is calmer in the house when I just do what he says and don't poke the bear." Embarrassed, admitting that to Matt, I broke eye contact as I felt the tears welling up in my eyes.

"Clearly, we need to have another conversation about that later. You are worth having your voice and opinions heard, Faith. Everyone is. Besides, I am not quite sure what you are doing with someone that doesn't support you. You are way better than that. Now keep going, I'm listening, what else do you got?"

As uncomfortable as he was making me in this instant, it somehow felt good to have someone paying attention to me, hearing me and really listening. I looked down for a moment as I shook my head and took a deep swallow.

Pushing slightly, he jumped in again. "Come on Faith, what else? What's the worst that could happen?" he said again, with force this time. "You're not selling me here on why you can't."

"What if I fail, Matt? What if it doesn't work?" I said softly as a tear rolled from my eye.

He laughed lightly before coming in closer, gently grabbing each of my arms and pulling me in, placing his hands on each side of my face and wiping the tears. "Hear me out here for a minute. You've been in staffing sales for 12 years, right? And you've been selling this entire time, am I correct? Did I understand that right?" he asked before lifting my face to make eye contact again.

"Yes."

He dropped his hands down away from my face and asked as he crossed his arms again, "Are you good at it?

"What kind of a question is that, Matt?" I responded, crossing my arms again.

"Ah, there you are." He started back in with a pleased tone. "I know quite a bit about staffing and from my understanding it's a real tough gig. Do you stop because you might fail or because someone might say no?" he asked.

"Heck no," I quickly responded, "I make more calls. And never end on a low note. That's the rule of thumb to keep the energy up."

Looking at me he asked, "Okay, so, what's the best thing that could happen, Faith?"

Don't do it Faith, don't do it I tried reminding myself. *You made your choice already. No turning back, remember?*

"Come on," he jumped in and said as he got closer to me.

I simply responded to him, "I could fly." Then I turned and started walking to the stream up ahead.

CHAPTER 14

Knowing that he had no idea how I intended that statement, I shook my head and thought about my final stop today. Doing so, memories drifted back to the year I moved back from Washington.

It was 1999 and I had been back for nearly a year. I was working as a restaurant manager at the local McDonald's. The comments and "I told you so's" when I moved back were hard. There wasn't a whole lot I could say in my defense. They were right; I gave up. The words from my sister and her friends when I moved back were probably the worst.

I could hear her like it was yesterday.

"I told you not to go. I warned you, Faith, there are some people who are meant to be heard and seen. You are not either of those people."

My heart sank in that statement. "Why can't she practice some empathy for a change?" I thought. "I wish she would just support me and practice a little kindness." Putting my head down I accepted her words yet again and said nothing in response.

She continued, "Your voice, well," she said with an arrogant tone, "nobody wants to hear you. Nobody cares what you think, that's the bottom line, and everyone knows but you. They are all just too nice to say it. You are meant to take the backseat and shut your mouth. Not seen, not heard."

With my body language shifting the longer she talked, I felt smaller and smaller. Shoulders folding in, my heart racing, face filled with heat and ready to cry. "At least I tried," I said softly.

She stood there with her arms crossed and said, "Ya know, Faith, even Mom and Dad have said it time and again. You were an accident, you were not meant to be here." Then she turned and started walking away, clearly knowing, once again, she got the upper hand.

That was the day I stopped shooting too. I decided it wasn't worth the pain or harsh reminders from her anymore. I had enough; they were all right. I didn't have what it took.

I owned those words that she reinforced that day, "Don't be seen or heard. Don't stand out. People don't care what you have to say." And I reminded myself of it frequently.

Daddy's words came in often too. "Keep your head down and work hard." That must have been what he meant all those years.

At the time, I was working 65-75 hours a week at the restaurant and going out dancing every night, drinking far too much. It was the only way I could shut everything off and be free on the dance floor. I made a conscious effort when I moved back to start eating healthy and held to it. All the added activity coupled with healthy eating led to a massive weight loss of over 118 pounds since moving back. Admittedly, looking back, I realized how good I looked then! Too bad I couldn't see it. When I looked in the mirror, I was still that fat girl.

Luke and I had been dating for nearly two weeks now. Tonight, he was making me dinner at his place. It was the first time I felt it. I should have seen it then.

The mood was perfect. He had candles lit everywhere,

music in the background. I truly felt special, not just to him, but as a person. I was sitting on the couch, and he made his way toward me with a drink, Amaretto sour, my go-to at the time. Bringing his hand to my face he gently pushed my hair to the side starting at my forehead then down to my chin. "Here you are, beautiful," he said in a soft and gentle tone as he lifted my chin and gently kissed my lips before handing me the drink.

With a bashful smile, I could feel my face turning red as I looked down then quickly looked up as thoughts entered in. "So, do you do this with all your lady friends?" I asked, in a serious yet sassy tone.

Looking back at me in silence he ignored the question, grabbed his drink and made his way back over next to me. "I do this for you, beautiful."

We talked, laughed, kissed and caressed one another for hours.

Laying there with him, I thought, "Is this really happening? Did I finally find someone who cares about me?"

I had messed around and had fun with other guys through the years, but they were all superficial. Luke was the first man to ever take me out on a real date.

Nearly eleven o'clock, still arm in arm, feeling safe, I quickly dozed off. I felt him get up before covering me with a blanket then gently kissing me on the forehead before falling back to sleep.

Sleeping there peacefully, I was abruptly woken up with him screaming at me, his face inches from mine. Instantly I was awake and quickly backed up as far as I could get from him on the couch. The more I backed up the closer he got. The smell of alcohol on him was overwhelming. Clearly, he went out after I fell asleep. Terrified, I managed to get the words out, "Luke, what on earth is going on, what's wrong?"

Barely able to stand up straight, I recognized he was drunk. He grabbed my arms on each side, lifted me to a seated position then grabbed my phone and started waving it in front of my face. "Who the hell is this, Chase, calling you at three o'clock in the morning?" He demanded an answer.

"Wait, Luke," I started.

Before giving me a chance to say more, he continued. "What, you decided I am not enough for you?" Slurring his words, he said, "Are you fucking around with other men?"

At this point, wide awake and frustrated with the way he was acting, I combated his comments. "Wait a minute, you leave when we were having a nice evening, go get lit up, come back and I did something wrong? How does that work?" I said.

"Don't even turn this around on me," he screamed back.

"What is this really about Luke, because a friend called me?" I asked.

"Men do not call women at 3 a.m. unless they want something. And, that something is what they cannot have from you, you're mine," he said with force. "I'll beat his ass if he comes near you again."

Seeing how mad he was and not knowing how he would respond next, I paused.

"Luke, why are you doing this? He is my friend, that's it. There is nothing more than that. I would never do that to you or anyone for that matter. And I was clear when we met, my best friends are all men. They cause way less drama."

Or so I thought.

His face got redder, and he was slurring more. It was as if he was getting more drunk the longer he stood there.

"You didn't drive here, did you?" I asked him.

"What are you saying, I can't handle my liquor? Of course I drove. I'm fine," he said, barely getting all his words out.

Shaking my head in the thought of him driving instantly reminded me of the people I'd lost to drunk driving. "Look, these are my friends," I reinforced.

Quickly coming in closer, he grabbed my arms again, tighter this time. "Look Faith, I said you're mine. If those guys come near you again, it's not going to end well." Then he picked up my phone and dialed Chase's number.

"What are you doing?" I asked quickly as I got up and tried to grab my phone from him. He pushed me back on the couch as he responded, "I'm calling this jackass to tell him to leave you alone."

"Luke, stop," I pleaded.

I could see the anger in his face. With the uncertainty about what he would do next, I backed up slightly. I waited and listened as I could hear the phone ringing on the other end, thinking to myself *Don't answer Chase, please just don't answer.*

Just then I heard it. "Hey Faith." In a sad tone.

"Shit," I said to myself.

"You are not getting my girl, leave Faith alone," Luke said to him firmly. "If I catch you calling her, seeing her, anything, you are going to regret it."

Not being able to hear Chase on the other side, I knew whatever he said just fired Luke up even more. He screamed, "She's mine, you dick; you better leave her the hell alone."

Sitting there on the couch, resting my face in my hands, I felt the tears welling up. "Why is he doing this?" I thought. "Is this normal?" came next. Feeling my throat tighten, I fought back the tears as I pulled my legs close to my chest.

"No man calls a lady at this time of the morning unless he wants a booty call, that's it, it's that easy," he said to him. "Like I said man, leave her alone." Then he hung up the phone and threw it at me. "I better not catch you talking to him again or we're done. You're mine. You don't need any other men in your life." Then stumbling over himself he made his way up the stairs without another word.

Tears started rolling down my face as he walked away. Uncertain in that moment how to feel or what to think, I buried my head, crying into the pillow. "Why?" I asked myself quietly. After some time, I grabbed my phone wanting to call Chase. Uncertain of how Luke would respond if he heard me, I simply texted him *I am OK, stop in tomorrow, I work the early shift.*

Sure, whoever this guy is, Faith, he's a loser, leave he quickly responded.

Gotta go I finished before quickly deleting the texts.

Laying there, tears continued to roll down my cheek. I thought about Chase's comments, then asked myself, "Why are you here?"

Quickly, I heard the answer: "He loves you and you love him. Besides, you might never find anyone that loves you like this again."

"I'll have to tell the guys I can't hang out anymore," came my next thought, not wanting to upset Luke while wanting to see where our relationship went. Leaving wasn't even a question in my mind.

"What were you thinking?" I said out loud to myself recalling that moment.

CHAPTER 15

"What do you mean, Faith?" Matt asked in response.

Trying to shake off the emotion that moment stirred up, I shook out my arms and upper torso. "Nothing Matt, just a thought I got stuck in about the past."

Still questioning myself I asked, "What would have happened that night if I would have stood up for myself? Would we have made it? If I would have shared how I really felt through the years, how would life have been different?" In those thoughts, appreciating the surroundings, the rocky cliffs off to our right, eagles flying overhead, the sun shining through the trees, I realized I was present in a way I hadn't been before. Then I heard it: "You threw the enjoyment of life away" as I shook my head.

Matt watched closely and jumped in. "Do you want to share what's so heavy on your mind right now?"

He really is paying attention. Is it that obvious?

"Oh nothing," I responded.

"Faith," he quickly responded, "you might be able to fool others with that, but I know you're full of shit. Talking about it could help. Get it off your head and heart so you can lighten your load up a bit. I may not have the answers but perhaps I will have a perspective for you to consider."

I looked at him for a moment with a partial smile, staying silent.

He continued. "Okay, let's just break it down, realistically. We may never see each other again. Am I right?"

Again, met with no response but a slight head nod. He continued.

"Okay, I'll take that as a yes, so if you decide to open up and share what's weighing you down, it could lighten you up and," he said with emphasis, "you can rest assured that no one you know will ever know." He laughed. "Wow that was a mouthful. But, seriously Faith, it's not healthy to keep it all inside," he said, slowing down his tone. "I know you know that. And, if it's judgment or embarrassment you're worried about, don't, I'm not here to judge anyone. I've done my own stupid shit." Then stopping mid-step, he grabbed my arm and pulled me closer to him. "But I do have to say I sure hope this isn't the last I see you," he said, looking at me as he held my hands with each of his before letting go and continuing up the trail.

Standing there, watching him walk away, I felt my heart racing. "Should I trust him? Can I?" I asked myself as I felt my body tingling as if it was telling me *yes, lean in*. I quickly ran to catch up with him. "Matt, here's the thing." I started, then stopped. "I guess, it's just ah," I groaned. "It's just hard to talk about. Ultimately, everything in my life, it's all been my choice. So, talking about it, what's the point? They're just life experiences that led me to today and admittedly there's a lot in life that I made heavy and it's too late to do anything about it."

"I gathered that Faith, and like you said, you're the one making life heavy. You also have the choice to lighten the load just by talking about it," he invited again.

With another deep breath, I let out a groan. "When I first met my husband, I was in love. Like, all the way infatuation, blinded by the fact that I finally had someone who wanted me for more than just a night of fun. I loved not feeling alone. He made me feel special and beautiful, it felt so good. Yet, looking back, I realize how unhealthy our relationship was. Like I said, I had blinders on. There are some things I should have seen and known."

Interrupting, he asked, "Why should you have *known?*" as he used his hands making quotes in emphasis.

"Well, huh." I responded as I asked myself *should I have known it?*

"Faith, when we have never been in healthy relationships before or if we haven't seen what healthy relationships look like, how are we supposed to know? Sometimes it's truly learning as we go."

"You have a good point, Matt. So, anyway, when Luke and I first met, most of my closest friends were men. They were just easier to be around. I never got into the drama stuff, they were clear, to the point, no bullshit. It really bothered Luke, he always thought it meant I was sleeping around on him, but I never did. He drove all of them away quickly and made it clear that I wasn't to go around them anymore. He also made clear to them that he would beat the shit out of them if they ever tried talking to me again."

Looking at Matt, I saw him shaking his head without a word. He looked back up at me with big eyes as if saying, "Really."

Then I continued. "They were my people and he forced me to make a choice, him or them. I reasoned with myself that this was his way of showing love. That I might never find anyone that loved me this much again."

With a brief pause, I let out a chuckle and shook my head.

"Truth be told, Matt, he was my very first boyfriend. Don't get me wrong, I had a lot of fun times and nights with other guys through the years before meeting him, but he was the first that actually took a long-term interest. It meant something to me."

"Taking an interest," he started with emphasis, "doesn't that mean loving who you are?" he asked with frustration.

"I get it. It's like I said, it was on me. I was so insecure at the time. The simple fact that someone wanted to be close gave me a feeling that I was someone. As I thought back to all those nights before meeting him, going out and partying, it's what I was always looking for. It was my own lack of confidence that prevented me from getting it and Luke saw beyond all that. I know it's dumb, right?"

"No, it isn't, not at all. Everyone deserves to have a voice and be seen," he replied.

"Looking back, I should have gotten to know myself and what I wanted before getting into any relationships. I didn't even know who I was at the time. And, to your point earlier, I never really saw a healthy relationship with my parents, aunts and uncles or anyone else for that matter. But I do believe that they were doing the best that they knew how. I definitely realize how much healthier they could have been in their own communication with each if they had known better." Taking another deep breath, I paused.

"Can you change it now?" he asked, then before giving me a chance to answer he continued. "Better than that, do you want to change it now? Do you want to fight for your marriage?"

Looking at him, feeling more connected than I've felt to almost anyone before, I connected eyes as if wanting him to read my soul. Feeling my heart thumping again, I quickly looked away then took another deep breath. As I forcefully breathed out, I said, "I don't know. I don't feel good with him. The thing is, he's just being him and doing the best he knows how. He had a rough life growing up. No one should have to see the things he did at his age."

"Wait a minute, wait a minute, wait a minute," he said as he waved his hands on each side of his face. "OK I get it, I hear what you're saying, I really do, but do you love him?" he asked directly.

"What kind of a question is that, Matt?" I responded.

"No, Faith, I am being serious. Do you love him? Better than that, are you in love with him?" he asked.

Instantly, tears started rolling down my cheeks. "I do love him very much. I care about every part of his well-being and his happiness."

Slowing down with a calmer tone this time, he asked, "Are you in love with him?"

Locking eyes with him yet again, I answered softly, "I don't know," as I felt my heart sink, my whole body feeling instantly relieved saying it out loud. "I've never told any-one that before, Matt. I've never told anyone about any of it. I never wanted to disrespect him. To me, talking about people behind their backs is just disrespectful. Well, unless it's good of course," I said with a *huh*.

"Talking about it is normal. When you don't, it gets stuffed and then worse things happen because you didn't deal with it," he responded.

"Can we not talk about him anymore? Please."

"OK, just one more thing."

"What?" I asked with a firm tone.

Grabbing my hand again, he pulled me over. "I'm right here when you need it." Then he gently put his hand on the side of my face. I leaned my head into it. He came closer as he wrapped his hand around my waist. "Faith, you are worth it, you deserve the most beautiful life." With his face just inches from mine, my whole body felt tingly. Then he quickly let go and backed up. "I'm sorry," he said, backing up further. "But, I meant it, I'm here."

Continuing up the path with an awkward silence for some time, he finally broke it. "Okay, well," said in a peppier tone, "so then what do you want to talk about?"

"Have you always been this enthusiastic?" I asked.

"Well, it's a relative question. I guess I would have to answer in two parts. The short answer is yes, absolutely. I have always been the optimistic one looking at the brighter side of things. It's one of my best traits, if I must say so myself. Based on our time today, I would have guessed it's one of your natural traits too, am I right?" he asked boldly.

"It used to be but time fades, and you see life for the harsh thing it really is," I responded.

"What on earth is that supposed to mean? Life is what we make of it," he countered.

Avoiding his comment, I responded, "So what is the other part? The other side of your answer?"

"Ah, the other side, well, the answer is no, I haven't always. I've had moments in life that took me down a dark path. I've had points that brought out things in me as a person that I don't want to be. When I was working at the law firm, there were some rough times. They had high expectations and that's great, I'm all about high expectations," he said as he waved his arms again, "but when they come at the cost of other people and businesses, or at the cost of pegging people against each other, I'm not okay with it. I'll never forget, I was about eight years in when it started getting bad. We all had some big names on our rosters. Each of us was responsible for securing a certain number of new corporate business accounts each year. Several of us had the same companies on the list. The way the owners looked at it was whoever could 'nail them down first, won.' They sure did get what they wanted at our cost. And at the company's reputation."

"That's too bad," I chimed in.

"It was. Part of it was on me really, I had a big ego then. Working at that firm meant something to the people in my world. Especially my dad. I wanted to work for a good company with solid values, of course, but also wanted to be seen and had my name known. Sounds familiar?" he asked, looking at me.

I smiled and looked back up at him.

"Anyway, the goals started bringing in some real sleazy sales practices. I started feeling more like a sleazy salesperson as opposed to a respected attorney." He quickly backtracked. "Don't get me wrong, Faith, I have a very high regard for sales professionals. We are all in sales, after all, but the ones who do things the right way. Not just trying to earn a buck. They have my true respect."

"I get it, it sets a poor standard for all salespeople when that happens," I responded.

"It's true," he acknowledged. "Chris, one of my colleagues, started just a couple years after me. He would do anything to look good without regard to our image, even lying or embellishing about what was possible from a legal perspective. I am not sure if the owners just didn't care or didn't pick up on it but it baffled me. As long as he kept bringing in new business, it's like they were turning a blind eye to how he did it. All the goodness we had done through the years and the community efforts I had become accustomed to somehow didn't mean as much, seeing what they started supporting."

"Yes," I said with emphasis, "I hear that too. I've been there before. Actually, I'm still in it," I said as I looked down and shook my head. "Why do we do it?"

"I'm not sure. Well actually, I am. It's like I said before, I was hungry, I wanted to be seen, I wanted my name known. To me, the only difference was that I acted with more integrity and people-focus than they did. And, no judgments, it's their business, they can do what they want. But I knew it didn't feel good for me. Anyway, I reasoned with myself, somehow told myself, this was the way people do business and to get ahead it's what you have to do. Boy, was I wrong."

He yelled out with a scream in frustration.

Watching him, shocked for a moment, I waited to see what was next.

"I can't believe I dealt with it for so long. There was this one time, we were going after the Nike account. The owners wanted it bad too. They often talked about how they would throw it in our competitor's faces when they got it. Whoever landed the deal with a one-year retainer got a $25,000 bonus. It was huge! We got bonuses often, but this was by far the biggest ever."

Shocked at the number, I reiterated, "Twenty-five thousand for a bonus?"

He chuckled. "Yep, it was crazy. The amount of money that gets tossed around for corporate business, it's insane. Like I said, though, it comes at a cost. Needless to say, Chris and I both were pushing hard to win that one." Stopping, he rubbed his forehead for a minute.

"You okay?" I asked.

"The things we learn in life, Faith, that's all." Then he continued walking as he finished. "The short of it is that Chris got the account by doing some very underhanded things. When the executives of Nike realized how much he embellished about what we could do they were livid and tarnished our names for a while in the market. After about seven months, they turned the account over to me to try to save it. I had a lot of pieces to pick up and groveling to do on behalf of everyone. I also had a part to own in all of it to the Nike people. Man, that sucked."

"I can imagine," I agreed.

"See Faith, but that's my point. It taught me so many lessons about staying true to myself and my values. Speaking up when I knew I needed to. And, more than any of that, looking back, it taught me valuable lessons I now use in my business that maybe I wouldn't have known otherwise."

I don't have any energy left for the fight I thought as he talked. *I'm just done.*

CHAPTER 16

I n that thought my memories took me back to all the energy and fight I put into the staffing company.

Working there for years now, the depth of knowledge I learned about people, business, leadership and myself was irreplaceable, although I didn't realize it then. There was always more work to do at the end of the day. Luke didn't like that I worked so much, although he hadn't liked it since Jake was born. I wasn't quite sure why; he got to stay home and watch him grow up every day. This day wasn't all that much different than the rest, and yet, it was a moment that has forever stuck with me.

It was nearly 6:45 p.m. and I was finally heading home. Although it was a long day, it seemed to go so fast. They all did. We hired out over 27 employees to various companies, not to mention the client conversations and other happenings of the day. The diversity of conversations kept the days interesting. On this particular day, I felt especially grateful to do what I do by the kind words and gestures of the employees.

My energy quickly shifted as I looked at my phone when I got into my car. Four missed calls since his last call about an hour ago.

"Where are you?" I heard in a firm, angry tone in his voicemail. "You should have left that place hours ago. Why do you keep choosing that job over our family?" came next.

My heart started pounding, and my stomach dropped as I thought about his comments. The dichotomy of wanting to be home with the kids yet wanting to stay at work to avoid him. "Please don't be angry at me," I thought in hopes of what his attitude would be like when I got there.

The next voicemail came. "My mom would have never been away this much. She was always home to provide for us kids, not neglecting us like you do." Those same words I'd heard from him over and over since Jake was born.

Then yet the next message I heard was, "I'm going to lose it with these kids if you are not home soon, Faith."

Instantly I hung up and called him. With the phone ringing I looked up at the sky as I said, "Take care of my babies." Then I blew a kiss.

He answered and I was immediately met with him asking "Where the hell are you?"

"I was working Luke; it's my job, remember? What do you want me to do?" Knowing as soon as I said it how frustrated he was going to be with me, I started preparing for his response as I shook my head.

"Get home," he said forcefully before hanging up.

Tears instantly started rolling down my face as I felt the anxiety build. "I wish he would just leave. It would be so much easier," I thought as I imagined what our lives would look like without him. "I can't handle this tonight," I said to myself.

Pulling in the driveway, I felt the heaviness in my belly. "Please don't be mad," I said to myself over and over. As I opened the door, instantly I was met with his voice screaming.

"Damn it, Douglas, what the hell do you think you are doing?" Luke said loudly.

Doug had just dumped out his tub of Legos on the living floor and came running up to me.

"I just wanted to play, Mommy." He looked at me with sad eyes.

"Get back in here and pick these up, you dummy. I told you there was no more playing tonight," Luke scolded. "Your mother is not saving you on this one."

Doug looked up at me with tears now rolling down his face. I dropped my bags then picked him up in my arms. "It's okay baby," I whispered in his ear.

Carrying him, I walked in by Luke. "Hi," I said with a cautious expression.

"Don't even think about it, Faith. These kids have been little brats all day. I would have never acted this way with my mom. They don't need a thing. As far as I am concerned, they can skip dinner and go straight to bed."

Lifting Doug's chin off my shoulder, I looked at him. "Were you listening to your father today?" I asked.

"I just told you he wasn't," he screamed back at me as he threw the Lego container across the room.

"I got that Luke, and he's only six years old," I responded.

"There you go, sticking up for him again," he screamed at me.

"Can we not do this tonight?" I asked him. "It's been a long day. I can get dinner started. The boys will get the Legos picked up. Then maybe we'll eat together and play a game as a family," I said in a soft tone, trying to calm him down.

"Oh, you had a long day?" He came in closer. "You had a long day? Well, there you go, I get it, it's all about you again isn't it, Faith?" he said in a more escalated tone as he threw his arms up in the air with frustration.

Hearing the yelling, Jake ran in the room and hugged me from the other side. He looked at Luke then back at me before laying his head on the side of my hip. Moments later, tugging on my shirt, he looked up at me. I glanced back at him and saw him waving his finger as if asking me to get closer. Then I kneeled down.

He came in close to my ear then said, "Can I tell you a secret?"

Not sure what to expect, I responded with enthusiastic hesitation. "Of course you can, honey."

"Daddy's having a very bad day. He's really mad. He even said I was grounded from going to the birthday party this weekend, Mom."

I saw Luke standing there with his arms crossed watching us out of the corner of my eye. Trying to keep my attention on the boys, I could feel the redness growing up through my neck as I wondered what was going through his mind.

Taking a deep breath with my attention on Jake, I looked back to Doug, kissed him on the forehead then gave my attention back to Jake. "Can I ask you a question?"

He nodded his head.

"Do you remember when you were playing with Isaiah a few weeks ago? The two of you got into an argument about your Tonka truck?" I asked.

"Yes, he was really mean, Mommy," Jake responded.

"Do you remember what you said to him when that happened?"

Taking a break for a moment, he looked down, then in a quiet tone said, "Yes."

"What did you say?" I asked.

"I don't want to be your friend anymore," he said quietly as he looked down again.

Gently lifting his chin up, I asked, "Did you mean it?"

"No," he said, "I was upset."

"See honey, sometimes we all say things out of haste," I said to him as I looked back up at Luke with an expression that implied I was talking to him. "See, we don't always mean what we say in those moments."

Watching him, I saw his face quickly turn red. "You're always sticking up for them. Just once I wish you would do the same for me!" he yelled, then he stomped his way down the hallway and out of the back garage door, slamming it behind him.

I felt a contradiction of emotions come over me. Gratitude that he just walked away and worried about what he was going to be like when he returned. Quickly collecting my thoughts for the kids, I smiled and looked at the boys. "Listen up you two, I expect you to be on your best behavior the rest of the night, is it a deal?"

With sad eyes, they looked at me.

"Come on guys. Let's not let it wreck our night," I encouraged them again. "How about some music?" I said with more enthusiasm.

Without another thought, I pulled out my phone, turned on my playlist and turned up the volume. Within minutes I watched as the kids' energy came back to life. We listened to music and danced around the house as Joy watched me cook dinner and the boys picked up their toys.

As we finished getting dinner ready and the table set, Luke came back in the house. "Turn that shit off. Why can't I just have a little peace in this house?" he yelled as he made his way from the garage door to the upstairs before slamming the bedroom door.

Shaking my head to myself, I turned off the music and tried to keep a positive tone with the kids. "Let's keep it down for Daddy, okay?

With no hesitation Doug responded, "Why doesn't he like us talking, Mommy?"

"It's not that honey," I responded. "He's just having a bad day."

"Every day is a bad day for him, Mom," Jake said abruptly. Without a response to his comment, I replied, "Let's go eat, okay?" Then I wrapped my arms around him, picked him up and squeezed him tight.

"Put the book away honey," I said to Joy who was already sitting by the table.

"Mommy, I am going to be a movie star when I grow up," she said with excitement in her tone.

Looking at her I could see the belief she had in those words and the sparkle in her eyes. "You are?" I responded.

"Yes Mommy, I'm going to be just like Cinderella," she continued.

Jake sat down next to her. "Princesses aren't real, silly," he said.

"Yes they are," she responded with directness, then looked at me. "Right, Mommy?" she requested confirmation.

I looked at Jake for a moment then looked back at Joy. "Of course, there are hundreds, maybe even thousands, of movie stars that we could call princesses, if we wanted to." Then looking back at Jake with a soft grin on my face, I requested acknowledgment. "Right?"

"Mom," he started with a scathing tone. Before saying another word, he saw the look on my face then paused, then looked back at Joy. "You are a princess, Joy," he said, then grabbed her hand and kissed the top as he bowed his head in the proper form for greeting a princess.

Watching him, I smiled. As he made eye contact with me again, I mouthed the words "thank you."

He shook his head and went back to eating his dinner.

Looking back at Joy I told her, "Baby, you can do anything you want with your life. You just have to stay focused and work really hard. All of you can," I said, looking back at the boys. "Always remember that."

"Like you do, Mommy?" Joy asked as she looked at me with the most heartfelt honest eyes.

Not realizing Luke was in the doorway, I was startled as he interjected. "Don't go filling those kids' heads with that rubbish. We work to pay the bills; it isn't meant to be fun. Dreams aren't real life."

"Luke," I responded with frustration.

"Mommy?" Joy said as she looked at me again with a question in her tone.

"Baby, I promise, you are smart, funny and beautiful. You would be one of the best movie stars ever, but like I said, it's going to take hard work and focus. Don't listen to Daddy, he's just being a grouch," I said as I turned and looked at him with a stern glare.

"You are going to regret talking to me like that," he yelled, then stomped away as he punched the wall and slammed the door behind him yet again.

"Is Daddy going to yell at you again tonight, Mommy? He scares me when he yells at you," Joy said with a sad look on her face.

"It will be all right, I promise," I told her with as big of a smile as I could muster in the moment.

"He's just mean, Mom," Jake added.

"He loves you kids very much," I said as I looked at all of them.

"Now go get washed up and put your jammies on while I clean up the kitchen." I started cleaning the table.

They were quickly off to their rooms getting ready for bed as I washed the dishes. Again, not hearing him come in the house, I was startled as Luke grabbed me from behind and turned me around forcefully. Squeezing my biceps, he pushed me against the wall. "What the fuck are you thinking, talking to me like that in front of my boys? What, I don't earn the money in the house, so my voice doesn't matter?" he claimed.

"You know that's not true Luke," I said.

"Don't you dare interrupt me," he reprimanded with his face inches from mine. "We are not raising them to be dreamers or to have their head in the clouds. We are raising these kids my way. Do you understand me?" he asked.

"My voice matters. They are my kids too, Luke."

He interrupted me, squeezing my arms even tighter. "Not in this house, you don't have a voice, we go by my rules."

"Luke, you're hurting me."

"See, you can't even fend for yourself when your back is against the wall, what makes you think you deserve a voice?" he said with scorn.

Shaking my head, I looked away from him. Wanting desperately to say something, I kept quiet to not escalate him further.

"Don't you look away from me," he scolded again as he grabbed my face with his hand to regain eye contact.

"Mom," Doug said from behind us in a worried tone.

"Let go of her!" Jake quickly jumped in as he pulled the back of Luke's shirt.

He immediately let go of me as he raised his hand as though ready to backhand Jake.

"Luke, don't," I said as I grabbed his arm watching Jake cover his head to protect himself. "Why!" I said to him forcefully, as I watched his arm come back towards my face.

CHAPTER 17

"**U**rgh!" I screamed out loud in frustration from that memory as I picked up one of the larger sticks and started hitting it up against a tree. Trying hard to release the anger, I didn't pay attention to the fact that Matt was standing back watching me unfold.

"Why?" I yelled as I dropped to the ground, pulling my legs in close and wrapping my arms around them. Resting my chin on my hands I asked out loud in a quieter tone this time, "Why couldn't you just love us?" Tears started rolling down my eyes as I asked, "Why couldn't you accept me, accept all of us for who we are?" Taking a deep breath, I wiped the tears as I sat there rocking back and forth. Then abruptly, I stood back up and looked at Matt. Our eyes connected. Watching him, it was as if he was feeling the pain and the hurt right along with me. I wanted so much for him not to be here right now so I could run off the cliff and just be done, finally completing my reason for being here today, ending the pain for good. Then it hit me, I had four videos left before I could go. Without a word to Matt, my whole body trembling, I made my way up to the stream and sat next to the water. *I let the stress and worry take over the enjoyment of my whole life.*

Tears started rolling down my cheeks. My throat tightened as I watched the memories of my childhood. All the times I felt defeated and alone. I felt the heat rolling up from my heart through my neck and up my face. These feelings were not new. I felt them for decades. It was almost normal to me at this point. "Let it out, Faith," I said aloud as I rested the side of my head in my hands.

I sat there, reflecting, and saw two beautiful red foxes not even twenty feet away. Symbolic of balance, inner strength, adaptability and the ability to find your way, my intuition was heightened at the sight. "What are you telling me?" I asked. "I don't have anything left," I said, as if wanting them to guide me.

Then I heard him, this man, watching closely. He quietly came up from behind as if not wanting to startle the fox. Then he sat directly behind me, folding one leg in and putting the other one out to the side as he gently put his arms around me and pulled me backward saying without words *it's okay*. I quickly let the tense feelings go and relaxed into his arms. Sitting there, I could feel my heart racing. Then the tears got stronger again.

He gently directed my head to his chest. "It's okay, Faith, let them come. Get it out."

Sobbing, the memories came fast and fierce. Every moment I felt voiceless, worthless and insignificant at work, at home, with friends, everywhere, they swarmed in. Holding me the entire time, he caressed my shoulder as I felt him kiss the top of my head.

After nearly a half hour the tears started to subside. With a steady breath, I wrapped my arm around him and squeezed him back. Then putting my hands over his, I looked at him as if saying *thank you* without a word spoken. My heart beat fast again for very different reasons this time. I gently placed my hand on the side of his face and turned around to fully face him. "Matt, I don't know what brought you to me today but I'm glad you're here. Thanks for," with a pause, "well," I breathed out again.

He stopped me mid-sentence. "Shhh," he said as he took a finger and put it over my lips. "It's okay. It's all going to be okay."

Instantly my throat loosened up, the pressure in my head lightened, and tears continued to subside as I felt that gentle tingling throughout my body again. It was as though it was telling me that he was right.

"What did he do to you?" he asked softly.

Looking at him with a pause, I replied, "We all have the choice in life, Matt. No one made me stay. I did it all to myself."

"Faith, I get it and I respect it. I mean the accountability you take in your life; you don't play victim and I love you for it. It's something you don't see often enough."

In those words, I looked at him, my heart fluttering. I felt more connected to him than ever.

Without giving me a chance to say anything he continued, "But here's the thing Faith, I believe people know or at least they should know how to treat other people. We should know how our actions impact others. We should know if what we are doing is right or wrong. Sure, maybe you had the choice, but it doesn't mean what he did was right."

Stopping him, I interrupted. "Maybe people shouldn't know, Matt. What if it was all out of love? Or, what if it was all out of fear? Or insecurity? What about the people who never learned how to treat other people? Are they wrong because of that?"

"You're a good woman, Faith. It's only taken me a few hours to see how kind, honest and faithful you are. But still, it doesn't mean you allow yourself to get hurt." Then grabbing my hands, he pulled me in closer. "It means you have the strength and the determination and the grit to know what's good for you. You know what's right and when it's time to finally throw up the white flag, say you're drowning and ask for help. He does not deserve you. You deserve way more from where I'm standing."

Trying to break the seriousness of the moment, I said, "Um, you're sitting" with a smirk.

He gave out a short huff then shook his head. Clearly, he wasn't amused. He didn't respond.

"Just lightening things up a bit, Matt," I said, then taking another deep breath, I gently pulled my hands away, brought my knees back to my chest and laid my head in my hands. After a moment I looked up at him. "Matt I need some time. There's something I need to do; can you give me some space?"

"No, I don't want to this time, Faith," he said firmly. "I don't feel safe leaving you like this. You don't have to do life alone, you know."

Looking at him, I said, "I do have to do this alone. Please."

With hesitancy, he looked at me, came in closer, then gently put his hands on my knees before rubbing them up and down the side of my thighs softly. "Tell me you'll be okay. Promise me."

Without a word, I shook my head.

He backed up then slowly stood and reached out his hands for mine, kindly pulling me to a standing position. Bringing me in close, he put one hand around my waist and the other around my shoulder. Holding me tight, I felt it again. Safety. My body felt somehow lighter in his arms. Lifting my head from his shoulder, I turned and looked at him, our lips barely an inch apart. With our eyes locked, he softly placed his hands on each side of my face. Gently brushing his lips against mine he paused, then tilted my head down and kissed me on the forehead.

Feeling a contrast of emotions, wanting to kiss him yet not wanting to betray my husband, I took my hand, put it on his heart and said, "Please, go."

He slowly let his arms down, grabbed his bag and said, "I'll see you again, right?"

I responded with a nod of the head.

"I'll wait for you at the pass," he declared.

"Ah-huh," I responded softly.

He slowly turned around and started walking. Looking back at me several times, I tried to ignore him. I sat back down by the creek. Positioning myself next to a large boulder, I grabbed my phone. Ignoring all the alerts, I unlocked the camera, propped it up and hit record.

Sitting there looking into the camera I waited and watched, then slowly started. "Luke, from the day we met, I was in love. You held me in ways I was never held before. You spoiled me with flowers and romantic baths and made me feel like I was the center of your world. And, it was totally unhealthy for me, I had blinders on to your control. You pushed everyone I cared about away. You made me choose between you and them. The worst thing is, I chose you and you still felt the need to control me."

Not realizing Matt was watching close behind, I continued.

"You had me. I gave you my whole heart. How didn't you realize it? Why did you make me your possession? Why couldn't you see me as your equal? Do you even realize it? You never gave me space to do anything. If I wasn't at work or with you, you called and called until I was home. I didn't see it then; I get it now."

Shaking my head as I sat there watching the camera, I paused.

"I was always on edge, thinking, wondering, worrying

about what I was going to come home to. You forced me to leave a job that I loved just because of the money. Don't you see how wrong that was?"

"And, when I talked, did you even listen? Did you even care what I had to say?"

With a huff in my breath, I shook my head again as I looked down, "and yet I kept loving you, every step along the way, wishing someday you would hear me, see me, and let me be me."

Placing my hand over my heart, I continued. "And, my babies, if I kept my mouth shut everything was fine but when I had a voice, you made me wrong every time. You were the one that was wrong for doing that, Luke, not me," I said with emphasis.

"The arguments and fights just because I wanted to be heard, it breaks my heart to know they saw that."

Tears now rolled down my face. I continued.

"Through it all, I stayed, I stood by your side. Yet, you still didn't see. You would listen to everyone but me."

Letting out another huff, the tears stopped as I grabbed some rocks from the ground and threw them powerfully to the trees. Emotions shifted instantly to anger.

"When the stress of work was finally too much and I just wanted your help to make the bills, you wouldn't. You never had my back. Still, I stayed, I kept fighting for us and I pushed every dream I had to the side. I learned to be silent around you, it somehow just became easier that way."

"Then, when the kids got older and you didn't let them have their own voice," I said, aggressively throwing more rocks, "I was disgusted, I was disgusted with myself for not stepping in and defending them. I'll never forgive myself for that. I am their mom, I was always prepared to stand up for them, but never thought I would have to do that with you.

Luke, you should have never put me in that position. They deserved to have their voices and opinions heard." I waved my hands in front of the camera.

I took another long deep breath as I paused to calm the anger. "We were supposed to share our lives together. It wasn't supposed to be us living the life you wanted us to."

Tears started rolling down my face again as I shook my head. "Well Luke, all the years of silencing, all the years of stress and anxiety. All the years of pain that I inflicted on myself over you. It's done. No more, you do not get me anymore. I'll always love you though, I know somewhere in there you have a good heart. I wish only the best for you and your life. I hope you find truth in the fact that other people also deserve the same level of listening and respect as you demand. Life doesn't revolve around you. I pray at some point you learn empathy and compassion for other people."

Pausing one last time, I looked again to the creek then back to the camera. "And, Luke, you better fucking start being better to my kids. This is their life to live as they want, not for you to choose. Goodbye Luke," I said before turning off the video.

"It's time to be done, Faith," I said to myself.

CHAPTER 18

Sitting there, wondering if those words would make any difference to him, my memories drifted back. It was summer of 2008. I just surpassed my one-year anniversary with the temp agency and was making my mark building the area. Continuing to feel out of place, I worked hard to keep to myself and hit my numbers so they didn't have the need to visit. We were a field-based company, so it was just me and my team unless people visited from the head office. Thinking back to that moment, it was no wonder why I felt that way. I set a very negative story in my head about my own self-worth after the initial interview with Ronald, the regional vice president, and the comments he made.

I remember it like it was yesterday. "You will never be a manager here," he said as he briefly lifted his head putting his nose up in the air to me. "We require more professional experience than your restaurant background. And a bachelor's degree. Are you sure you want to take a step back knowing you have no room to grow here?" he asked in the interview boldly.

I remember looking back at the HR manager, Shelia, who was in the interview with us. She had a snarky smirk on her face in response to his comments. I felt like I was in high school being judged by the cool kids.

Needing a job at the time, I quickly defaulted to a "Watch

me!" mentality. "No one is going to tell me what I am or am not capable of," I thought. I knew that anything with my name on it at work was going to do well.

Remembering this moment now, a smile came over me. I was reminded of the level of confidence, grit, determination and resilience I had then. "How didn't I see it?" I wondered.

What I wasn't aware of when I was hired was that the location had been a money-losing office for the past fifteen years. There were talks of them shutting it down if we didn't get it to profitability. Ronald, the regional vice president, had already ruled me out as being able to make that happen. He was planning their exit strategy from the market. When I learned of this it motivated me ever more. There was no way I was going to lose this job; I was the sole income earner and didn't need Luke on my ass if it didn't work out.

Quickly after starting, I built a strong reputation in the market and secured four new businesses. I was hired on the recruiting side but soon jumped into the business development side of things. Within the first six months I tripled our sales. Corporate was noticing too. There was no assigned manager at the time, but the team and clients all leaned on me with questions or concerns. It often frustrated Ronald. He would redirect my team and even the clients to come to him with questions. He wasn't very fond of me, and that was fine, I didn't care much for him either. I felt that he was always minimizing my ability because of my lack of degree, the way I looked or because I didn't do it 'his way.'

Ronald had been with the company for nearly twelve years and made sure everyone knew his history in the industry. On this particular day, he decided to drop in for an unexpected visit.

I was making calls in my office when he got in just

after 9 a.m. When I heard his voice, I instantly felt my chest tighten and voice weaken to the client I was speaking with. My heart started racing as I felt a bead of sweat drip down my back. Hearing him make his way down the hall, flirting with the girls and shooting the shit with the guys, was distracting and made me even more anxious at the thought of him coming into my office. I got up and closed my office door to keep focused on Bill, my client on the phone.

Ronald fiercely swung open my door. "Doors do not belong closed in this office, Faith. What are you hiding for?" he said loudly.

With a snarky expression, I pointed to my headset, telling him without words, "I'm on the phone."

Rolling his eyes and shaking his head he said in a quieter yet firm tone, "Your door is to be left open." Then he plopped himself down on the chair and started playing with his Blackberry. Ronald was a middle-aged, heavy-set man with graying hair. He huffed and puffed a lot when he didn't get his way. This morning as he waited for me to get off the call it was no different. Looking at his watch every couple of minutes then back to me, he was making it very clear he wanted me off this call.

I could feel my body continue to react to his sitting there watching me, finding it harder and harder to talk as my throat tightened and feeling as if the temperature in the office was getting hotter and hotter. I wasn't sure if I wanted to run away, quit or stand up and scream at him for being such a tool with how he treated people. I worked hard to hide any physical signs of frustration and discomfort. There was no way I was going to let him see anything but strength, grit and focus.

I finished my call, hung up the phone, then turned

Created

and greeted him in a firm, direct, yet friendly tone. "Hello Ronald."

"What were you doing on that phone for so long? This isn't your time to chit-chat you know; we have a business to run here," he declared.

"I'm fully aware of that Ronald," I replied. Before I could get another word out, he interjected.

"This office is never going to get to profit if you are bullshitting with all of our customers," he said.

Shaking my head, I took a breath. "This is exactly how we build, Ronald," I said with my hands in front of me. "People want to do business with people they like, not just sleazy salespeople trying to make a buck," I said with a tilt of the head and a glare back at him. "Besides, I was closing the deal. They just signed the contract. The team will be starting on new warehouse positions today. Building relationships is exactly what this branch has been missing and it's how I've pulled in new clients in the last year."

Seeing him glaring back at me from those comments, I knew I was in for it. "Don't you -" then he stopped immediately as Zach came into my office.

Turning his attention to Zach, he asked, "Hey man, what do you need?"

"Umm," Zach responded with hesitation. Then avoiding his question, he turned to me. "Faith, can you give me some ideas on how to handle Zip Corporation? They're being overly critical with my candidates. I can't get them to understand the skills don't match what they're asking for."

"Why are you asking her?" Ronald said, irritated. "She's not your boss, I am."

Zach looked at me with wide eyes, then back to Ronald, then back to me.

Seeing his discomfort, I interrupted. "Ronald, I know this

account and have worked with it closely since securing the business. Zach asking me means nothing more than me knowing the people he's dealing with and how to communicate with them. We all know who the boss is. You make that very clear."

Again, he glared at me without a response.

I took another breath and looked back to Zach. "How about if we talk through some ideas after I wrap up with Ronald?" I asked him with a calm demeanor and a slight smile.

"Thanks, Faith," he responded, then quickly walked out of the room.

Looking at me as Zach left, Ronald shook his head, then stood and leaned his hands on the front of my desk.

Unsure what he was about to do, I scooted backwards as much as I could in my chair.

"Don't you dare ever talk to me like that again in front of this team. This is my region and my office; we do things my way. If this team has issues, you direct them to me. Do you hear me?"

Before giving me a chance to respond, he continued.

"You are not the manager here and you never will be, Faith. Companies want to work with men who know how to deal with this kind of stuff, not someone like you," he claimed as he waved his hand up and down in front of me. "This is a man's world, lady, you'd better get used to it." He pounded his fist on the desk.

With a brief pause, he stood up and looked out the window in my office. "And don't you even try thinking you had anything to do with the growth of this office. It's only because of my leadership and direction that you are seeing any kinds of results."

With a sarcastic huff, I crossed my arms and shook my head, still sitting there watching him. "You are such an asshole,"

I thought. Feeling my chest tighten as the heat rose into my throat, I wanted to scream at him in that moment. *Does he even realize how much of an ego-driven douche he is?*

I took another breath then said to him, "Ronald, with all due respect, I've done a lot of work to build this office, build community awareness and build relationships to secure new business. It is my direct efforts on the business development side and my teams' efforts on the recruiting side that has us growing our numbers. Can't you even acknowledge the work we're all doing here? I mean, quite frankly, all our work has you looking really good to your boss."

Still standing there over me, his face turned bright red. "You actually think you made an impact here, don't you? Look here young lady," he said as he pointed his finger at me. "We don't need you here. All of this could have been done without you."

With another chuckle under my breath I said, "I don't doubt that other people could have easily done the same thing I have, Ronald. Hands down there are a lot of amazing people in this world that know how to build relationships just like I do. But I can say this, this will be the first time in fifteen years that this office has made money so yes, I am damn proud of the work I have done," I said as I pointed to myself. "Is there anything else, or can I get back to work now?" I said in a curt tone.

Not sure how he was going to respond, I sat back in my chair. My heart was racing. *What did you just do, Faith?* My stomach started churning. *How is Luke going to respond if Ronald fires you? He's a total jerk, Faith. Who cares what Luke thinks, you need to start sticking up for yourself to him, too.*

With impeccable timing before my thoughts could get any more out of control, Meg stopped by my office. Not realizing Ronald was still there she asked, "Faith, can you call Boost for me? They have a…, oh, um," she stopped herself as she saw Ronald. "Um, actually we can talk later, no problem," she tried redirecting.

"Wait one minute Meg," he stopped her. "Continue, what position do they have?"

"It's fine Ronald, we can work on it later," she replied.

"No, we can discuss it now, this isn't Faith's job," he asserted as he looked at her, then at me, then back to her. "Now out with it."

"It's okay, Meg. What's the role?" I encouraged her with a positive tone trying to ease her nerves about the situation. Then I made eye contact with her with a soft smile.

Looking at me she started to share. "They have a Center Manager position open. Faith I have some really good candidates for it."

Ronald jumped in again. "I'll take care of it, Meg, it's not Faith's job," he declared while glaring at me.

"Um, Ronald, Faith is really good at this stuff. The clients like her," Meg said, trying to reason with him.

"Yeah, sure they do. It'll be better if I call, trust me. I've been doing this far longer than she has. Is there anything else you have to say, Meg?" he asked her.

Instantly she looked deflated and was clearly upset by the situation.

I stood up, reached over my desk and grabbed her forearm to get her attention as she started walking out of my office. "Meg, you did an awesome job identifying the candidate and finding a job for them. We'll help get it done for you. Nice work." I showed as much enthusiasm as I could muster in the moment. "I'm proud of you."

"Thank you, Faith," she responded before putting her head down and walking out of the office.

Looking at Ronald, I immediately started in. "You didn't have to talk to her like that. Fact is, it's all of us here every day, not you, and we've found a way to work really well as a team. What we're doing is clearly working. Just look at our sales reports." Then crossing my arms again, I held eye contact with him and asked, "Is there anything else, or can I get back to work?"

"We'll be done when I say we're done and don't you talk to me like that. I've been doing this far longer than you have and know way more than you ever will."

"All right then, there you go, you do it then," I said to him as I threw my hands in the air and sat back in my chair.

He continued for another fifteen minutes telling me everything I should have said differently in the call with Bill, then drilled me about how I approached cold calls in the field. I sat back and listened to him criticize everything I was doing, thinking to myself, "Is this really what business life is like?" Finally, he came to a close with his rant just as he stood up, hovering over me again.

Pounding his finger on the desk he said, "If this team has questions from now on, you have them call me, you are not their boss."

Knowing full well I wasn't going to follow his direction, I simply responded, "Are we done?"

Hesitantly, Meg came back into my office. "Um, Faith," she started, "Right Industries is on Line 2 for you."

"Thanks Meg." I looked at Ronald again. "Are we done? Can I get back to work now?"

With a huff and wave of his arms he walked out of my office.

My thoughts came back to now, but I felt a sense of pride as I remembered the confidence I had with Ronald that day. "How didn't I see it then?" I wondered.

CHAPTER 19

S itting there next to the stream with my back up against the boulder, the memories faded and I was brought back to the present. A slight grin came over me as I saw the confidence and grit I had talking to Ronald all those years ago. Emotions quickly shifted to those of frustration and disappointment. "Why didn't I see it then?" I asked myself again. "I was so strong and confident in my demeanor and my voice. Why did it feel so hard then?"

Looking off to the left, I saw Matt hovering in the distance. Disappointment quickly built to anger. He caught me looking at him and quickly walked in my direction. I wiped the leftover tears from my face, stood up, then grabbed my pack. Throwing it over my shoulder, I crossed my arms and looked at him with a glare.

"It's the right choice, Faith," he said, then asked, "Are you okay?" He reached out his hand, trying to console me by touching my shoulder.

I quickly backed away from him as I said with a loud tone, "You were listening the whole time?"

People now filled the area along with us. He instantly responded "shhh" as he looked around to see who was watching.

In an uncaring tone, I said, "No, don't Matt." I quickly snapped back. Pulling back up even further to get space between us then breaking eye contact, I said, "I told you I needed space, I trusted you."

"Faith, wait, I was worried about you. I'm sorry," he said with care in his tone as he tried to grab my arm again.

"Matt, knowing you heard most of what I said to my husband, you now know I felt small and insignificant for years with him. I've spent decades of my life not being heard by others, putting myself in situations where my voice, opinions, perspectives and desires weren't listened to, respected or valued. I'm not doing it anymore, especially not today. I thought I could trust you; I really did." Then looking down, I shook my head again, feeling the tears start to build. "Clearly I was wrong," I said in a quieter sad tone. With my eyes holding the tears back, I said, "Just go," pushing him away. "Matt just go," I said again.

"Faith, come on, don't do this, I made a mistake. I care about you, I was worried," he said with sincerity.

"I've heard it all before, Matt. One minute apologizing, saying you care, the next minute actions showing otherwise. I'm not doing it again. No more," I said with emphasis. "Just go," I said again more forcefully this time. Turning around, I walked past the boulder and toward the cliff, then looked out over the view. Not looking back, I felt the tears starting down my face.

"Faith, please don't do this," he said again.

Discreetly wiping the tear then turning around, I looked at him. "Go, please, just go," I said one final time as I turned back around and felt the tears start coming in stronger.

"I thought he cared," I said to myself. "I thought he was different." I took a deep breath, watching the view. "Don't let him be there when I turn around, please. I can't do it." With my chest tingling, I could feel my throat tighten. I tried to hold back the tears. "I am not crying over another man in my life."

"It's almost over, Faith; a little way to go and then you can be done," I reminded myself as I backed up and leaned against the boulder. I waited there with the hope that Matt would be far enough up the trail that I didn't have to see him again. Listening to the surroundings as I stood there, I could hear children laughing. The park was getting busier. In that instant, it hit me. "Please don't let them see me when I go. They don't need that childhood memory," I thought. "Shake it off, Faith, let's go" came next, then I grabbed my pack and turned around. Matt was nowhere to be seen. Thankful in that moment that he was gone, a small part of me felt sad that he didn't stay and fight for me. He didn't stand by in the hard moment. "Yep, he definitely wasn't who I thought he was," I reinforced as I started up the trail.

Looking off to the creek, the two beautiful foxes still hadn't moved much but they were acutely aware of my presence. "Trust your intuition," I reminded myself. "Thank you," I said to them gently as I blew a kiss up to the sky.

Moving along up the trail I came to the fork in the path. I veered right to go the long way around as I was met with the rock staircase. Nearly 100 stairs beautifully formed with rocks and small boulders, not for the faint of heart. With a steep decline on one side, large steps and quick inclines, attention is a must. One step after another, I gained momentum as my legs started burning. I reminded myself in that moment how much strength and determination I had. I said to myself, "You got this, Faith, keep going." With that thought, I caught it. "You got this, Faith, keep going." I stopped nearly halfway up the climb. "No, no," I told myself, "You made your choice, what's done is done." Leaning over slightly and putting my hands on my knees I tried to catch my breath as I stood there with that thought. Just then, a family with two young children started heading my way from the opposite direction. Seeing them smiling and giggling all the way down the stairs, I put on the mask I've put on so many times before.

"Good morning." I greeted them with a smile.

"Good morning to you." They returned the greeting with a smile and a nod. "Have you been out here long?" the lady asked.

"Yes, I've been here since dawn. How about you?" I replied.

"Oh no, we just got in. We came in the back route to skip the inclines," she said as she pointed in the opposite direction, then continued, "It's still a bit too much for the little ones. They're not quite ready for the whole trail."

"Yes I am, Mommy," the young girl pleaded.

Gently rubbing her on the head, her mom looked at her with a smile.

"Well," I interrupted, "it's a beautiful day to be out, you guys, stay safe," I said. Then turning my attention to the kids, I added, "and you guys have fun."

"Thank you," they responded shyly.

The smiles and conversation reminded me of all the years I wore that same mask. That smile was my mask when I was frustrated and when I was angry. It was my mask when what I really wanted to do was scream. That smile was my mask when I wanted to cry. What I needed to do was cry. "I showed up and I smiled and I gritted it out, maybe that's it," I said to myself. "Maybe I needed to smile less and show my feelings more."

"Stop Faith, it's over, it's not worth it," I told myself again, more forcefully this time as I shook out the thoughts, took a breath and continued up the rock stairs.

Making my way up the rest of the trail, I was met by three other passersby coming from the opposite direction. I greeted them one at a time with a smile, a nod and a "good day." As I came to the top of the trail that met another large opening giving a full view of the park, I saw him waiting there, sitting on the bench with his elbows resting on his knees and his head between his hands. Slowly, I approached. He looked up and immediately came to his feet when he saw me.

Before I had a chance to say a word, he stopped me. "Just hear me out," he said. "Please." Then he paused.

I thought, "He's here, he stayed, he didn't leave, what does this mean? Luke never stayed. I always made the first move to rectify things. He never came back until I apologized. Nobody did. I've always made the first move."

Then without a word, an expression of wonder came over me. I nodded at him as if telling him, "Go ahead, keep talking."

He came in closer. "You're right, I was watching, I heard a lot of what you said and I'm sorry. It wasn't to betray you, though, it wasn't to watch over you." Then he paused and backtracked. "Well, it kind of was to watch over you, but it was only because I was worried about you. I care about you, Faith, I don't want to see you hurting, I, I..."

I quickly interrupted, not certain if I wanted to know what he was going to say next. "Matt, stop. Why did you do it? Why couldn't you just listen?" I asked.

Shaking his head, he looked down. "I was wrong."

Taking a breath, I continued to watch him. Clearly remorseful; it was something I hadn't seen often. "Faith, this is your chance to be rid of him. He doesn't need to know how your day ends. You don't need to hurt anyone else. Don't put him through it. You are getting too close" came one thought after another. I walked towards him, then put my hand on his chin to lift his face and made eye contact. Our eyes connected and I was filled with relief at his sight yet again. My whole body quivered. "It's been great getting to know you today, Matt. Perhaps this is just the way it was supposed to be."

"Give me one more chance," he pleaded.

What do I do? What do I do? What do I do? My heart started racing. "You need him here, Faith, he's good for you. Trust him." The thoughts rushed in.

"You don't need to hurt anyone else" came the other voice, reminding me again as I sat down on the bench. I put my hands on my face and closed my eyes trying to center my thoughts.

"What does it matter anyway? I'll be gone at the end of the day. I might as well enjoy his company," I thought.

He kneeled directly in front of me, placing his hands on each side of the bench beside me. Then he lifted my chin. "I swear to you, I'll never betray you again. I promise to always honor what you feel and what you think. And I promise to always support you. Please give me another chance to show you," he pleaded.

In that moment, my thoughts drifted back.

CHAPTER 20

I was eight years into my career with the staffing company. The company nearly doubled in size since I was hired and it continued to grow rapidly. My office was in the top three of all fifteen locations week after week for sales. We were frequently leading the charge in first place. Over the past few years, we were awarded sixteen record-breaking sales awards. We were also building a solid brand in the community. We had become the go-to staffing company in the market, frequently winning business even over the national names.

I was awarded the Sales and Service Award for the company three years in a row. I remembered how strong and proud I felt at times, yet that humbled voice kept me grounded. The other voice showed up regularly. "Who do you think you are?" When I heard it, the nerves surged throughout my body. "You can't possibly keep this up." My heart was beating fast. "They will eventually figure out that you have no idea what you are doing. Then what?" I wondered how Luke would respond if I lost my job. Each time it showed up, the anxiety and nerves got worse.

With all the growth the company had seen, they decided it was time to add a second Regional Vice President. When I saw the posting come out, I instantly asked myself, "Should I apply?"

"No, you're not qualified for that," I quickly responded.

"You could show everyone what could actually be done in this role," reasoned the other voice.

I read through the description and saw that they were requiring a bachelor's degree. "I knew I wasn't qualified," I reinforced to myself again. "Besides, Ronald would never let that happen. To be his equal? I don't think so."

Contemplating applying for it, I decided to bring it up to Luke and his mom during dinner that night. They listened as I shared all the reasons that I was not qualified. Then as if defending myself to them they listened as I shared everything I could do in the role if they would consider me.

"Sounds to me like you already ruled yourself out, Faith. Besides, I am not sure it would work with you being away all the time. Who would take care of the kids?" Luke said.

Looking at him, puzzled, I asked myself, "Did he really just say that?"

Then I responded with hesitancy, "You're here, Luke."

"Sure, put more on me," he responded as he got up from the table slamming his chair down and pushing it in.

"If you feel you're not going to get it, why did you bother continuing to talk about it?" Monica, Luke's mom, said brashly. "Besides, you don't want to be away from the kids that much, do you?" she asked with judgment in her tone.

Monica was as feisty as they came. A rather attractive woman, she never left the house unless she was fully put together from head to toe. Married four times, she swore she knew everything about what didn't work in a marriage and constantly told me everything I should and should not be doing in mine. Having been in sales her entire career, she also claimed to know everything about how to build a successful career. She often shared her stories about outselling everyone in the companies she worked for. Sometimes I wondered how much truth was behind it all.

Luke came back to the table. "What's the salary for this role?" Clearly, he rethought his last comments.

"It's not all about the money Luke." I replied. "But it is substantial. It would be more than double what I'm making now."

"You better apply for it, Faith, we could use that money." He quickly changed his tone. "But you need to figure out a way to take care of your responsibilities here at home too. I'm not picking up the slack," he said with emphasis.

Shaking my head, I thought, "How much more do you want from me, Luke?"

After several weeks and more conversations with Luke and Monica, I decided to apply.

Within days of turning in my resume for it, I was invited to the corporate office for an interview. Two long grueling interviews with the executive team later, I was in the final consideration for the role. I was uncertain if the CEO was trying to find a reason to hire me or trying to find a reason not to hire me at this point. He asked me to go to lunch to further discuss it.

Corey the CEO was a tall, good-looking man. He was still young for his role, just over 40. He was a rather fit man who clearly took care of himself. A family man, I knew from brief conversations we had through the years that he was married with two kids himself. Corey had been in the staffing industry since college. This was all he knew. It came with a lot of benefits and he seemed to truly care for his employees. But, with the amount of time he had in the industry, it also came with some drawbacks. I often wondered if he knew how much recruiting had changed through the years. Was he aware of all the changes our industry had gone through and what was needed for us to stay up with the times?

There we were sitting at Benvenuto's Italian Eatery

for my final interview. It was meant to be a more relaxed conversation, but I was more nervous than I had been in the previous two. I could feel my heart racing. It coursed through my whole body. Throat tightening, I started worrying if I would be able to get a word out, clearing my throat over and over as I took a sip of water. The sweat dripped down my back, palms sweating. I had a clear view to the door. "I could slip out of here pretty easily," I thought.

"Don't screw this up." I heard Luke's voice ringing in my head as I sat there.

"Faith, we've never really had the opportunity to get to know one another. Tell me a little bit more about yourself," he asked.

The question I dreaded more than any other. I never quite knew how to respond. "Why would anyone want to know a thing about me?" I wondered every time someone asked me this question. Quickly in default mode, I responded, "It's a pretty broad question, Corey. What is it exactly you want to know?" I said, with a slight hesitation in my voice.

I was reminded of how much I still hated that question even now. "Such a loaded question," I said to myself.

The memory continued.

With a slight smirk, he responded, "Why don't you tell me a bit about your family. Do you have any kids?"

"Wow!" I thought. "Eight years I've been here, and you don't even remember my kids."

Shaking my head for a moment I paused, took another drink of water and responded. "I have three kids, Corey. My two boys, Jake and Doug, and my baby girl Joy."

"Remind me, what does your husband do again?" he asked.

"At least he remembered you were married," I thought.

"He better, he met Luke several times at the Christmas parties."

"My husband is a stay-at-home dad. He picks up projects here and there for a local construction company but with the hours I work it's easier to have him home," I responded.

"Hum, that's right," he replied with a question in his tone as he rolled his eyes and shook his head. He leaned in. "And tell me the truth, are you okay with that? I mean, men should work."

Instantly I could feel my eyes widen. "Yes!" I quickly responded, defending him. "Corey, with the number of hours I put in growing the office, there's no way I could do it if he wasn't at home with the kids."

"There is such a thing as childcare," he interjected.

Shaking my head, I thought, "Is he really that oblivious to what he's saying?"

"Corey, I believe parents should be present for their kids. He can be there for their sporting events, help with their homework, take care of the house, and everything else that comes with having kids." In the back of my mind as those words crossed my mouth, I thought, "Even though I do most of it when I get home every night."

"You do realize this position involves a significant amount of traveling, right? I would guess you are going to be traveling two or three, sometimes even four days a week, overnight in hotels away from your family. I'm not quite sure this position is right for a mom with three kids at home."

"Did he really just say that to me?" I thought.

Shaking my head, I responded, "Corey I'm quite confident that any mom with kids at home who is focused can do any job a man can do."

"Oh wait, I didn't mean it like that, Faith, don't take me wrong," he quickly retracted.

"Take me wrong?" I thought.

"Is there a right way to take that comment?" I responded, as I placed my hand on my heart. "Corey, I'm very confident that I can handle this position, while still making sure that my family is taken care of. The last eight years is a perfect example. I have built a highly successful office while not losing touch with my responsibilities at home. They always have been and always will be my number one, and they know that." In that moment I felt the confidence course through me. No hesitation in my tone or tightness in my throat. I was clear and concise.

"All right then," he responded. "You should know this is a lonely road, Faith. Most days you will be on the road by yourself, no longer having a team to collaborate with daily." Then backtracking immediately, he continued, "Well, I'll be here to support you however I can. And the executive team is your new team. I need to know you are going to have our back and support our decisions."

"Won't I be a part of those decisions?" I promptly interrupted.

"Well, um," he paused. "Of course, we want to hear your insight, but some things are just going to be the way they are, and I need to know you are going to support how we want things done. When you disagree, I need to know you are still going to hold your teams to whatever we decide."

Pondering that comment, I thought, "I am going to be a pawn to hold my teams' hands to what everyone else thinks they can do? Is that really what you want, Faith?" I asked myself.

"Here's the thing Corey," I said. "I believe I will absolutely still have teams; it just looks different than before. My teams are now just spread out around the area."

"Well, yes, I guess you can look at it like that," he replied.

"But," I continued, "I must admit, I am not a fan of just holding people's hands to something I think is dumb, or something I don't believe in, especially if there are other ways to move the ball forward. I didn't necessarily always follow every little thing corporate told me to do in my branch and the results have been fantastic, wouldn't you agree?" With an annoyed look on his face, he looked at me. Before giving him a chance to respond I continued.

"Besides, I work very independently," I said to him as I wondered *why is he pushing so hard? Is he trying to get me to take myself out of the running?* Looking at him again, I asked, "Corey, you've made clear you're not sure you want me in this role, so why are you making me jump through all these hoops? If you don't want me in the role, just say that." With a shocked look on his face, he quickly backtracked. "Faith, that's not even it, don't go putting words in my mouth," he defended.

"Well then, help me to understand. I mean, you have said more than once in my presence that you know within a few minutes of interviewing someone if they're right for the role. Yet here we are on interview number three and you're still hesitant. So, what is it?"

Looking at me, I was met with silence yet again.

"Fair enough," he started back in as he pulled out an offer letter from his padfolio.

Just then my thoughts came back to the present.

CHAPTER 21

S itting on the bench, Matt still holding my hands, he asked, "Where did you go?"

He noticed my mind drifting. "Oh, nowhere," I responded.

"Well, I know that's not true," he replied, challenging me yet again. "Where did you go?"

I looked at him with a smirk as I shook my head without a word.

"So what do you say, Faith, can you forgive me? I know I was wrong," he said with sincerity. "And honestly, I knew you didn't need more to stress about today, yet I added to it anyway. It won't happen again; I promise you that," he said as he squeezed my hands tighter, then leaned in. "I care about you. I want to keep learning more." Then with emphasis, with our eyes locked, he moved his hands to my thighs. "I want to know everything about you, Faith," he pleaded.

I took another deep breath, leaned back against the bench and closed my eyes. Completely in this moment of thought, the people passing by became almost non-existent. Reminding myself that I didn't want to hurt this man, I sat back up and looked at him. "Matt you need to know something. If I look past it and we keep hiking together today, at the end of the day that's it," I said, then looked down for a moment. He grabbed my hands again. "We'll never see each other beyond today. We each have our own lives and we each have our own paths to lead. It would just be easier to part ways now before we get any closer."

"Why does it have to be like that, Faith?" he replied quickly.

"I'm not prepared to take on anything more right now. It's all I have to give. All you have is today, take it or leave it," I said to him with a shrug of the shoulder, gently chewing my bottom lip.

With our eyes continuing to meet, he tilted his head back and forth. "There is no changing your mind, is there?"

I shook my head.

"I'll take as much time with you as you'll give me," he said.

"One more thing Matt," I said.

"What?"

"You need to honor when I need time to myself. No more looking over my shoulder or we're done," I said with directness.

"I'll never break a commitment to you again Faith. You have my word," he replied.

Breaking eye contact then looking away, I caught a glimpse of the group of teenagers walking by and gave them a soft smile then a nod of the head, saying hello without speaking a word. In that moment, I imagined my kids taking the same hike now without me. "Will they still enjoy it?" I wondered. Not wanting to bring up the emotions of that thought, I stood up. Matt stood right along with me. Inches from each other, he gently put his hand around my waist as he took his other hand and put it softly on the side of my face. I could feel my body tingling as he got closer, our bodies gently touching one another. I put my hand on his elbow as I felt the heat of my body rise, tingling all over as if seeing the love of my life for the first time. A contrast of thoughts passed through my mind, wanting to kiss him yet not wanting to break my vow to Luke. He gently tilted my head as he brushed his lips up against mine. Lost in the moment, I closed my eyes then quickly opened them and backed away.

"I can't Matt, it's not right," I said to him, then grabbed my pack and continued up the trail.

The vision of the trails was breathtaking: small purple flowers, hints of red coming through, multiple shades of green moss on the trees and rocks. The boulders and rocks around us created their own unique rainbow of colors. Hues of red, orange, brown and tan. Coming up just beyond the halfway mark, a large opening gave way to a clear sightline to my destination. I could see the very tip of it. Devil's Doorway. My chest felt full as I stopped, took a breath, looked at it and thought, "Are you sure? Do you have any more fight left?" Looking back to the trail then back to Devil's Doorway, I reminded myself, "It's time, Faith."

As I stood there watching, contemplating, Matt came up from behind, gently placing his hand on the middle of my back. "Are you all right?" he asked softly.

Looking back at him I quickly responded, "I'm fine," then continued on the trail.

"Faith, can I ask you a question?"

"Sure, but it doesn't mean I am going to answer," I responded, trying to lighten the tone.

"Ha, ha, ha. But for real though, what were you thinking about before when you were sitting on the bench? You were clearly in deep thought, and it looked like it was something heavy."

"It's nothing Matt, just memories of the past, that's all." I gave him a soft smile.

"You know Faith, memories of the past offer insight into the growth of our future. It's every one of those moments and experiences that build us into who we are today." He paused. "What was it that brought such a powerful recollection to you?"

Shaking my head, I looked at him with a smile as I kept walking up the trail. Contemplating if I wanted to share, I reasoned with myself, "Maybe he has some insight. Not that it really matters at this point."

"I remembered when I applied for the vice president position."

"That's your current role, right?"

"Yes. There was a huge mix of emotions. I hesitated even applying for the position in the first place. It was clear that the CEO and entire executive team doubted my ability and fit for the role. I still don't know why they offered it. Probably because they thought they would lose me if they didn't. But -" I continued, "that's no reason to promote someone." Shaking my head, I continued. "It was clear that the CEO never really trusted me for the role. I still question if he does." Putting my head down, I kicked around the rocks on the trail while we walked. "My husband and mother-in-law were really pushing for me to get it too."

"'*You better get this job,*'" Luke would say," I said with emphasis. "'*We need the money,*' he said over and over."

I looked back at Matt. "We didn't, though, he just didn't want to go to work. He was really pushing me to go for it."

"Is it what you wanted?" he asked.

"You know, looking back, I'm not really sure, but it doesn't really matter at this point."

"Well, that can't be true. Your happiness matters. So, what did you really want?" he asked boldly.

"I wanted to travel," I said, looking at him. "I wanted to take my kids on every adventure possible, showing them the world while creating and meeting people along the way.

I wanted to find unique people, places and creators and promote them so the world could see them. For years, I imagined starting a blog and magazine about different places in the country." Then with an expression, I said, "*Come visit beautiful Sandusky, Ohio,*" with my arms extended bringing emphasis to that moment. "*And be sure to check out little Annie's Café in downtown just off 3rd Street where you'll find the best chocolate chip cookie you have ever had. When you do, take the short drive to Pikes Peak, the view is breathtaking.* And to be able to bring that all together with my writing and photos. I'd be living the dream, for real!" Taking in that moment as I shared my thoughts with Matt, I felt the excitement in my body just talking about it. Then looking back to him I said, "Can you imagine?"

Looking at me with a smile, he responded, "I can." Softly then, he said, "Faith, why don't you go for it?"

Instantly the weight of life filled in. I could hear the comments from Monica, Luke, my family, then shook my head. "It's a pipe dream, Matt. You can't make a living like that. Believe me, I've had plenty of people reinforce that. I'm sure they were right though. It's not what a married mom of three should be doing to take care of her family."

"Have you ever thought about doing it on the side, maybe going on some weekend excursions to get started? Starting the blog to go with it." Then with clear excitement he stopped himself and looked at me. "Oh Faith, I got it, we could build your website to be all-encompassing, selling your shots like we talked about before and blogging about people and places along the way. It would be perfect. And I'm sure your kids would love to be a part of that."

Shaking my head, I said, "I don't have the time for that. There's already so much to do on the weekends, and I work most of them already. Being a VP is not a 9 to 5 job, that's for sure. Besides, Luke would never go for it," I said with a sad tone as I looked down again.

"Faith," he said with a strong direct tone, "why are you doing this?"

I looked back at him with questions in my eyes. "Doing what?"

"Why are you selling yourself short? We get one round, one moment, one journey in this lifetime. You lit up when you were talking before. Why are you stifling your dreams?" he asked.

"It's just not the right time, and besides I let all my dreams go a long time ago," I responded.

"Are you serious, Faith? See, this is exactly why you need me in your life. I'm not going to let you throw your dreams away. No one in your life should let you settle. Do you really want to look back and say you settled for life? Do you want to be 80 years old sitting on your deathbed wondering *why didn't I do that?*" he asked.

Looking back at him as I bit my lip, I thought, "It's over anyway."

He continued. "Or," as he grabbed my arms and pulled me in front of him, gaining full eye contact. "Or would you rather risk it? Go for it? No matter what happens, at least you tried, right?" he said powerfully. "And, I have to say, you have a very clear vision that lights you up. It's really half the battle, you know. When we know what we want and why we want it, we can do anything."

Biting my lip, I turned back around without a response as I started back up the trail. Shaking my head as I looked down at my feet, I said, "It's just too late. It's fine though, it wasn't meant to be." Then I looked at him for a moment. "Can we please stop talking about this?"

"Okay, but I just have one more question before we do."

Pausing for a moment, he looked at me as if he was waiting for my response. "Fine, what?" I said.

"If Jake or Doug or Joy were in their mid-30s, early-40s, and they said, 'Mom I'm so miserable, I don't know what to do. Every day I go to work dreading it, I just wish I could…'" then he put his fingers in quotes as he said, *"fill in the blank* with whatever their true dream is, what would you do? What would you tell them? Would you tell them it's too late? Would you tell them not to go for it?" Then he stopped and put his hand on my chest, stopping me, now directly in front of me, looking at me directly in the eyes. "Faith, would you tell them any of that?" He stopped and waited, then bringing his other hand to the side of my face, he asked, "or, would you say *babe you gotta go for it, no matter what happens. I'll have your back."*

My heart was racing as we held eye contact. I felt as if he was talking directly to me and my dreams.

"Live your life, you're worth it. Is that closer to what you would say?" he asked.

The emotions continued to rush through me as I sat with his words. I could feel my chest getting warm then going straight up my throat and into my face. Tears started welling up. Breaking eye contact, I looked down then back up. "You know I would encourage them," I said with passion. "What kind of a question is that?"

"Then why don't you do it for you?" he asked softly.

Abruptly backing away, I started walking up the trail as I wiped the tear from my eye. "I'm not talking about this anymore," I said forcefully just as another couple walked by, overhearing the conversation.

"Are you okay?" the young lady whispered to me as she slowed down.

I nodded my head as if to say I was fine.

Quickly catching back up, he grabbed my hand. "I'll stop, I won't bring it up again; well today, anyway. But when you're ready, just know, I'm here to help every step of the way. I have your back, Faith," he said.

In silence we continued up the brief incline in front of us as my thoughts drifted.

CHAPTER 22

I t was February 2013, just months after the promotion to vice president of the Western Region. I had been sick on and off for what felt like years. Month after month it would get more prominent, breathing difficulty, tight throat, coughing and wheezing. One doctor visit after another, each one told me in their own way that it was all in my head. Luke had his own moment in life. It was as if I was on an emotional rollercoaster and all alone taking care of it all myself. Day after day, the fatigue built, never quite feeling like I could catch up on sleep. But I kept pushing. There was no other choice, until that Saturday morning I couldn't do it anymore. I could barely breathe that morning. I was coughing to the point of nearly throwing up. I knew something wasn't right. "There's no way this is all in my head," I thought.

"I'm going to run over to urgent care. Something isn't right," I said to Luke.

"Maybe you just need to go lay back down. You were just at the doctor's office," he responded.

Jake ran in the room. He had always been observant of others. "Mommy, are you okay?" he asked.

"I'm all right baby, no worries about me. Your mom is one tough cookie," I said with a smile. "Mommy is going to the doctor. Can you help Daddy while I'm gone?" I asked.

Looking at me again with sadness, he asked yet again, "Mommy, are you going to be okay?"

Seeing the tears brewing, I mustered up a big smile as I tried to hide my discomfort, then got down on my knees and brought him in close. "Honey it's just a cold. I'll get some medicine and be all better, I promise. We can watch a movie when I get home together, maybe build some Legos?"

"Can I come with you?" he asked softly.

"Enough Jake," Luke chimed in directly. "Go play with your brother and let your mom get out of here."

I gave him a hug and whispered, "I love you baby. Mommy is going to be okay. Go play now."

He hugged me back tightly then turned around and left the room.

As I stood back up, I started coughing again, over and over, gasping for air. I could feel it, the heat of the redness in my face, trying to catch whatever breath I could.

"Go get something to drink," Luke said.

Shaking my head as it started subsiding, I held my chest, feeling the discomfort. "That's not it, Luke." I got out slowly. Exhausted by that moment, I said softly, "I'm going."

"Are you sure you're okay? Do you want me to drive you?" he asked with care.

"I'll be fine. There's no sense in dragging the kids out in this weather," I responded as I rested my hand on his shoulder.

"Let me know when you get there," he requested, then pulled me in close. "I love you, beautiful," he whispered as he hugged me.

"I love you, Luke," I gently responded, then I let go of him, grabbed my keys and my purse, and headed out the door.

It was sleeting outside and just below freezing. I knew the roads were going to be treacherous at best. Driving to the clinic that morning, my thoughts drifted. I worried about what this was. "Did all the smoking finally catch up with me? Is this what stress does?" My thoughts shifted again as I thought to the week ahead. "I don't have time for this. I have to feel better by Monday. I have a lot going on this week." I thought again about the three-day trip I had planned to my offices.

Before I knew it, I was at the clinic. It was slow there that morning. I checked in and was instantly seen by the medical assistant. There were no doctors on staff that morning due to the weather and thankfully so.

"You look very uncomfortable," she said. A nice young lady named Lori. She was about 5'4", short brown hair and beautiful blue eyes. Her demeanor instantly came across as one of caring and composure. I would never forget her. The woman that finally took me seriously.

She took my temperature, blood pressure, looked in my throat, nose and ears then started poking around my neck. She took her hands from one side to the other then stopped at my neck. Continuing to poke around, I watched as her tone changed to that of concern. "Um," she said with hesitation. Then she stopped, looked at my chart and continued. "Has anyone ever addressed the nodule in your throat before?" she asked.

"Nodule?" I asked.

Without a response, she placed her hands back on my neck and observed it further.

"What's going on, Lori?" I asked.

"Um." She started again. "I don't want you to worry."

With that comment, the worry instantly began. "I knew there was something wrong," I thought. Then I said to her, "Lori, what is it, a nodule, you said?"

"Faith, there is a significant lump in your throat. When was the last time you were seen by your doctor?" she asked.

"I was just there last week," I responded, shaking my head as I looked down.

Watching her tone again, it looked as if she was asking herself *how did they not find this?*

I continued. "They said it's all in my head," I said with a smirk as I smiled back at her.

Backtracking, she said, "Well, now, I'm only a medical assistant, let's not get too far ahead of ourselves. I'm going to get you scheduled for a scan first thing Monday morning."

"Is there any way I can go today? I have a busy week ahead and a lot on my plate at work," I said.

She turned back over to me and slowed down. "Look Faith, I get it, you have a lot going on. I'm sure your job will understand."

Seeing the concern in her face and hearing her tone I instantly felt the seriousness of it. "Isn't there a way I can go today?" I asked again.

Watching me in that moment, I was certain she saw the thoughts running through my head: worry, concern, stress, anxiety and a whole gamut of other feelings rushing in. She said, "Let me see what I can do. Give me a few minutes." Then she went back over to her desk and picked up the phone.

I listened as she pleaded with the hospital staff to get me in immediately for an MRI. Hearing her genuine care about my situation and what I was feeling, I wondered what she had been through to bring this much protection to another person. After a few minutes, she hung up the phone. I watched as she made some notes then she made her way back over to me.

"All right Faith," she said, "you better get moving. They're going to take you in right away. In the meantime, I want you to take these," she said as she gave me a prescription. "They'll help you breathe easier," she said.

I looked back up at her, wanting to say so many things. Someone finally acknowledged that it wasn't all in my head. "Thank you," I simply said.

"You're welcome. Now go," she said with emphasis.

I had several tests, starting with the MRI that day. It was followed by an ultrasound and a biopsy. Within days they had my results. I'll never forget that moment when the doctor called. We were in the F-150 headed home from grocery shopping. Luke was driving, the kids were in the back seat. He pulled over into a parking lot when he saw it was the doctor calling. Then he turned around and watched me as I spoke with him.

"Okay, I understand," I said to the doctor. "I'll wait to hear from your office." Then I hung up the phone, dropped my hands to my lap and stared out of the windshield.

"What did he say?" Luke asked.

I looked over to him and shook my head. "We can talk about it later," I responded, then looked back at the kids. "We should stop and pick up dinner on the way home, what do you think, boys?" I asked in a fun, uplifting tone with a smile on my face. Then looking over to Luke, I said directly, "I'm not cooking tonight."

"Faith, what's going on?" he asked again.

"Luke, not now," I said more forcefully this time. "Let's go so we can get home." I looked back out the windshield.

Without another word, he turned and started driving.

We picked up dinner and were quickly home. I set up a picnic for the boys in the living room, turned on a movie, then Luke and I went in our room to talk.

"Faith, what is it? Tell me already," he said with emphasis in his tone.

I took a deep breath then sat down on the floor, leaning with my back against our bed. Hugging my knees in close, I rested my forehead on them. I could feel the tears starting to build. "Let it out, Faith," my body was telling me.

"Faith you're worrying me. What's going on?" he asked again.

With my face still resting on my knees, I said softly, "It's cancer." My comment was met with silence. I looked up at him. "I have a four-centimeter cancerous tumor in my thyroid." Then I watched as his face turned pale, and he leaned against the wall then slowly sat down. In silence we both sat there.

Continuing to watch him, emotionless, I heard that voice from inside. "You can fight this, Faith. It won't beat you." Then I said to him, "They're going to schedule me for surgery to remove it. I'll be fine, Luke." Looking back over to me, he made eye contact. I saw the swelling in his eyes as he clearly held back tears. Then I reinforced, "I'm going to be fine."

Without a word, he stood up, made his way over to me, kissed me on the head and quickly made his way out of our room.

"Wait, where are you going?" I asked him.

"I can't, Faith." he said as he continued out of the room.

Sitting there, the tears started falling. In that moment, needing someone to be there with me, I asked aloud, "Why do you keep leaving, Luke?"

Then I heard Jake from the living room. "Mommy, come eat with us."

"Your kids need you, Faith," I reminded myself. "Nothing is going to beat you. You got this." Then taking another breath and pushing it out with force, I wiped my face, slowly made my way up and headed to the living room.

Just then, my thoughts came back to the present.

CHAPTER 23

Heading up the trail as my thoughts came back from that moment, I started gasping for air as I felt the emotions from all those years ago. With shortness of breath, I could feel the pressure come over my whole body as if one of the boulders was sitting on my shoulders. It was the same heaviness all over again. Stopping, I put my hands on my knees then tried to re-center myself. The heat in my face grew as my eyes watered. Matt stood behind me with his hand on my back.

"Faith, are you okay? What's going on?" he asked.

I waved my hand as if saying *back off*.

Continuing to breathe as I let those memories go, I was reminded of how lonely life is and why I was here today. "I don't want to feel this way anymore," I said to myself before taking another big gasp of air. Then I stood back up, turned and looked at Matt. "I need a few minutes," I said to him."

"Faith," he said with emphasis.

Before he could get another word in, I put my hand on his chest. "Please," I said to him. "I need this."

"What is it Faith, what happened? Are you honestly okay?" he asked again.

"Matt I just got stuck in a thought of the past for a minute, that's it, I'm fine," I said. "I need some time to process it."

"What is it? How can I help?" he asked.

Shaking my head, I let out a brief *huh* as I looked back up at him. "Give me a few minutes. Give me some space, please Matt, I just need some time."

He came closer, grabbed me around the waist with one hand and put the other on the side of my face. Pulling me in, he pressed his lips up against mine. Before I had a chance to think about what was happening, I felt my body melting in his arms as he kissed me. Getting lost in that moment I wrapped my arms around him and held him tightly. Locked arm in arm, I felt completely safe.

Then in an instant, I realized it and released my lips from his. Standing there, still arm in arm with my heart racing, eyes watery, looking into his eyes, I felt it: connection, safety and love coming from him.

"Let me stay, Faith," he said.

Breathing easier now, I gently put my hand on the side of his cheek and rubbed my thumb across his lips. Then I softly brought both of my hands to his heart. Vaguely, for a moment, I saw a couple off to our left, appearing to be watching the view but I sensed they were watching us. I heard the birds chirping. Completely present to everything around me, I asked myself, "Why didn't I meet him sooner?" Then looking back up to him, I said, "I just need some time Matt, please?"

Without words, he tilted his head back and forth before placing his hands on each side of my face. Then he pulled my head down, kissed my forehead and without a word turned and walked over by the clearing not 50 feet away.

Standing there, I closed my eyes and put my head back as I relived that kiss. Then bringing my focus back to why I was here, without giving attention to him watching me, I turned and headed to the cliff just in front of me. A line of beautiful full weeping willow trees lined the edges. I saw two trees with full vines hanging all the way to the ground, perfectly spaced apart. I got closer to the edge and saw the waterfall off to my right. Taking in a breath, the air smelled fresh and fragrant. It was a sweet smell coming from all the blooming. Looking down over the water by the beach I saw the kids playing. Then in my view back to the sky, I saw a swarm of beautiful eagles and hawks surrounding me. It was like the perfect picture.

In that moment, I saw a flash of my babies standing over my casket. It played through my head like a movie. I watched as they visited me in the cemetery. I could see their pain. I felt it. "They will understand," I told myself. "They're old enough, they'll be okay, Faith." My eyes started watering, tears rolling down my face. I could feel the pressure coming back to my chest. Then I took another breath. "I love you kids," I said aloud as I let those thoughts pass. Pressing my hand up against my lips, I blew a kiss to the sky. "Take care of them for me, Daddy. Let them know I always loved them."

I took two more steps getting even closer to the edge with my toes gently hovering over. I looked to the left, grabbed the vines from the weeping willow tree and wrapped them in my hand. Then to the right, with the other tree perfectly spaced, I reached out, grabbed the vines and again wrapped them around my hand. I gave them each a gentle tug as if in that moment wanting the safety to not go over yet. Then I gently put my head back and I leaned forward, holding the vines tightly. I went up to my toes, getting as little ground as I could under me. Feeling the wind, hearing the water, I felt free and embraced it.

Not hearing anything around me, my emotions quickly went to shock as Matt grabbed me around the waist, squeezed me tightly and pulled us both back. We fell to the ground behind us. "What the hell, Faith?" he yelled at me.

Jen Zahari

Just as quickly, he got back up off the ground then stormed back over to the clearing, now empty of any other visitors. I watched as he picked up some of the larger rocks and forcefully threw them over the clearing. "Ahh," he yelled, looking back at me. "What were you thinking?" He yelled again in an angry, firm tone.

Saying nothing, still laying there on the ground, I watched him. Seeing his emotions, I thought, "He really cares about me."

He hit the leaves with his hands then picked up a large stick and started hitting the tree, over and over, as he scowled and groaned.

"There must be something more to this," I thought. "This can't be all over me."

Watching him continue his rant, I sat up, rested against the tree behind me and grabbed my phone. Pulling my knees in close, I pressed my elbows on them, holding my phone steady in my hands, opened it and hit the camera ignoring all the messages once again. I switched to video and instantly hit record.

With a soft smile in the camera, I started. "My baby girl, Joy. You, my sweetheart, are such a bright light. All you have to do is walk in a room and you light it up. Honey, from the day you were born I knew you were going to be my dreamer. You have always brought laughter, fun and light to everyone around you. You are a gift. Do you realize you can completely turn someone's day around just with your presence?" Then looking away for a moment and looking back I said, "I will always be watching over you." Taking a deep breath, I looked away again and back with a smile. "When you air in your first movie, I'll be watching. Please don't let this slow you down. Stay focused, travel, see the world. And don't let anyone stop you from living your dreams. You have a chance to really shift communities and bring a light to people." Stopping again for a moment, I looked up at Matt. Watching me, he looked calmer now. I caught eye contact with him and instantly looked back at Joy. "I love you," I said to her. "I'll always be listening. You can talk to me anytime. Live your dreams, baby girl," I said one last time then brought my hand to my lips and blew her a kiss. "I love you," I told her one final time before turning off the video and dropping my phone between my knees. Then resting my elbows back on my knees, I gently put my head in my hands as I played Joy's life back in my mind. A gentle smile stayed across my face as I thought of all the beauty she had brought to me. "She is going to be okay," I reminded myself.

Lifting up my head, I took my hair tie out and ran my hand through my hair. Seeing Matt standing there watching me with his hands in his pockets, I made eye contact with him again. We watched each other for a moment as I thought, "Go talk to him, Faith."

Clearly frustrated with me, he turned his view from me to the clearing yet again. I slowly got up and made my way over to him.

I got just a few feet away when he turned around and looked at me. "What were you thinking, Faith? Do you know what could have happened?" he asked.

"I just wanted to feel free for a minute," I responded.

His tone escalated slightly. "Do you know what could have happened?" he said again.

"Matt, I'm fine," I said with haste.

Shaking his head, he picked up the large stick again and started hitting the tree with force. "Faith, you could have died. What would have happened if you lost your balance? What if the vines broke? What if something scared you and you accidently let go?" Then he scowled again, turned and took a few steps backward.

Saying nothing, I stood there and just watched.

He turned back around then quickly came closer to me and grabbed me around the waist. "I'm not ready to lose you. I can't do it again."

"Again?" I wondered. "Do I ask him?" came next.

Letting go of my hands he turned back around, Matt picked up more rocks and threw them over the ledge with more force, one after the other.

"I can't do this to him. I have to end it now," I said to myself.

"Matt," I said softly. Without a response, I waited for a moment, then said it again, in a louder tone. "Matt."

He came in closer. With his hands back in his pockets, standing there in front of me, he shrugged his shoulders. "What?" he asked.

"I'm going to just go. I told you earlier, beyond today." Then I stopped myself, shook my head and looked away. *Don't lie to him Faith, don't lie to him.* "I told you, we won't see each other again after today."

I watched as his tone changed from one of anger to one of sadness.

"Matt, clearly this isn't healthy. I don't want to hurt you. If we stay together today, we are just going to get closer and that will make it harder for both of us. We should just go our separate ways now; it will be a lot easier that way." Then I took my hands, pulled my hair up and put it back in a ponytail.

"It looked great down," he said.

With a soft smile and a blush, I continued. "I'm going to go." Then I grabbed my bag, threw it over my shoulder and made my way over to him. Gently putting my hand on his arm, I looked at him. "I will never forget you." I went on my tiptoes and kissed him on the cheek. "Thank you for everything today." I turned around and quickly made my way down the trail. *Let him go, Faith, let him go.* I felt like I was walking away from someone who actually loved me.

I made my way down the decline and just around the fork as my memories drifted back.

CHAPTER 24

I t was April 2013, just weeks after having a complete thyroidectomy. I was emotionally exhausted. Luke and I just returned from my follow-up visit. The doctor advised me that my vocals were nicked during surgery. I might never get my full voice back. Since surgery, my voice was raspy and soft-toned at best. I could barely talk at half my regular tone. Thoughts spiraled through my head as I sat on the living floor. I was scared.

"What am I going to do without my voice?" I asked myself.

"How am I going to work? My voice is my job" came next.

The kids, hearing we were back home, swarmed around me. They were clearly excited that we were back. With a soft smile, I embraced them.

"Mom, will you come play Legos with us?" Doug asked.

"Leave your mom alone, she needs some rest," Luke snapped.

Instantly I saw the sadness come over his face. I pulled him down closer to me. Then with as much voice as I could muster, I said to him, "Dad and I need to talk, honey. Maybe after lunch and a nap we could play."

Snuggling his head into my chest, he looked at me. "Okay, Mommy," he responded, softly hugging me tightly.

"Hey now," I started in response. "Don't be sad. We

have a whole lifetime to play. Sometimes we just need to rest, right?" I said to him. "And," I started again, "if I get some good rest, we could even build the ship you got for your birthday and maybe even watch a movie when we do. How does that sound?"

"Really, Mommy?" he responded quickly.

"Yes, but I want you on your best behavior until then. Is it a deal?"

Without a word, he responded with a slight nod of his head.

Having no idea at the time what the kids were feeling, I wrapped my arms around him tightly. "It's all going to be okay, honey," I said softly to them as I tried to convince myself of the same, wondering if it really was going to be okay. Looking up, I saw Luke getting more frustrated the longer I sat with the kids. Arms crossed, he sat forward. Then he started waving his hand as if to say, "Let's go, move along."

"Boys, you heard your mother, we need some time, now go play," he said in a scolding tone.

I gently put my hand up at Luke as though telling him to stop. Exhausted and not ready for an argument, I looked back down at Jake then brushed my hand through his hair. "Daddy and I will be quick, I promise. Then we can snuggle. I'm not going anywhere."

Looking back up at me he asked, "You don't gotta work?"

"Not yet sweetheart."

He squeezed me again, then got up.

"Now go have fun," I said to him with a smile as I patted him on the tush when he walked away.

Sitting there, I leaned back against the couch, pulled my knees in close, then put my hands on my forehead. As I did, thoughts continued yet again. I wondered what the future held for us.

"Do I have it in me to keep going?" I wondered. "I don't want to do it all alone anymore" came next.

With the stress of everything weighing on me, I imagined what life would be like if I quit my job. "There's no way he would let that happen," I thought. Anxiety built quickly as I thought about work. My throat tightened as I struggled to get a deep breath. Tears started rolling down my face as I thought back to the last eight years with the company. "They never really cared about me," I thought.

Luke watched me and chimed in, "It looks like you have a lot on your mind, babe. Care to share?"

"Say it, Faith. Say it," I heard over and over in my head. "Tell him that it's been long enough." My stomach started churning at that thought as I felt the pressure build straight through my chest and up my throat. I could feel my face turning red, palms sweating, and body shaking. Working to be as direct and sure of myself as I could, I looked at him and said it. "I can't do it anymore, Luke. I have been pushing too hard for too long. This is a wake-up call. It's time to change something."

"What are you saying, Faith?" he asked bluntly.

Feeling his negative energy, my heart started racing even faster. I looked down then looked back up at him. "Luke, I don't want it all on my shoulders anymore. I don't want to be the only one working. If you found work, I could slow down and maybe even find something I enjoy. I could finally take a break."

"You're just tired," he responded. "You just need rest. You'll feel better in a couple days when your voice comes back," he pleaded.

"You're not listening, Luke; I don't want to do this anymore. I want more time with the kids. And besides, sales has never really been for me. It's all just too much. You know I love talking to people but if my voice doesn't come back, well." I stopped and looked down, not wanting to think about that possibility. "Besides, they don't really like or appreciate me there. I'm just one of the puppets in their game to make money."

"That wasn't the deal, Faith. We made a deal; you would take care of us, and I would take care of the kids. We're not able to change that right now and besides, I wouldn't even be able to make half of what you make. It wouldn't make any sense for you to leave your job."

"But that's the thing. We could do it. If you went back to work, I wouldn't have to make as much money. Then we could both be happy. And I could be here more with the kids," I pleaded with him.

"The kids need their dad here; we have been through this before, Faith," he said.

I reasoned, "Jake is in school now and we could enroll Doug in early pre-K. It would be healthy for all of us. And it would get the kids more social interaction."

I watched his face getting redder as he raised his tone. "You don't think I'm doing good enough, do you? Is that it? I'm not good enough to be here taking care of my kids?"

"Luke, that has nothing to do with it. I need you to have my back. I do not want to be solely responsible for us financially anymore, that's it, that's all there is to it. I've been unhappy for a long time. This just brought it front and center," I replied.

"Oh, come on, there wasn't any sign, it was cancer, that's it," he said in an annoyed tone.

Getting more tired sitting there arguing with him, I thought, "He's never going to change," as I felt myself backing down yet again.

"What if I did it on my own?" I thought as I saw an image of raising the kids on my own.

Then my attention went back to him. I knew how much pain and hurt he would feel if I left. "I can't hurt him," I thought. "It's the life you chose, Faith. Deal with it" came next. Pressure moved through my eyes as I felt more tears coming. I reached over to grab a Kleenex as I looked up at him and said, "I just want you to have my back."

As soon as the words came out, I knew he wasn't going to respond well.

"What are you saying, I don't have your back? So, nothing I do around here matters?" he snapped back at me.

Shaking my head as I sat there, my heart was racing and my throat was tightening. "You should have kept your mouth shut Faith," I thought before replying to him.

"That's not what I'm saying, Luke. Financially speaking, this is supposed to be the two of us. You told me you would always have my back. To me that means financially too," I said passively, actively trying not to frustrate him. Then I said it again. "I just don't want to do it alone anymore."

He stood up abruptly then walked by me, stomping through the house. I heard him slam the door as he walked out. Tears started falling down my face as I hugged my knees tightly to my chest. "What am I going to do?" I asked myself again.

Over the next couple of days Luke barely spoke two words to me. I tried to keep as much energy and light-hearted conversation around the house so the kids didn't worry.

Monday morning, the day I was scheduled to return to work, came quickly. It had been three short weeks since my original surgery. Despite the work I was doing to restrengthen my vocal cords, my voice was still scratchy and low. Day after day, I would practice talking and leaving voicemails to regain strength.

Getting ready for work that morning, I remembered

thinking to myself, "You have to do this, Faith. Your family needs you."

"Mommy, I don't want you to go," Doug said as he ran in the kitchen and grabbed my leg. "Can't you stay home?" came next.

Tired and still emotional, I could feel the tears well up in my eyes. I desperately wanted to tell him, "Yes, baby I'll stay home." Yet the voice in the back of my head screamed at me, "Suck it up. Your family needs you to show up and do this." With one knee down on the floor, I said to him, "Sweetheart, I'll be home before you know it. Do you want to help me make dinner tonight?"

His tone changed as he looked up at me. "Really, Mommy?"

"Yes, of course honey, we can do it together."

"Me?" he said with emphasis. "I can help make dinner? Can I cut the vegetables?" Getting more excited he continued. "Mommy, can I use that big knife like you do?" he asked.

Luke, hearing us from the other room, responded, "Absolutely not, you're too young for that. You could cut off your fingers," he said in a harsh tone.

Redirecting and ignoring Luke's comments, I looked back at Doug. "Honey, I have a very special knife that you can use. We will do it together, okay?"

Looking slightly less enthusiastic, he replied, "Okay, Mommy."

"Now give me a hug," I said, then reached my arms out and brought him in close. Then with as much voice as I could muster, I called for Jake to say goodbye before I left.

Slowly making his way downstairs, Luke chimed in, "Come on, move it, she needs to go."

I made eye contact with him as he walked into the

kitchen. Then I gave him a big smile and a wink. Opening my arm wide, I brought him in close as I continued to hold Doug on the other side of me. "I love you boys, always remember that. I want you to have a good day today."

Jake started pleading with me. "Can you please just stay home for one more day?"

"I'll be home soon," I replied as I kissed his forehead. "Now go eat your breakfast."

Luke made his way into the kitchen. We looked at each other without a word. I grabbed my keys and my purse, threw my briefcase around my shoulder, gave him a half-hearted smile and started making my way out of the door. With each step I felt questions swarm in. "Why am I doing this? I hope the kids are okay today. This job is so not worth it." The dreary day and chill in the air further built on my discomfort and sadness leaving that morning.

The further away I got from the house, the more sadness grew, as I felt the tears welling yet again.

I can't do this anymore, I thought.

CHAPTER 25

The longer I continued down the trail away from Matt, the emptier I felt. "Why are you walking away from this man who truly cares about you, Faith?" I thought. "He clearly is interested in you and what you want in life." Comparison started creeping in as I thought back to that time with Luke in 2013. "I wish Luke would care like that."

Shaking my head, I made my way down and around the back end of the trail that led to the waterfall. Walking, I found myself in a moment of true appreciation, enjoying the view as I soaked up the fresh air. Then the thoughts quickly came in again. "What did I do wrong? Were my expectations too high?" I wondered.

"It's your responsibility" rang through my head. Then quickly came my response to myself. "Was it, though? Did I really take that on?" Memories ran through my head as I tried to answer this question. "Maybe I should have just backed off and let him be?"

Looking back as I pondered these thoughts, I saw the shift cancer had in my life. It all quickly started weighing on me.

I saw it so clearly now looking back: the kids begging for more time from me after my promotion and our move. "How did I miss this?" I thought as my heart sank.

Then another vision. I saw again, clearly, the toll that it took on my body, emotions and energy level. No longer having a thyroid took a major toll on my hormones. The constant push to do everything right at work didn't help. I gave all the energy I had not to slip at work yet lost so much focus on the kids and Luke.

Everything I did, I questioned myself: "Am I doing it right?" There was so much more on the line now. The constant worry of losing this job had me edgy all the time. I felt it in that moment like never before. "What did I do?" I thought, throat tightening, heart racing again.

I saw other park patrons coming toward me and mustered up as much of a smile as I could. I put my sunglasses on so they wouldn't catch wind of my emotional state. Greeting them one after another, I wondered, "Are they really happy in life or are they putting on a face just like me?"

The more interaction I had the quicker I realized that it was time for Doug's video. I headed down the decline that had big, well-spaced out rock structures for stairs. The trees mixed in between the boulders gave a beautiful setting to walk into. "It's the perfect spot," I thought as I looked up at the sightline which reinforced the choice. Looking straight up through the trees, the sun peeked through. Then, I saw it, a tree stump as if calling my name, that was spaced perfectly in between another tree that gave the ideal setup for my phone. I watched as the occasional passerby looked at me with curiousness and I greeted them each softly with a nod. Continuing my observation of the people walking by, I grabbed my phone. I saw 32 messages. A combination of texts and calls. Against my better judgment I looked at the calls first: Luke, Jake, Luke, Mom, Jake, Jake, Jake, Luke...my heart sank as I thought about Jake calling. Taking a deep breath, closing my eyes and leaning my head back, I thought, "Forgive me, Jake." Then bringing my head back up and putting my hands in a prayer position, I sat there thinking about him and his life.

After some time, I said aloud, "I love you son, never forget that." Then I looked back to my phone. Text upon text from everyone: Jake, Luke, Mom, Doug and even Joy. Shaking my head, I thought, "Why is he getting them all worked up?"

Then I saw it, from Luke. "I love you Faith, please come home."

"Yeah, if you love me so much why didn't you let me have my voice? Why didn't my thoughts and feelings matter to you?" I thought.

"He's just not strong like you, Faith" came the other voice.

"I can't do it anymore" came the next.

"You could just leave him" continued the internal dialogue. "You don't have to end it all."

"He would never let that happen."

"You know you'll never leave him; you love him too much. This is the only way."

"If only he cared as much about me as I do for him." Back and forth some more.

My heart sank more with every word. Tears swelled up as feelings of sadness, anger and frustration all hit me at once.

"Why can't he just see?" I asked myself. "If you only knew, really knew, how much I cared, maybe then you would treat me as a partner rather than a pawn."

As the thoughts continued to fill my space, I scanned through more texts.

I saw the message from Jake. "Mom where are you? I'm worried. I knew something was wrong this morning when you left. Please answer me. Are you hurt? Are you okay?"

I saw the next from Luke. "I'm sorry."

I saw another message from Jake. "Mom, I don't know

where you are, just please, tell me you're OK. I know you said you were going to the lake, but Dad said something was wrong. Are you coming back? I don't want to do life without you."

Crying at that thought, I said out loud, "Dammit Jake, you had better keep going when I'm gone."

I read the message from Joy. "Mom I miss you, when are you going to be home? Everyone is freaking out here. I told them you'll be fine. You are the strongest woman I know. You are always OK; you are OK, right?"

I saw the message from Luke as my whole body felt the emotions run through. "I know I haven't always done well by you. I've made mistakes, I've hurt you, I've hurt the kids, I got it, but don't leave, we need you. I'll do better. I promise, I'll work at it."

"I've heard it all before," I said to myself as tears continued down my face.

In that moment, a group of women walked by. I quickly wiped my face as I saw them stop and turn around. "Shit," I thought. "Don't talk to me, not now, please."

They made their way over to me as I looked away from my phone and mustered up as big of a smile as I could.

The woman standing tallest and behind the others, clearly in good shape, leaned in. "Are you okay?" she asked with sincerity in her tone.

Giving a slight smile and giggle, I said, "I'm good, just having some memories pass, that's all."

The redhead lady, standing shorter, off to the left of the others, looked at me. She tilted her head, then brought it back to center. "I know the emotions of memories very well. We have good ears, we can listen," she offered as the other three women shook their heads in agreement.

Why do you care? No one ever cares. No one has ever asked quite like this before. I looked at them with a puzzled look.

With silence I felt the emotions as those thoughts came back quickly, straight up my belly, into my chest. Then the heat in my neck. *Don't do it, Faith. Don't do it. You have to stay strong; you have a plan.* Taking a deep beath, I did my best to hide it. "I'm okay." Instantly in that response, there was no hiding it, tears started rolling down my face again. I wiped them away just as quickly.

The women come in closer still.

The tall blonde with gorgeous blue eyes sat down directly in front of me as she gently placed her hands on my knees. "Can we stay with you for a while? We need a break anyway." Then she looked back at the other women as if telling them to gather around. They each found a place to sit.

"Who are these women?" I asked myself.

Quickly the initiator who sat down first introduced herself. "I'm Shelly." Before giving me a chance to respond she continued to introduce the others. "This is Nancy, that's Rachel, and that's Beth. What is your name?" she asked.

"I'm Faith," I responded with tears continuing to roll down my face.

"Do you want to talk about it?" Shelly asked gently.

"Nope, I sure don't," I responded.

"Oh, I get those days, we've all had those, haven't we girls?" Shelly asked for agreement.

Instantly the other three women acknowledged her comment, then one after the other started sharing their stories. Experiences of failed relationships, stories about self-criticism and faults, the shit they put themselves through for mistakes they thought they made with their kids, and stories about regrets.

Sitting back against one of the boulders, Rachel leaned in. "They were all lessons," she said boldly.

"Isn't that the truth?" Beth agreed. "Some of the lessons sucked, though."

Laughing, Nancy chimed in, "You're not kidding there."

The other girls shook their heads in agreement.

They continued with the stories, but with a new twist, laughing at themselves and shaking their heads at the pain they put themselves through, the growth these women had over the years watching as their children and relationships developed.

"How long have you all known one another?" I asked.

"Oh, what is it now, girls? Seven or eight years ago?" Shelly said. "Rachel and I met first."

"Then we met Beth at the local coffee shop. We overheard an argument with her and her boyfriend at the time," Rachel chimed in.

Shaking her head, Beth added, "My boyfriend left me there as he screamed walking out of the shop. Everyone was staring. Shelly and Rachel came over and sat with me almost instantly. We talked for hours."

"Yeah, and we've been stuck with her since," Rachel added with a sassy tone as she playfully bumped Beth on the shoulder.

Shelly jumped back in. "We met Nancy hiking. She was out with her kids."

"It was such a horrible day until I met these girls. They made me feel a bit more normal. Like I wasn't completely screwing up my kids," Nancy added.

"It's really great you have each other," I replied.

As they continued talking about their experiences together, I saw Matt out of the corner of my eye coming up the trail. His head was down kicking around the rocks with a solemn look on his face. Instantly I felt it. My whole body tingled. "Will he stop?" I thought.

I'm not sure what caught his attention, the girls talking or a natural instinct that we were here but, he looked up. As soon as he made eye contact with me, he stopped. Waiting there, watching, saying nothing, as if we were talking through our eye contact.

I felt it, throughout my entire body yet again, warmth in my heart, racing, in a good way. Wanting desperately for him to come and hold me one more time. I felt myself biting my lower lip. Then it hit me. "Don't do it, Faith. Let him go." And I looked away.

The girls watched the entire scene playing out and got defensive as they watched Matt. I could see the look on Nancy and Rachel's faces. They were ones of protection, a "don't mess with my girl" type of look.

He looked at me then over to the girls and back at me, giving a brief nod. Then he put his hands back in his pocket and continued down the trail, both of us tried catching glimpses of one another as he walked by. My heart screamed at me. "Don't let him go, Faith. He's good for you."

As he continued to walk up the trail, Shelly looked back at me, "Is he the reason? The one that has you so emotional today?"

"Nah, I just met Matt this morning. He's a good man. He will make someone very happy someday."

Nancy intervened with a snarky tone. "It sure looks like he wants to make you happy."

Just as quickly Rachel looked back to her watch. "Girls, we gotta keep moving," she said. "You are welcome to join us, Faith. There is always room for one more."

"Thanks Rachel," I replied, then looking up at them, I said, "I need some time to myself. I appreciate you girls, thank you for stopping and all the perspectives."

Reaching in her bag, Shelly held out her notebook. I

could see her writing. Then I watched as she passed it to Rachel, Nancy and Beth before ripping out the page and handing it to me. Written on the page were each of the girl's names, numbers and email addresses.

"It would be great if you stayed in touch, Faith," Shelly said as the other girls chimed in in agreement. "You heard Rachel, there is always room for one more in our tribe. And Faith, you would make the perfect addition. Us girls need to stick together," she finished.

Then Beth added, "Always remember, we all have bad days, we all have bad moments, some days just suck. But, the smiles on our kids' faces, the laughs with girlfriends, the joy in those big wins, it all makes the bad days suck just a little less. Not to mention the handsome men we meet while out on a hike who clearly want our attention." She finished with a smile as the other girls laughed in agreement.

Shelly knelt right in front of me again, and with direct eye contact, said, "Focus on the good today, Faith." Then she leaned in and hugged me.

One after another the other girls came in for a hug, then made their way up the trail.

"Take care, Faith," they said as they waved.

Reflecting on what just happened, I looked up to the sky. "Today, really?" I shook my head and opened back up my phone. Ignoring all the messages this time, I turned on the camera, put the phone up against the tree just across from me and hit record.

"Doug," I said with a pause, "my baby boy," I said as I let out a sigh. "Son, you have such a gift. Your awareness of people, circumstances and environments is something most people only dream of having. You are natural with this gift. Your ability to understand what people are honestly saying as opposed to what is just coming out of their mouths is uncanny. You have the ability to see the unseen. Lean into it, okay? And when things get hard, do not give up. Lean into your dreams. You know what you want, go for it. Keep going for it. Dad might give you some resistance. Don't give in, he will eventually understand. Doug, I am so proud of you, just know I will always be watching out for you. I may not be here in person but I'll be here in spirit. And always remember how much I love you. I'm sorry it had to end this way. I just don't have the fight anymore, but this has nothing to do with you, nothing at all, this was all me. Keep shining bright, baby, I love you." Then I blew a kiss to the camera and gave him one last smile before turning it off.

Sitting there, I thought, *that's it!*

CHAPTER 26

The awful feeling of what most mornings felt like post-cancer hit me in an instant as I sat there.

I was taken back to a morning in late 2018.

Waking up that morning, I felt like I was about 1000 degrees and exhausted, as if I didn't have a wink of sleep. Head and sinus pressure against the right side, fuzzy eyes. "When is it going to end? Why can't I just feel good?" I asked myself. Day by day it seemed to be getting worse. And the more I focused on it, the more I felt it. The last thing I wanted to do was get up, much less go do my workout. I wanted to crawl back under the covers and not wake up again. Sitting there, I started reasoning with myself. "Come on, Faith, get moving or you'll run out of time." Thoughts shifted to what I would feel like if I didn't get my workout in - sluggish and lazy. The constant worry about my weight and looking in the mirror came to mind. In that instant I took my Levothyroxine and chugged back the water next to the nightstand. Then without a breath or another thought, like a zombie, I got up, grabbed my gym clothes, changed and made my way downstairs.

Standing there in the kitchen taking a couple of sips of coffee, I continued to think about how lousy I felt, contemplating the option of calling my boss and telling him I couldn't come in. The conversation in my head had become a morning ritual. "You know you are never going to call in,

Faith," I thought, before chugging back the rest of my coffee and heading downstairs to the gym.

In what felt like robot mode, I turned on the news, hopped on the treadmill and quickly got in 3.2 miles as I drowned myself in the happenings around the world. As I did, the thought of the day crept in. Anxiety growing significantly worse than ever before, I felt an all-the-time need to perform. Saying it right, doing it right so the boss would be happy with the numbers. Feeling the constant need to pressure my teams for better, stronger numbers, knowing full well they were all doing their best every day. It was a continuous fight of my own integrity having to have those conversations, knowing full well how hard my teams were working.

In that thought I felt myself running faster as I thought to the last board meeting, listening to them minimize the teams and the work they were putting in. "Perhaps we need a day in their shoes to really see what is going on from their perspective." I recalled the words coming out as I got glares from the other VPs. I wasn't exactly liked at the company. My hard work was the only thing that kept me here. They never really wanted my opinions or thoughts.

As I ran harder, those memories came in faster.

Having to listen to them cut down tenured staff members for a simple difference of perspective.

Sitting there, they passed by every thought I had on how to bring back the sales numbers. I knew full well they didn't want me there and truth be told, I didn't want to be there either.

One leadership team meeting after another I was left wondering "What am I doing here?"

Shaking my head at those moments, my treadmill started winding down, telling me that my run was almost complete.

"What's the point in all of it?" I asked myself again, "I am just their frickin' pawn, anyway," I said out loud as I hopped off the treadmill and slammed the heavy bag with my fist. "Urgh!" I screamed as I hit it in frustration.

Quickly I changed gears to get my strength training in. Leg day. The frustration of thoughts from work had me pushing even harder than usual. I put an additional 20 pounds on my sets as I did weighted squats. With each drive of the thighs back up I felt it, pushing out every ounce of anger and resentment. "Why don't you fucking listen," I said out loud. "Why doesn't anyone listen?" I said on the next set, a little quieter and with less force this time as I felt the rush of sadness come over me.

"Stop, Faith!" I instantly demanded of myself.

My alarm sounded, warning me that it was time to get the kids up and get ready for work.

I pressed the weighted bar up over my head and gave it a couple of overhead presses before returning it to the stand. Then, stopping for a moment, I rested my hands on my hips and took a breath. "Is this all there is to life?" I thought. "Playing a role in other people's games? Are you kidding me?"

In that moment, I felt strong, like I could conquer anything. Then reality quickly set back in, and I was reminded of everything holding me back.

As I stood there pondering, I heard it, screaming through the house, Jake's alarm clock. The second sign that I needed to get moving. I turned off the lights, ran back upstairs, then peeked in his room. "Jake, Jake," I whispered with a tone to try to get his attention. "Shut your alarm off, you're going to wake Dad," I said to him. He turned for a moment then fell back asleep. "Jake, come on man, shut it off." Not moving. I snuck into his room trying to be quiet to not wake Luke myself, I shut off his alarm then shook him. "Jake, come on, it's time to get going. I'm running late, we don't have time for this today. Let's go."

"Urgh, Mom, come on. Give me just fifteen more minutes," he responded in a gruff tone.

"I'm going to shower; you'd better get up when your other alarm goes off or your father is not going to be happy," I warned.

"I will, geez," he responded.

Making my way up the hall, I peeked in Doug's room first. He was already sitting up in his bed. "Good morning," I whispered.

"Morning Mom, can you make me breakfast?" he asked immediately.

"It's that kind of morning?" I asked.

"Yah, I didn't sleep good," he responded.

"All right, well, get moving and help Joy get ready and I'll get breakfast going as soon as I'm done, deal?" I asked.

"Sounds like a deal, thanks Mom," he replied. Doug had always been a good riser in the morning.

Next, I made my way into Joy's room and sat on the side of her bed. "Good morning, my baby girl." She slowly opened her eyes as I brushed the hair out of her face. "It's time to get moving, I'm jumping in the shower. I'll make you some breakfast as soon as I get out."

"Mommy, can I just skip it today? I'm tired. And the girls at school aren't so nice," she said.

"What do you mean, honey?"

"Some of the girls pick on me and Jill. They said our clothes are funny and out of date." Then she looked at me. "I like my clothes, Mommy. Why are they mean?" she asked.

Shaking my head, I thought "already?" "Honey I was hoping not to have this conversation with you for at least a few more years. It stinks, and I'm sorry to say, some people are just mean," I said.

"Oh, you mean like Daddy?" she questioned.

My heart sank in that moment. "Well, no, a different kind of mean. Daddy just gets stressed and doesn't always know how to communicate it. These girls sound like they do it more for fun or to take the attention off themselves," I said, trying to explain it to her respectfully. "But honey, you need to know whatever they say to you, it means nothing about you, do you hear me? It only says a lot about them and who they are."

"But why do they do it?" she asked again with curiosity.

"I am not exactly sure, honey," I responded.

"Maybe I should just ask," she responded boldly.

"My girl," I said with a smile as I shook my head in delight.

Just then, I heard Luke coming down the hall.

"Could you guys be any louder, geez!" he scolded as he hit his fist against the wall.

Jake's alarm started sounding as he walked by. Anticipating the frustration, I started shaking my head.

He backed up quickly to Jake's room. Pushing the door open abruptly he said, "Hey, turn that shit off. Don't make me tell you again."

Looking back at Joy, I said gently, "Let's get moving, okay?"

"I know, Mommy, don't poke the bear, right?" she spoke.

Jake, Doug, Joy and I finished getting ready to go and were making lunches as Luke made his way back in the house.

"You could be a little quieter in the morning, you know. Some of us are still sleeping," he said.

"What are we supposed to do, be completely silent?" Jake said under his breath.

"What did you say to me?" Luke asked him bluntly as he got in his face.

"Nothing, sir," Jake responded.

"Come on, if you have something to say, at least say it to my face." He egged him on. "You don't have the balls," he said.

"Mommy, is this what you meant?" Joy whispered in my ear.

I gently shook my head to her as I tried to break up what was happening with Jake and Luke. "Come on guys, not this morning okay, please," I pleaded with him as I gently placed my hand on Luke's forearm. He quickly pulled it away.

"You're always sticking up for him. When are you going to start sticking up for me?" he claimed, then he stomped his way back outside again.

"I don't get it, Mom," Jake said.

"Honey, don't start, okay?" I asked.

"Can you guys go get in the car? I am going to say good-bye to your father," I said.

Making my way out back to Luke, I stepped in his garage as I was greeted by a poof of cigarette smoke. "We're leaving. Are you going to say goodbye to the kids?" I asked.

"Tell them I said to have a good day, I'm sure they don't want to hear from me right now," he replied.

"I'm sure they would," I countered.

"Just go, all right?" he said forcefully.

"You know Luke, some day," then I stopped myself, shook my head and slammed the door behind me as I walked out.

Walking around the back of the house towards the car, trying not to cry, I shook my head as I wondered if this was what all relationships looked like.

Is this it? I asked again as I got into the car.

CHAPTER 27

Continuing to sit there on the tree stump, the videos I made today replayed in my head. "That's it, I completed them all, it's time to go," I said to myself. "There is nothing left to be said or done. I am complete." I felt my body react at the thought of ending it all. "It's really over."

As that thought hit me, Matt came back into my head. "I need to say goodbye the right way," I thought. Then without a second thought, I stood up, threw on my pack, wiped my eyes and abruptly made my way up the trail. "I hope I catch him," I said to myself.

Walking up the trail each year of my life started playing in my head. From my youngest of years that I could recall, the ones when I started building the story. One of disempowerment. That of a girl not having a voice. Having to watch every word she said. Then shifting to the weight I carried, quite literally. An obese girl. Why on earth would anyone listen to her?

Moving into young adult years, drinking, parties, I was finally starting to be seen. It was fun, it felt good. Looking into that part of my life now, I realized, I wasn't really seen, I was fake, drunk, playing a part. They never liked me. As long as I was buying everything and giving it up whenever they wanted I was able to be a part of their world. And if I didn't, well, then I didn't matter to them. They were moving onto someone else.

"Shit, how could I be so naïve?" I asked myself.

Then it happened. I met Luke. Our first year together, the laughs, the giggles, the love I felt from this man. His holding me, romance, drawing me baths, music, flowers, candles, I turned a blind eye to the fact that he, too, disregarded my voice. The other things made me feel finally seen in a way I had never known before.

Then our baby boy, Jake, came into this world. And everything started shifting. I could see the stress in him. He wanted to do everything right. Our relationship shifted. I often wondered if he really wanted to be a dad. In this moment, I finally realized he was simply scared and unsure. The older Jake got the more I saw him question himself and it came out towards me and Jake in a very harsh way.

My legs kept getting heavier with the memories as I got closer to the falls. It took me nearly twenty years and now I finally started uncovering what Luke was really feeling all those years. Shaking my head, I looked up yet again. "Really, now?"

The memories continued when Doug came along. Luke pulled away even more. I saw it again, his discomfort and uncertainty. "He was wondering if what he was doing was ever right," I said to myself in that moment. "How didn't I see this before?" I never saw it from that perspective until now. As the boys got older and we had Joy, it became even more prevalent. He had this little girl to protect now. Looking in on our life, on him, his responses, the frustration, his anger, I shook my head at the thoughts. "I missed it."

It hit me, all the stories of when he was a little boy, him and his mom. How many times he was silenced by one of her boyfriends after another. The violence he witnessed. The beatings he and his mom endured. "He never healed," I thought. "He was trying to protect us the best way he knew how." My heart was sinking more with each thought.

"He never healed," I said to myself again.

In that instant the memories dissipated as I saw the waterfall. Then I saw Matt sitting on the bench. My heart started racing, butterflies in the stomach, my whole body reacting as if I was seeing him for the first time. This man who had encouraged and challenged me the entire day, sitting there again in front of me as if he were waiting for me to go by.

He looked my way, made eye contact and came to his feet. Coming closer with hesitation, he put his hand out. "Faith, please just listen."

Knowing in that moment I had no intention of walking away from him this time, I simply replied, "I'm listening." I walked closer and listened.

"I know I came out strong when we met. And, perhaps, I overstepped a few times, but it's only because I care about you. I see you, Faith. You have so much life in you, yet it looks like you are ready to throw in the towel for all of your dreams," he said as he stood there.

I shrugged my shoulders and gave a half-agreement type of smirk without saying a word. Now almost directly in front of him, I kept listening.

"I want to know you more. And I know I said that earlier, but I really believe that I can help you get started. It wouldn't be hard and it's worth a chance, isn't it? I could help every step of the way." He paused as if he was waiting for me to say something.

I tilted my head and kept listening.

"You could finally get out of that job you dread," he added. "Come on, you aren't going to say anything, really?"

"You waited?" I said. "You knew I was going to stop at the waterfall. Were you waiting here for me?"

Looking at me square in the eyes, he nodded his head. "I was." Then he grabbed my hand. "I had to know you were okay. You looked really upset when you were sitting talking to those women. And they made it noticeably clear that I better not be stopping by you," he said. "I care about you, Faith. Don't you see?" He grabbed my other hand.

Closing my eyes, I shook my head slowly in wonder as I thought, "Really, today?" Then I opened them back up as I regained eye contact with him. Gently I placed my hand on the side of his face, then softly pressed my lips against his.

He quickly wrapped his arms around me and pulled me in close. Kissing each other passionately, I melted in his arms. My body felt safe, protected and tingling in ways I hadn't felt in years. He softly caressed my back before bringing his hand up around my waist. Then he stopped, bringing his hand to the side of my face. "Faith, what are we doing?"

"Um, we're kissing Matt, I thought it was pretty obvious," I replied with a sassy tone and a smile.

"You know what I mean Faith, come on," he replied with irritation.

"Matt, I can't tell you that we will ever see each other after today. But I can tell you that I am very attracted to you. You have made me feel special in ways I haven't felt in years. You gave me back a bit of me today that I haven't felt in, well," pausing, I shook my head, "in longer than I can recall in this moment."

"Then what are we doing here if I never get to see you again? I don't work like that," he said.

"I feel safe with you and completely connected. But I can't give you any more than today. That's the best I've got," I said as I let go of him and started backing away.

"Faith, why?" he asked.

I sat down on the bench and started taking off my

sneakers and socks. Then slowly I looked around to ensure there were no rangers walking into the creek to get to the falls.

"What are you doing?"

"What does it look like I am doing?" I replied.

"It looks like you are about to get us kicked out of the park," he said as he started taking his shoes off.

"Nah, they might make us get out of the water, but I haven't been kicked out yet," I replied. "If you follow me in here, you need to know, today is all I have to give. Please don't push for more."

He paused, then stood there watching me.

I gently put my hand under the water before laying my head back and allowing the water to hit me. Taking a deep breath, I thought, "Let me be free." Getting lost in time, I was slightly startled when he put his hands around my waist. Pulling me in closer, he guided my head to rest on his chest, then held me as he kissed my neck. Feeling my body quiver, reluctantly I turned around, kissed him softly then grabbed his hand and guided us to the sitting rocks behind the falls.

Looking at me, he smiled before clearing my hair out of my face. "This space is amazing, Faith. How often have you done this?"

Giggling, I responded, "Never, this is the first time. I have always wanted to and just never took the time. Today is a great day to take the time to do it all," I said before reaching my hand out to catch a drop of the falls.

He reached out his hands, grabbed me on each side and pulled me in closer. "I want more of you," he request-ed. "I know you said today is it, but what will it take? How can I convince you to see me again? I don't know what this is yet and I know you're married but isn't it worth a second date?"

"Date?" I quickly replied before backing up. "Matt, this is hardly a date."

"Okay, fine, a day together. Isn't it worth another day together? Is that better?" he reframed it.

"I'm going away for a while Matt, not sure if I will be coming back. It's time to get out of here." I told him.

"What do you mean, what about the kids?" he quickly responded.

"They will be okay; I've made sure of it. They are old enough now to take care of themselves. But enough about that. Can we just enjoy this moment?" I asked.

"No, Faith. Where are you going, can I come see you?" he asked again.

"Matt, I told you, this is all I've got right now, please," I pleaded with him as I held eye contact.

He reached out and pulled me in again. "Tell me you're going to be okay?" he asked as he softly put his hand back on my face and put his lips closer to mine.

Avoiding the question, I met his lips with mine. Getting lost in the moment, I raised one leg over his to sit on top of him and embrace even closer. He softly reached his hand under the back of my shirt and started his way up my back. Lost in the moment, we were both abruptly interrupted as we heard children coming down the trail. I quickly got up, tucked in my shirt and started walking out of the water. I made it a couple steps out from under the falls then I looked back at him and quickly ran back for one last kiss, then made my way out.

Not saying a word, we walked out of the water just as the family got there. With his hand gently on my back, the woman with the kids gave me a soft smile as I watched the man give Matt a head nod as if saying "way to go" in guy's code.

"Mommy can we go in too?" one of the children quickly asked.

Looking at me, she shrugged.

I responded, "There is no sign saying not to" then I shrugged back and winked. "Have fun you guys," I said as I grabbed my shoes and backpack, then started my way up the trail.

"Aren't you going to put your shoes on?" Matt reasoned.

"Nah, they can wait." I responded.

Walking for a while with no words between us, I thought *it's time to let him go, Faith.* Turning to him, I stopped. "Matt, this was a lot of fun today. Thank you for bringing me back to me. I really needed it. You are a gift and someday there is going to be a very lucky lady by your side," I said.

"Why does this feel like goodbye? Can't we at least spend the rest of the hike together?" he pleaded.

"I need the rest of the day for me, Matt." Then dropping my shoes and pack I got closer to him. "I will never forget you. You made me feel alive today. And, pissed me off a bit. And, showed me that people still know how to care. Thank you." Then I got in close and kissed him before gently rubbing my fingers against his lips. Smiling, I gave him a wink then reached down to grab my things.

He abruptly pulled me back up and close to him again. Wrapping his arms around me he said, "What if you are the one that is meant to be by my side?" Then he kissed me yet again, first starting on the lips then making his way down my neck. Tilting my head back, I briefly got lost in the moment.

"Matt," I said softly as I looked at him and gently licked my lips, then smiled at him. I kissed his cheek and pulled away, holding his hand for another moment as I did. "Till next time." I left it with a wink, then grabbed my things and started up the trail.

I felt him watching as I walked away. Without looking back, I continued on the trail.

"I think I fell in love with you today," I said to myself as I walked away from him, shaking my head again in disbelief of everything this day had brought.

CHAPTER 28

Walking in silence for the first time in what seemed like years, maybe ever, there were finally no thoughts, no pondering, no wondering if I was making the right decision. It was my time.

Then, as I stopped to look up at the climb to get to Devil's Doorway, life crept in. I felt it. Jake came into my thoughts like a storm. It hit me so powerfully. Looking up to the climb, nearly 1500 feet in elevation to get there, I felt it, every emotion in my body. My eyes started watering, then I took a deep breath, put on my sunglasses and started the climb.

Getting to Devil's Doorway was a steep climb up, made of large boulders for rocks. It wasn't for the faint of heart. There was an easier way around through the woods, but I'd always preferred the climb that kept my heart racing. It was my final day here. "I am not missing this last climb," I thought.

With each boulder I stepped onto, a new memory of Jake came into my space. First, in the birthing room the day he was born. Twenty-one hours. It was exhausting and painful but when I saw him, all my worries, stress and pain instantly went away. The days of sitting on the living room floor building Legos with him for hours on end. The walks to the park. Swinging with him. Running around in the backyard with cups of water for water fights. Then my heart racing the day I took his training wheels off. And again, even more so the first time he drove away without me in the car after getting his license. I loved all the kids but there was a certain connection I had with him. "Forgive me Jake, please, I love you. Keep leaning in and go after everything you want in life!"

With tears running down my face, sweat dripping down my back, I continued the incline. The usual soreness in my thighs wasn't present. Looking up, the most beautiful view. "Kids, you would love it here right now," I said out loud, not giving a care of who was around to hear me. The beauty of the rocks, splashes of red, orange and yellow with some dark brown mixed in between, and the sun hitting it perfectly to bring out the shine. It was breathtaking!

Then as quickly as the memories of Jake started passing, Doug came into my mind. He was such a peaceful baby, the easiest of all my pregnancies by far. And delivery was a matter of hours. Looking at him in the delivery room that day was instant peace. Doug had always been naturally creative. As soon as he could hold a crayon, I saw it coming through. The three of us would sit at the kitchen table for hours drawing, coloring and painting. Jake and I would often look at Doug's work with amazement. It seemed like he was doing it for decades. Then when he started school, his natural demeanor towards defending others shone through. He joined the debate team early on. Doug had always been more internal and introverted than Jake, but when he got to that podium, nothing was silencing him especially when it was a topic he was passionate about. His words flowed as if he practiced for days. Doug had often naturally defended everyone. Looking in, as I climbed, it made perfect sense why he and Luke had always been closest. Doug had always seen him, not the anger or frustration, but he had really seen the heart behind it all. "I love you Doug, so much. Never let anyone take away your kindness."

Nearly halfway up, memories shifted again. I saw her, my baby girl. At that moment, I chuckled in recollection of her birth. Instantly she smiled and giggled as the nurse put her in my arms. We all looked at each other as if thinking, "Did that really just happen?" She could walk into a room and bring both peace and light at the same time. Her laugh could lift anyone's spirits. All the other kids in the neighborhood had brought her their 'problems' since as early as I could remember. She and her friends would sing and dance out on the front lawn for hours on end. The boys and I would watch her in awe of her natural showmanship. When she was five, Jake turned a song on the radio. She instantly started singing as if she'd heard the song a million times before. It was in perfect tune, too. She hit nearly every word. Joy had often struggled to keep up in school, but her creative side sure did make up for it. "Joy, keep singing, keep dancing, enjoy your life, experience life and have fun with it. I love you my baby girl and I promise I'll always be the angel over your shoulder. Call on me anytime you need me."

With only a couple of hundred feet left to the top of the cliff, Luke came to the front center of my mind. Clear as day. The love of my life. I thought about the moments where I was truly happy with us. The times when he let his guard down and genuinely let me in. Those moments out at his parents' house tossing around the football. The family cookouts. With each spark of good times that came in, the hard ones came in right behind them. "I can't keep it out, Luke, I've been looking for the negative for far too long, it's too late. I hope you take another chance, find someone who can love you the way you need. And, take good care of my babies. You are a good man, Luke. Find a way to stop letting yourself down. And, don't you dare let my kids down, Luke."

In that moment, I stopped with just a few feet left, looked up to the sky and said "help him see Lord, please, help him see. I'll always love you, please know this wasn't your fault, it was all created by me."

With that thought, I tilted my head back one more time, took a deep breath and paused as I felt the air breeze in. Then bringing my focus back to the rest of the climb, I made the final few steps up and onto the landing directly across from Devil's Doorway.

The onlookers sitting on the side rocks now made into seats stared at me as I arrived.

"Hello," I greeted them.

"Hey yourself." I was met with a reply. "How was your climb up?" came the next question. I took a deep breath and stopped for a moment as I looked over to the Doorway then up to the sky and back at them. "I've done this climb countless times and today was probably one of easiest I have ever done."

"Easy?" one of the men said, sitting there. Then he looked at the people he was with in disagreement. "I don't know anyone that would ever call that climb easy. Who are you kidding?"

The woman by his side backhanded him.

Shaking my head, I replied, "Well, look at that, you just met the first person who would absolutely call it easy," I said boldly then turned and raised my arms up enjoying the view from the top.

"I've let jerks like him shoot my voice down for decades. There's no way it's happening today," I said to myself.

Then I turned back and looked at the group sitting behind me. The man who made the remarks avoided eye contact. I gave them a gentle smile before walking toward Devil's Doorway.

The Doorway was breathtaking. Made from quartzite rock, it was believed to be formed by water freezing and thawing in the cracks during the glacial period. Standing nearly fifty feet, this rock formation was one of the most captivating I had ever seen. As described in the name, the formation gave way to a large opening in the middle, the "Doorway." I'd climbed into the Doorway a couple times through the years but never had the nerve to climb on top of it. The park strongly cautioned against climbing any part of the Devil's Doorway. From the time I knew it was over, I knew this was where I wanted to spend my final time.

I looked back to the crowd, then back to the Doorway. They didn't look like they were leaving anytime soon. Not wanting to delay further, I took a drink of water from my pack then returned it and started climbing in. The right side of the Doorway offered more grip to climb. I'd watched a handful of experienced climbers make the trek and was trying to mirror their way up.

"Lady, I wouldn't do that if I were you," one of the onlookers called out.

In silence I continued.

Left hand, then right, nestling in my feet wherever I could find, my heart was racing. It felt good, exhilarating. No fear of what might happen, I knew this was the end today anyway. If I was taken a little sooner than expected, oh well. "Maybe then they would think it was just an accident," I thought for a moment. "That could be easier on the kids" came next. "Nah, they will know from the videos, Faith" the internal dialogue reasoned yet again.

"Keep your focus," I said to myself out loud.

I was so close, within ten feet of reaching the top.

"Oh my gosh, be careful, Faith" came a lady's voice.

"Who is that?" I thought. Wanting to look, yet hesitating so I didn't lose focus, I kept going.

The next reach was a stretch. There I was on the side of the Devil's Doorway, now with a small audience watching, stuck. Where do I go? My left arm reached as far as I could grasp onto the edge of the rock. My left toe was barely nestled in a rock sticking out. My right hand had nothing to grab onto.

"Focus, Faith." I told myself. "Take a breath" came next. Then I heard it.

"Move your left foot about three inches to the left, there is a more stable rock there." It was Matt.

Peeking over my shoulder I saw him watching, evaluating the structure and ready to tell me my next move. I regained focus and moved my foot to where he said, then looked at him again.

"Do you want to go all the way?" he asked.

"Yes," I replied without a look.

"See, she got scared, I told you she couldn't do it," I heard the man from earlier say.

"Oh yeah, she has bigger balls then you do, dick" came another woman's voice. "Keep going Faith, you got this," she continued.

It dawned on me; it must be one of the women from earlier. "Are they all here watching now?" I asked myself.

"Keep your focus, Faith." I heard Matt. "Can you reach your right hand about five inches to the right?"

I tried to make it but couldn't quite get there. Maneuvering around I tried moving my left hand slightly to give me more space.

He interrupted. "Stop, you'll lose grip. There is a beautiful rock about four inches down from where your right hand is right now. If you grab that, can you loosen your left."

I loosened and wiggled my fingers then took a breath. Then following his instructions, I reached for the grip to my right. It was a nice-sized rock with the perfect placement for my fingers. Instantly I could feel it allowing my left hand some relief. Instinctively I moved my right foot down slightly to a rock I knew was there from earlier. Then I was comfortably on the side of the rock shaking out my left hand. It gave me the perfect break to look up and see what my next move should be. Then without a second thought, I made three quick moves, first my left hand up and over, then quickly followed with my feet and right hand again.

"Nice move Faith." I heard Shelly this time from the crowd.

"Hold it steady, Faith, take your time. You are not in a rush today, remember," Matt reminded me from our conversations earlier.

Then with what felt like a second wind, in six easy moves I made it to the top and instantly laid out over the top of the Doorway. Hearing the crowd clapping I sat up and gave a gentle wave. "Please leave now," I thought, knowing what was next for me.

"Nice work, babe," Matt said softly from below.

I looked over and caught eye contact with him. "Thank you," I mouthed without any voice behind it.

He nodded, then went over to the side of the Doorway and sat down on a large boulder.

"Faith, that was scary. Why would you do that?" Beth said aloud.

"And, awesome," said Nancy just after her.

"It was pretty awesome," Rachel agreed.

"Faith, I wish we could stay to see you down safely, but we are already late for something. Are you going to be okay?" Shelly asked.

"I'm not going anywhere until she's down safe," Matt chimed in.

"Thanks Shelly, I'll be good. You can all go," I said with emphasis as I looked at Matt. "I'll be fine."

Shelly looked at me then at Matt and back at me. "Is it okay?" she mouthed.

I nodded to her in acceptance.

She blew me a kiss then winked as she looked at the other girls. "All right girls, let's go."

"I'm not leaving you up there, Faith," Matt demanded.

Shaking my head, I stayed in silence.

The rest of the crowd started their way down the trail too, leaving only me, Matt and one other onlooker, all in silence.

Sitting at the edge of the rock with my feet hanging off, hands perched behind me, I thought, "This is the best view here. I could stay here forever."

At peace, I realized my breathing was more comfortable than it had been in years, decades, maybe. With every look around the park, I was in appreciation of the colors, the eagles flying ahead, the trees, the laughter I could hear from afar. There were no worries, no second-guessing, no frustrating conversations. Peace, complete and total peace. I closed my eyes, tilted my head back and saw everyone in my life, the smiles, the laughter, the love, the moments. A light smile came over me.

Then I stood up. I saw Matt out of the corner of my eye stand up just after me.

I brought my feet to the very edge of the front of the rock which gave way to the view for miles and miles off in the distance.

"Faith, that's too close!" he yelled.

Ignoring him, I reached my arms out as wide as I could, laid my head back and perked my chest out forward.

"Faith, be careful!" he yelled in another, stronger tone.

Leaning just a bit more forward, I felt the breeze up against me. I was in total peace and serenity at that moment. With complete and total gratitude for my life, I was ready.

And in that instant from off in the distance, I heard it just as I leaned forward a bit more.

"Mom."